TO CATCH A THIEF . . .

Raised as an English country girl, Bororavian princess Lily Bancroft simply *cannot* wed her detestable, power-hungry cousin. Yet she dares not refuse—and that's where Kit Fox comes in. This charming, disarmingly attractive thief-turned-British spy would be the ideal partner to help divest her of unwanted royal obligations by "robbing" her of her innocence. But first the gentleman rogue will need some "convincing"—a prospect Lily finds somewhat frightening . . . and deliciously stimulating.

. . . FIRST STEAL HIS HEART

It could not be more perfect! Kit's liege has assigned him to investigate dark doings in the Bororavian court—and now the true heiress to the throne is offering him entry! Lily's seduction is his sworn duty, her passionate manipulation his sole aim. But what is this feeling in his heart the exquisite lady inspires—this sensuous need and unbidden tenderness that threatens to blossom gloriously into love?

SUSAN SIZEMORE

Captured Innocence

An Avon Romantic Treasure

AVON BOOKS
An Imprint of HarperCollinsPublishers

This is a work of fiction. Names, characters, places, and incidents are products of the author's imagination or are used fictitiously and are not to be construed as real. Any resemblance to actual events, locales, organizations, or persons, living or dead, is entirely coincidental.

AVON BOOKS
An Imprint of HarperCollins*Publishers*
10 East 53rd Street
New York, New York 10022-5299

Copyright © 2003 by Susan Sizemore
ISBN: 0-06-008289-5
www.avonromance.com

First Avon Books paperback printing: January 2003

Avon Trademark Reg. U.S. Pat. Off. and in Other Countries, Marca Registrada, Hecho en U.S.A.
HarperCollins® is a registered trademark of HarperCollins Publishers Inc.

Printed in the U.S.A.

10 9 8 7 6 5 4 3 2 1

For Nan Burridge and Marj Ihssen,
who have taught me a great deal about friendship—
and what little I know about sheep

Prologue

London, England
1854

He'd been told it'd be hard, but it wasn't like they had dogs or anything. He had a sore on his leg from the last house, where they'd had plenty of dogs. Usually he scrambled up drain-pipes and such to the upper stories where it was easier to get in the windows. No luck with that to-night, for the sore leg left him weaker than he thought. There was no way he could beg off the job, not if he wanted to eat. No one slacked in his master's shop. Besides, he had his pride. Given a job, he did it. The question was, how?

It was a good night for it, dark as pitch, with a hard, steady rain coming down to mask any noise. Not that he made noise. He cursed the rain because it soaked through his thin clothes and left him shivering. Since he couldn't go up, he made a careful circuit of the house, discovering that the windows on the lower levels were securely barred against criminals such as himself. The locks were tricky. The householder obviously didn't have a trusting soul.

"It's down the coal chute for me," he decided when he could find no other way in. He had to leave most of his clothes on the wet ground. He was thin enough to shimmy down the narrow chute full of coal dust and total darkness. It was a quick trip, but it left him shivering with fear and wiping black dust mixed with tears from his face when he reached the cellar storage bin. He wasn't scared, he told himself sternly. Not of the dark. There'd be hell to pay if he didn't bring back what he'd been told. That was an acceptable fear, and it drove him up the cellar stairs.

He made quick work of the lock on the door, and moved silently through the pantry and kitchen and up to the ground floor. He went through the rooms on the main floor quickly, pausing only long enough to pocket a few expensive trinkets for his own reward for the night's work. It would have been safer to leave now, but he'd been told to fetch a box of papers kept in an upstairs room, so up he had to go, quiet as a mouse. Or so he would have been if every other stair didn't squeak the tiniest bit at his step. It was torture, but no doors had been flung open by curious servant or householder by the time he made it to the landing. He kept his lock-pick tight in his fist, ready for use as he moved from door to door, but each knob he tried twisted easily open. He searched quickly, with brisk fingers and eyes accustomed to the dark, but did not find what he was looking for until going through the third room of his hunt. The box he'd been told to find rested on a table in a room full of books. He breathed a sigh of relief, snatched up the box, and turned.

"Hello," said a little girl in the doorway. She wore a lacy white nightgown and carried a candle.

The girl with black braids standing beside her was younger than the one with the candle. "Hello," said the smaller girl.

"That's Mum's," said the girl with the candle, looking at the box.

"I'm Harry," said the little one. "Who you?"

"Harriet, say 'who *are* you,'" corrected the woman who joined them.

God! He was caught and no mistake! The way was blocked, but he ran toward the doorway any-way. He was quick as a monkey. Maybe—

The girl with the candle tripped him. The woman saved him from a fall by grabbing the back of his shirt. The box went flying, broke open, and papers scattered across the room.

"That was not polite, Lucy," the woman said. "But it was very good work, my dear. Thank you." The woman tightly held on to him. Her hands were not soft, as a lady's should be, but her grip didn't hurt. She ignored his squirming and kicking, and knelt in front of him. "My name is Hannah Gale," she said. "Who might you be, young man?"

"He's a thief," a harsh woman's voice spoke from the hallway.

"That's obvious, Aunt Phoebe," Hannah Gale said. "But that only explains what he is, not who."

The old woman moved nimbly into the room and turned on the gaslights. "Filthy bugger. Must have come in through the coal chute."

"Don't swear in front of the children, Auntie."

"Bugger," announced Harriet loudly.

"You see?"

"What's this, Lady Hannah?" yet another woman asked. He looked up over his captor's shoulder, to behold a stick-thin woman glaring down on him. He gulped in terror.

"Another charge for the nursery, I believe, Mrs. Swift," Lady Hannah answered. "What are you lad, about six? Seven?"

"I don't know!" he couldn't help but answer, though he'd been told never to talk if he was caught.

"And what is your name?" Lady Hannah persisted in her gentle, but no-nonsense way.

"Kit," he answered. "Christopher." Somebody had called him that when he was little.

"Kit? Like a baby fox?" Lucy spoke up.

"You going to keep him?" Mrs. Swift asked. She didn't sound at all happy about it.

"He's a thief, Hannah," Aunt Phoebe pointed out. She held up papers she'd gathered from the floor. "And look what he took."

"I doubt the lad's aware he was committing treason, Aunt Phoebe." She examined him while she spoke. "He's covered in bruises. Someone has treated him very badly. Of course I'm going to keep him."

"Then I best get a bath ready," Mrs. Swift said.

"We have a brother, Harry," Lucy announced to the younger girl.

"A thief in the family might come in handy," Aunt Phoebe decided.

"Bugger," Harriet said.

The adults laughed, before correcting the little one's language. "A *brother*, Harriet."

At no point did anyone ask Kit what he wanted, but he was caught, good and proper for the moment. He'd try to make his escape later, but right now he judged it was best to keep quiet, and suffer through having a bath.

Harelby House
Yorkshire, England
1854

"You have a beautiful daughter," the midwife who opened the bedroom door announced. She held a newborn wrapped in a soft blanket toward him.

"A girl," Maxim said, scratching his graying curls. "How very interesting." It took him a moment to work through whether or not he should be disappointed at this dynastic setback, and he decided that he did not mind at all. He took the baby into his arms and examined it with a solemnity that soon turned into wondrous joy. She had her mother's coppery hair, not as much, of course. "Peach fuzz," he murmured, running his thumb across the top of his little girl's tiny head. "And how on earth did she get such perfect little fingers?"

"They come that way," the midwife answered, and stepped out of the doorway so Maxim could carry the child into the bedchamber, and the waiting arms of his darling wife.

Eleanor was sitting up in a nest of pillows in the center of the wide canopied bed. Though she looked tired, her beautiful youthful face shown with pride and love. "My dearest, you make me feel young again," he said, settling down beside her, carefully handing the bright-haired bundle to her lady mother. He brushed her lips ever so gently with a kiss. "Now you have given me a princess," he whispered. "You have my heart and my gratitude. I pray that someday you will also have the gratitude of the Bororavian people."

Even flushed with pride and love for the child they had created together did not stop his lovely wife from turning a stern look on him. "We've discussed this before, Maxim."

He sighed. He felt like winter faced with the adamant heat of summer. Though he was only fifty-one, persistent illness made him feel much older. "My dear," he reminded his wife. "She *is* a princess."

"Yes, she is, if you must be technical about it," Eleanor conceded. "But it would be very dangerous for her to be proclaimed crown princess of Bororavia, now wouldn't it?" She gazed lovingly on the babe. "Do you know how relieved I am to have a daughter? You have enemies, Maxim," she reminded him. "I want our child to inherit your intelligence, your gentle wisdom, and your beautiful eyes. I do not want her to inherit the enmity of your vicious nephew. I certainly don't want her to be put in danger by a claim to the inheritance of your lo— of your kingdom."

"Of my *lost* kingdom." He added the word for her. Maxim loved Eleanor for loving him as a retiring scholar and country squire rather than as the exiled King Maxim IV of Bororavia. She loved *him*, but it also saddened him a little that she was so adamantly opposed to even a hint of anything that might put him—and now their child—in danger from international intrigue. "It is not as if I am going to try to raise an army and overthrow the usurper in my daughter's name," he pointed out to his wife. "By the way, what is her name? Perhaps Princess Soforonia Ikaterina Elisabetha? That would satisfy tradition and the shades of several of my illustrious female ancestors. Perhaps we should add 'Victoria,' to flatter the good queen who allows me to reside as a guest in her country. What do you think of Soforonia, my love?"

"Lily," Eleanor replied. "I want to name her Lily."

"Lily?" He stared at the bundle in his wife's arms. The baby lifted its red and wrinkled face and yawned. "What sort of name is Lily for a princess?"

"Lily," Eleanor persisted. "Lady Lily Victoria Bancroft. I think it sounds like a lovely name for a simple country girl." She turned her stern look upon him again. "Don't you?"

He did not think so at all. Bancroft was his English mother's name. He had used it when he fled his throne and homeland after being overthrown by his usurping nephew. Eleanor first knew him by that name. As much as he might wish to disagree, he reluctantly saw the wisdom of protecting his child from the dangers of political intrigue. This little one was likely to be the only child he ever sired. She was precious, evidence of the love he and his young wife shared.

"Lily is a very pretty name," he finally agreed. He took the baby from Eleanor's arms and smiled upon her with all the love in the world. "You shall be a good, simple country girl," he declared. "And never give a thought about being a princess at all."

Chapter 1

London
1880

"Dance with me."

Beside her, Lady Ornov huffed in shock, but Lily was so taken by the shape and beauty of the hand held out to her that she was barely aware of the effrontery of the request. He was not wearing evening gloves, this man who'd approached her from out of the crush of the crowded ballroom. It was an utterly masculine hand, but long and slender-fingered, made for elegant, graceful gestures, yet without concealing inherent strength. Her fanciful imagination told her that this was a hand that was as at ease holding a weapon as it was being held out in a gesture of request.

"Dance with me," he repeated.

As no one had ever asked Lily to dance before, the words seemed almost foreign to her, but the rich timbre of the stranger's voice sent a deep shockwave through her. She'd run through quite a gamut of emotions recently, among them grief, fear, and helpless fury, but her reaction to the man's voice was certainly something new. And she liked it, strong and vivid though it was.

She couldn't help but smile. She couldn't help but look up into dark, dark eyes, and say, "Gladly."

Lily shifted her gaze quickly after that bit of boldness, but she didn't back out of the agreement to dance, though she knew the action might cost her. She thought Lady Ornov might actually grab her by the back of her ball gown to keep her from stepping away from the wall, for the lady took her position as chaperone very seriously. Whatever her chaperone might have done was quite swiftly moot, for the stranger whisked her onto the dance floor with a grace that masked the amazing speed of the movement. When they began to whirl in time with the music, it was magical.

Well, it would have been more magical if she had not stepped on her partner's foot first thing.

"You dance beautifully." Her partner lied without even a wince.

"I hope I didn't hurt your toes too badly."

"A tiny thing like you? Doubt you even scuffed the shoe leather, my dear." His fingers shifted subtly on her waist, to control her movements better, Lily supposed.

Though she was slender, she hardly thought of herself as little, for she was rather tall for a woman. Willowy, was the term her mother used, countering her father's contention that Lily's stature was regal. Her cousin Gregory called her a skinny roan colt, which she didn't mind hearing from him at all. She didn't want compliments from King Gregory of Bororavia.

"You look suddenly sad." Her partner's concerned voice broke into her thoughts. "Are you worrying about my shoes? I beg you not to give them another thought."

"I was not thinking about your shoes," she answered, trying to adopt his teasing tone while cursing her inability to hide her emotions. She had thought she was quite good at schooling her features to keep her thoughts to herself until this moment. Perhaps her partner was more discerning than most, or his charm made her guard slip. She'd have to be more careful. "I'm not used to dancing so quickly," she answered as they twirled deeper into the swift-moving crowd.

"You've never waltzed before?"

"Oh, yes. But never with anyone under sixty," she confessed.

"How do you know I'm under sixty if you won't look at me."

"I suppose I could be wrong in my estimation, but you don't feel . . . wrinkled."

He laughed, and the infectious sound drew Lily's gaze to his face for the first time. If she'd thought his hands, eyes, and voice attractive, they paled in comparison to the entirety of the smiling countenance before her. How dark eyes could be so bright, she did not know, nor did she understand the thrill of excitement they communicated to her. The twinkle of roguish merriment lit up his whole face. It was a long face, with sharp, chiseled cheekbones and a wide, mobile mouth. His hair was a rich, dark brown with a hint of red in it, very thick and a bit too long for fashion. It was probably auburn in the sunlight.

His smile flashed bright white teeth, and he asked, "Whatever are you thinking, my dear?"

"That you do not look quite *reputable*," Lily answered, speaking her mind before she could stop herself.

"Quite correct," he replied before she could draw breath to apologize for such an outlandish statement. "Very discerning of you."

Lily wanted more than anything to laugh, but she managed to control the impulse. Still, she was a bit breathless when she said, "First I trod on you, now I've insulted you. You really don't have to put up with this."

His smile was mellow and warm, as was his

voice when he answered. "Every action has a price, my pretty. I didn't expect to dance for free."

Lily did not at all know how to take this comment. Was this handsome stranger insulting her? Teasing her? She was a person used to plain talk and plain actions. That she now had to navigate her way through a world that was anything but plain and simple did not exactly confuse her, but she often found the necessity of always being on her guard quite irritating. Once one learned guile, how did one unlearn it?

She did agree that this dance came with a price for her, but a scolding from Lady Ornov was a fair enough punishment for this small act of rebellion. She felt as if she hadn't moved in weeks, but now she was being rushed along into a new world of warmth and color. She was used to plenty of fresh air and movement, but even a brisk walk on a cool, bright spring morning had never afforded anywhere near the stimulation she was receiving from a few minutes in her companion's arms. She felt as light as air, caught up in the music and her partner's smile, dazzled by candlelight and the rich colors worn by the other women dancing around them. She had never felt like this before, and never wanted it to end.

"I could dance with you forever," she said, her thoughts slipping away from any restraint once again. Where had all her newly found caution gone?

He looked thoroughly surprised at her words, as well he should be. But the hand on her waist moved to draw her closer. "Forever will last only a few more minutes," he told her, his voice low and compelling. "Alas."

A shiver went through her. Her answer was a whispered, "Alas, indeed." Then Lily laughed, trying to make her declaration seem like a sophisticated joke. "This is my first proper waltz," she explained.

"I'm sure it will not be your last. Princesses are often called on to dance."

His tone made no pretense at this being a simple statement, but this time Lily's reply was as regal a nod as she could manage. If she spoke, too much might spill out. He was, after all, a stranger. Just because he was handsome, broad-shouldered, and a fine dancer was no reason to instantly trust him. She didn't even know why she wanted to. Perhaps it was the smile. "What is your name?" she asked. "I don't believe we've been properly introduced."

His dark eyes glinted with mischief. "Improper is ever so much more fun, isn't it?"

"I wouldn't know," she answered primly. "Princesses are not allowed to be improper."

Somehow, they were even closer together than they'd been before. "Then why are you dancing with a stranger?"

He had long legs, and Lily was more aware of the muscular thighs brushing against hers than anything else in the world. She tried to ignore the not unpleasant sensations stirring her blood and made herself concentrate. "Because you asked," she answered. "Why did you ask me to dance?"

"This is my favorite waltz," he replied. "And you were the only lady under fifty that seemed to be without a partner. It seemed a logical choice."

She accepted the prick of disappointment, and managed to nod again. "Yes. I can see that."

"Why were you without a partner?" he asked. "Were you waiting for the king?"

She couldn't stop the caustic burst of laughter. "Gregory? Oh, no. Gregory's off somewhere smoking cigars and plotting ways for Bororavia to conquer the world." He cocked a quizzical eyebrow at her, and she conceded, "All right. Not the entire world. I'm sure he doesn't have any ambitions to rule the British Empire."

"I'm happy to hear it."

"So am I. I'm quite used to Queen Victoria's silhouette on the coinage and postage stamps. I still don't know your name." What she did know was that this man tempted her to commit all sorts of indiscretions. She should not have spoken of the king of Bororavia in public to a stranger, and certainly not shown her lack of respect. What if someone overheard, and reported her joking words?

"Don't you?"

She almost jumped, but his hands held her still and steady. "Don't what?" she asked in confusion.

"Know my name." His eyes crinkled and he tilted his head to one side. The effect was both charming and teasing.

"You aren't going to tell me, are you?"

"You speak English very well," he said, "with a delightful accent."

"I sound like I stepped off a Yorkshire sheep farm, you mean. I have a dreadful country accent and know it."

"Nonsense. You have a lovely grasp of the language."

"I should hope so. It's my Bororavian that's a bit rusty. Fortunately, I don't have to speak my father's native language here in London."

"Ah, London," he said. "My native soil, though I don't come here often. Of course, I find that after I spend a few days in London I tend to start dropping *H*s. It's the company I keep in town, I'm afraid."

"One does meet the wrong sorts of people at embassy balls," she agreed. "Cutpurses and pickpockets—"

"Cardsharps and ruffians of all sorts," he added. "I can't imagine what a lady such as yourself is doing in such company."

"I had to come," she told him. "The ball's in my honor." She found herself leaning close to whisper in his ear. Her cheek brushed against his, and the effect was quite extraordinary. Her breathing was a bit ragged when she whispered. "I'm really quite old for it, but this is my coming-out party. I was quite firmly on the shelf until tonight."

"And now here you are dancing with a rogue and ruffian."

She looked his face over carefully. "No visible scars, so at least you don't look like a ruffian."

"The scars don't have to be on the outside, my dear."

"How true," she agreed solemnly. Then she made herself abandon the sudden understanding seriousness that seemed to have taken hold of both of them. "What an odd conversation we're having. And what is your name?"

The teasing look took over his features again. "Does her highness command?"

Her highness would like to command that this dance go on for the rest of the evening. Her partner confused, amused, and stimulated her. She had never been so drawn out of herself before. His bold touch was quite unlike anything she'd ever felt; it had led her toward an unexplored world. There was mystery here, and excitement. She wanted it to last.

"Her highness does not command," she finally answered, looking into his eyes. A smile tilted up his wide mouth, and she wondered what it would be like to experience her first kiss from those lips. Wondering about it would be something to keep her company in the future. "Her highness thinks you should tell her your name—when next we meet." Even though a second meeting was unlikely, it would give her something to look forward too.

As the music stopped, they came to a halt in the middle of the dance floor. He took a moment to kiss the tips of her gloved fingers with the merest brush of his lips. "I promise you a name when next we meet."

Then he was gone—

And Lady Ornov was suddenly there, insisting that Lily return to her place by the wall. Lily sighed, and obediently followed her chaperone and stood rooted in place beside that formidable lady, being seen but not approached, until the last guest was gone from the ball. In all that time Lily did not catch a glimpse of her mysterious dancing partner again.

Chapter 2

Well!" Lady Ornov said, not for the first time. "Well!"

Lily sat quietly in a deep chair near the sitting-room fire and watched her chaperone, or lady-in-waiting as Lady Ornov preferred to be called, pacing the rather threadbare carpet. Lily's own feet ached from an evening of standing in a pair of pretty, but uncomfortable, shoes, so she found herself almost wincing in sympathy for every agitated step Lady Ornov took.

Personally, Lily was more than happy to be sitting, though the chair was a bit lumpy. The furnishings in the residential area of the Bororavian Embassy were not quite shabby, but they shared nothing of the grandeur of the newly refurbished public rooms. At another time Lily might even have found this room rather comforting and homey, but sitting here in her magnificent ball gown and jewels, she felt more out of place than ever. The dress was a silvery blue confection, beaded and embroidered and draped with matching lace. The pale color of this magnificent creation was certainly suitable for wearing to an embassy ball. The dressmaker had specially designed it to show Lily's complexion, hair, and form to perfection. Lily had to admit she felt beautiful in the gown, but—

It should be black, Lily thought with a surge of guilt and grief. Or if not black, at least dark gray. And she should not be attending balls yet, even if Bororavian mourning customs were not those of England, as Gregory had gruffly explained to her. She smoothed a wrinkle in the heavy fabric. Despite the king's command to her to think otherwise, she felt English, and English custom suited her fine. But it had only been eight months since her father died. *This is wrong. I should still be at home, still in half mourning instead of attending parties.*

Yet if she hadn't attended the ball, she would not have met her mysterious stranger, she would not have had those few minutes of swirling pleasure to hold in her heart as a bit of light in this dark time . . .

"Oh, please," she whispered under her breath. "A little less melodrama, if you please, Lily Bancroft."

That she was unhappy went without saying, so she made herself stop feeling guilty about the impropriety of ignoring mourning customs when her present actions were no fault of her own. And she would save any romantic fantasizing about her dark-eyed dancing partner until she was quite alone. If King Gregory of Bororavia—her distasteful and treacherous cousin—wished to see her, she had best keep her wits about her.

So she kept still, and simply tried not to be noticed while her chaperone continued to pace and mutter. Lady Ornov had insisted Lily wait here, "at the king's pleasure." Lily had only seen her cousin once this evening, and from a distance, at the very beginning of the ball. She would be perfectly happy to keep it that way. Seeing Gregory even once a day was more than enough.

What she desperately wanted was to be alone, to go to bed, to be out of sight, and out of mind of all the strangers who filled her life. She had shared laughter for a few moments tonight, and experienced a rush of unfamiliar pleasure from a touch, a smile, a flirtatious glance that took her mind off her troubles. Lily wanted to go to sleep thinking about the ball, at least dwelling on the pleasant moments of the evening—dancing, for instance, with a handsome, charming—

"Well!" Lady Ornov said once again, louder than before.

Lily looked up to find Lady Ornov staring at her with deeply concentrated annoyance.

"Whatever is the matter?" Lily asked.

"You were smiling," Lady Ornov declared.

"Was I?"

"Yes. Dreamily." Lady Ornov shook a finger at her. "Don't think I am unaware of what you were thinking, Highness."

"I was thinking about getting out of my corset," Lily confessed. "And into my nightgown."

"Shameful!" Lady Ornov declared. "Wicked! I knew I should have stopped it. I knew it."

"Stopped what?"

"I have more discretion than to say."

Lily's temples began to throb, confusion added to the tension and exhaustion that already plagued her. She'd had quite enough. So she stood and started toward the door.

Lady Ornov put herself between Lily and the exit. "Where do you think you are going?"

"To my room. I am going to bed," Lily asserted. She tried to speak with high-handed imperious-ness. Lady Ornov did not look impressed, no one ever did when she tried to be regal. Lily wondered if she got the tone wrong because she was so tired. Possibly it was because she was a very improper princess. It was the lack of training, she supposed.

"I am sure that whatever Gregory wants can wait until tomorrow," Lily pleaded. "I'm certainly not going anywhere. Besides, he's probably forgot-ten whatever it was."

What she meant was that His Royal Highness had probably drunk himself into his usual evening stupor by now and was happily snoring on the bosom of some temporary mistress. She knew about his penchant for women; Lily even knew about the official mistress back in Bororavia. Or was she in Paris at the moment? Lily had over-heard a snatch of conversation between Gregory and Lady Ornov about Countess Irenia that indi-cated the mistress *en titre* was closer to the proceed-ings in London than Gregory would have liked.

Lady Ornov considered Lily's reasoning, and for a moment it looked as if she was going to waver, and let Lily out the door. But before she made up her mind, the door opened. King Gregory entered, but not alone. Two men and a woman followed him into the large sitting room. It was the woman who slammed the door dramatically behind them.

Lady Ornov gasped and whirled around. "Ire-nia!" She put her hand to her heart. She put herself between the woman and Lily. "You should not be here. How dare you?" Lily had no trouble looking over the smaller Lady Ornov's head to see Count-ess Irenia's reaction as Lady Ornov scolded, "You will leave at once. I insist!"

"Oh, do be quiet, Mother," Irenia answered. "I have made up my mind to be at my beloved's side. He agrees. Don't you, Gregory?" the mistress de-manded of the king.

Gregory looked pained. Lily hid a smile. She was used to Gregory being bullying and beastly. It would be nice to see him being bullied for a change. Lily was a bit embarrassed at Countess Irenia's barging in, but more for Lady Ornov's sake than for her own. For all that these people had thrust her into the center of their lives and intrigues, she tried to avoid personal involvement. She tried to remain aloof, to guard her heart and soul from them. She wasn't very successful at it, of course, but she did try. She was growing fond of Lady Ornov, for example, because the lady tried so hard to be a proper chaperone, companion, and teacher of Bororavian ways. Lily knew that proud Lady Ornov felt ashamed and heartsore from her daughter's fall from grace. But it was an "honor" to serve the king. And from what Lily gathered, Irenia had been serving the king for at least ten years.

What an unkind thought, she thought, and smiled, only to realize that she was being observed by her other cousin, Duke Michael. He was leaning against the mantel, attempting to be inconspicuous, as usual. And, as usual, he held a wineglass in his hand. Michael was another member of the Bororavian court Lily had trouble being indifferent to. She quite liked him, though she wished he didn't drink so much.

The family connection was complicated. Her father had a half sister, the Grand Duchess Sofia. Sofia's first husband had been a Russian prince, and their only child was Gregory. After the prince died, Sofia followed her heart and married Bororavia's greatest general, only the general happened to be a Gypsy. Despite the large Gypsy population in Bororavia, the marriage was considered a scandal, though apparently it was a very happy marriage. Michael was the couple's only child. He was only a boy when Gregory usurped the throne. Like Lily's father, Michael was sent into exile. However, when Gregory's late wife did not present him with any heirs, Michael was eventually recalled. Michael was the closest thing to heir presumptive—and Gregory hated the idea of the throne not going to a full-blooded Bororavian. The country's nobles didn't much like the notion either, and revolt was threatened if Gregory didn't remarry and father an heir.

Which was where she came in.

Lily knew that she was, technically, the real heir to the Bororavian throne, which she didn't want and hadn't asked for. She had two estates in Yorkshire and Northumbria to manage, along with a great many sheep. She had many progressive plans for those lands and the sheep. Gregory didn't care. He wanted a legitimate son, and Gregory had an unfortunate tendency to get exactly what he wanted. By any means necessary—which meant taking Lily as his bride.

"So *that's* my replacement."

"Don't be ridiculous, Irenia. I have no intention of replacing you."

"Highness—" The third man in the room spoke up, his reedy voice high-pitched with shock. He was a thin, pale, old man with a long silver beard, dressed in black priest's robes. "Be careful what you say, sire," Bishop Arkady, the Metropolitan of the Bororavian Orthodox Church warned. "There are impediments enough to your betrothal without any declarations of insincerity of intentions."

Lily watched in dread as Gregory whirled to face the old priest. "Insincerity? Impediments? I'm determined to marry the girl." He pointed at Arkady. "I don't want to hear anything about impediments!"

"But they exist," Arkady persisted. "There is the matter of faith. No ruler of Bororavia may wed a member of another religion."

"You're here to see that the girl converts."

"*If* she professes a true wish to practice the faith of her fathers. There is also the matter of her godmother's approval to be obtained."

"Why?" Gregory apparently was not aware of this new diplomatic wrinkle in his plans.

"Her godmother is Queen Victoria," Michael spoke up.

Lily's only contact with the Queen had been at her baptism when she was a month old, so she had no memory of the occasion. Victoria had acted as godmother as a mark of favor to the exiled king living in her country, and now it seemed that small political favor might act as some protection against Gregory's plans. She wondered how Michael had heard of her connection to the Queen.

At Gregory's glare Michael took a sip of wine, and began to explain, "Head of the Church of England and—"

"I don't really care." Gregory made a dismissive gesture, and Michael concentrated on his glass once more.

"There is also the matter of consanguinity," Arkady went on relentlessly, not ready to concede to the king's temper. "You and the princess are first cousins, sire."

Gregory's face was red with rage, but he replied calmly enough. "My mother was Maxim's half sister. Surely that makes us less than *first* cousins." He smiled coldly at the head of the Bororavian church. "Besides, haven't I already ordered you to issue the official dispensation so that we can marry?"

"Marry!" Irenia shouted. "I think not!"

Irenia's angry pronouncement brought Lily's attention back to the recently arrived mistress. She stepped away from Lady Ornov's protective shadow and faced the woman on the other side of the room. "Good evening," she said politely. "I trust you had a pleasant journey. May I ring for some refreshment?"

No one ever bothered to ask Lily's opinion of the king's wedding plans so she concentrated on trying to be civilized when she would much rather have squared off against Gregory and shouted as loudly as he did. Shouts and defiance might have provided some emotional satisfaction, but they would do no good. Lily knew that what she must do was tread carefully while appearing to be a mild as milk, pliable miss.

The countess, who was really a very beautiful woman despite her furious expression, snickered. It was not a pleasant sound. "Refreshment? I've already had my *refreshment* for the evening." The glance she turned on the king was one of such obvious sexuality that even someone as innocent as Lily could understand the meaning. "As soon as I arrived I was welcomed into the arms of my be—"

"Enough," Lady Ornov interrupted her daughter. "You were not invited to join the king here in England and have no—"

"Yet I came! And he welcomed me back to his bed. Didn't you, Gregory?"

"It wasn't a bed, Irenia—but you entertained me far more this evening than those vapid English nobles could."

So that explained Gregory's absence during the ball.

As though reading Lily's thought, the king ignored Arkady and Lady Ornov's gasps and turned on her. He demanded, "What's this I hear about you scandalizing my guests?"

So that was why he had wanted to see her, to reprimand her because she had dared to dance while he could make love to his mistress and brag of the act. Lily fought off the temptation to sigh, as she'd known she'd have to pay for her tiny indiscretion sooner or later. Better sooner, she thought as she folded her hands in front of her and tried to look puzzled. Gregory was a tall, heavily built man, broad-shouldered and thick in the middle. He never hesitated to use his physical size to intimidate. Lily always tried to pretend that she didn't know exactly what he was doing when he loomed over her like he did right now.

"Scandalizing?" she repeated. "I am sorry, sire, but I do not understand what I could have done to displease you—"

"You danced with a foreigner," he interrupted, his large hands held in tight fists at his hips. "And far too close for propriety's sake."

"Oh, dear," Lily answered. The person that was far too close was the king, but she babbled on as though unaware of his closeness. "I didn't really consider that he was a foreigner. He was a guest, and I tend to think of myself as English—which, of course I am not, but I do forget when I get flustered. It was my first ball. I am not at all used to such social occasions. I certainly meant no impropriety."

"It was only the one dance," Lady Ornov pointed out. "Her Highness was the soul of discretion through the rest of the evening."

"Do you want to see my bride tainted? To ruin my reputation?" Gregory shouted—Lily wasn't sure at whom.

He *was* quite the high-stickler about notions of

purity. Other people's, not his own. Lily had heard quite a bit about his demands for an unsullied, virgin bride since her arrival at the embassy. There'd even been a medical examination.

"And it wasn't all *that* close," Michael added. "Your spy made the tale up. I saw the dance from across the room, and it was perfectly innocent."

Lily didn't dare glance at Michael to show her gratitude. Michael wouldn't want any more attention than he'd already drawn to himself. She couldn't help but wonder if he was in his cups, because he'd spoken to Gregory twice in the last few minutes, and that was not like him. Lily was well aware that Michael disliked Gregory as much as his half brother despised him. Michael was simply more civil about it.

"If you saw her dancing, why didn't you put a stop to it?" Gregory demanded.

"Dance with your intended myself before you, you mean? Oh, no, not likely." Michael held up his glass. "Besides, like you, I found a distraction early in the evening. Unfortunately, we both ignored our dear cousin. I think it is we who owe her an apology."

"Apology!" Gregory thundered.

"I don't want an apology," Lily told them. "All I want is to go to bed. And . . ." She hesitated as Gregory glared darkly, but finally worked up the courage to say. "I would like to see my mother, if you please."

Gregory's florid face went even redder. He took a deep breath, as though he was getting ready to shout again, but the bishop said, "That is certainly a reasonable request."

Gregory gulped, and he glared, first at the elderly clergyman, then at Lily. "Perhaps you may have a visit with your mother next week."

Next week. She wanted to protest, but the cold look in his eyes kept her from pushing the issue. She nodded and said, "Thank you, sire."

"Go," he answered, and stepped aside to let her make her escape out the door.

Chapter 3

"I'll bid you good night, Aunt," Kit said, and kissed her swiftly on the cheek.

"Not so fast," Lady Phoebe Gale said, and grasped the lad's wrist before he could slip away with complete impunity after escorting her home in a hansom cab. "Come along with me, my lad."

She led him into the sitting room off the front hall, where a warm fire and golden lamplight waited. It was a room full of flowers and china figurines, a place suitable for a little old lady who gossiped over needlework. It was, in fact, the headquarters of an espionage network Lady Phoebe had overseen for much of her life. She employed many members of her extensive family in this patriotic enterprise.

Once inside the sitting room, she took her favorite seat, put her tired feet up on a footstool, and regarded the young man who hovered near the door. He looked very much as though he wanted to be elsewhere, rather like a defiant schoolboy waiting for a dressing down by the headmaster, she thought. Just when she thought he was being petulant, he tilted his head to one side, and gave her a devastatingly winning smile.

"Hmph. I am not easily won over, if you recall," she responded, and couldn't help but smile back.

Slippery was one word that defined the charming Kit Fox MacLeod very well, but Phoebe was a creature of steel-covered velvet, with ice water in her veins. The ice melted occasionally for members of her family, and this particular great-nephew tended to warm her more than most. She was especially fond of this lad that her niece Hannah had adopted. He was a rogue and a charmer, and she'd seen to it that his talent for taking things that belonged to other people had been trained and polished until he was the finest burglar, pickpocket, and all-round thief in the British Empire. He served the Queen, of course, as did every member of the MacLeod clan, but no thief was ever completely honest. In Kit's case a streak of deviltry came out in a tendency to be a thief of hearts, kisses, and maidenly virtue. He was quite the shameless plunderer when it came to the ladies, preying on affections with casual impunity.

"You are not getting away with anything this

evening," she informed him, and gestured for him to sit. He declined with a shake of his head.

"What have I done?" he asked. The look of puzzled innocence was most fetching on his long, sharp-boned face. Oh, he was a handsome child.

"If you weren't perfectly aware of exactly what you have done, you would not ask."

"Did you have an unpleasant evening?" He put his hand over his heart. "Was I inattentive?"

"You were not supposed to be attentive to me, and in that you were admirably successful. I wanted you to enjoy yourself."

A dimpled smile lit his face, and a thick strand of dark hair fell becomingly across his forehead. He looked like exactly what he had always been, a rogue, a rascal, and a bane to all convention and good sense.

"Whatever were you thinking when you approached that girl?" she demanded, her tone as severe as it could possibly be.

"I was thinking that she was the prettiest girl in the room," he replied, as insouciant as he could possibly be.

"She is a princess."

His smile only widened. "If a cat can look at a king, Aunt, I don't see why a fox may not dance with a princess."

He did it out of boredom, she thought, because the embassy ball had certainly not been the most stimulating event. He did it because he could, she knew. Well, the girl certainly hadn't said no. Scandal generally required the cooperation of both those involved. *Two cooks to brew a scandal broth*, as her mother always said—after Phoebe managed yet another escapade all those decades ago.

Phoebe's expression softened the tiniest bit as she looked at Kit. She was not reckless and in love with walking on the edge of danger anymore, but there had been a time . . . She and the lad were a great deal alike in spirit, even if they shared no blood connection. "I'll grant that hardly any harm was done, Kit."

"Hardly?" Kit protested. "I wanted to dance. The lass wanted to dance. We made quite a nice couple on the dance floor, I thought, and I didn't steal any of her jewels. I admit I was tempted to take at least a ring as a memento, but a good look at her jewelry showed that what looked like diamonds were paste."

"You never steal anything but the best," she agreed.

"She was the prettiest woman there," he went on. "Lovely, I thought. I always pay court to the prettiest, now don't I?"

"Your attention has made—and almost ruined—a few debutantes," she agreed.

"It was her coming-out ball," he went on. "She told me so. A girl, even a princess, deserves a dance at her first ball."

"It was hardly your place—"

"No one else paid her any mind." He chuckled. "It was like she was a jewel set on a high pedestal, meant to be admired but not touched. How could I resist snatching a jewel, if only briefly? She reminded me of a ruby. Or a pink diamond. It's not fashionable, but I like red hair, and hers is red enough to light the room." He grinned shamelessly. "Of course she did step on my foot at first, but with a few private lessons I'm sure I can have her dancing to my lead quite—"

"No," Lady Phoebe interrupted. She waggled a finger at him. "You are not to approach the young lady again."

"Why not, Aunt?" Though Kit's tone was as light as ever, there was something dangerous in his eyes.

"Because it would not be—"

"Proper?" he interrupted.

She was surprised by the tension suddenly radiating from him. Whatever was the matter with the boy? "Perhaps *politic* is a better word," she answered.

"I see," he said. There was cold fury in the words.

She rose and took a step toward him. "What is the matter with you, lad?" He drew himself up stiffly, obviously not wanting any physical contact. This was very unlike the affectionate Kit. "What have I said to set you off?" she asked.

"The very fact that you feel it necessary to give

me a lecture sets me off," he answered. "You are the last person I expected to ring a peal over me because I dared look above my station for a few minutes."

She laughed. "*Ring a peal?* I haven't heard that term since my mother's day."

"It's a term *you* used to use all the time."

"Really? I don't remember. I do try to move with the times, Nephew. Now, perhaps when you were a child—"

"I was a nameless, homeless, thieving ragamuffin," he reminded her, with a bitterness she'd never heard from Kit before. "Now you see fit to remind me of my lowly birth."

Phoebe bridled. "Do I?" she asked, reaching the edge of anger herself. "In what way? Why would I?"

"You clearly don't feel that a man such as myself is fit for a princess such as—"

"Good, lord, what's gotten into you?" She eyed him critically. "Don't tell me you're attracted to the girl?"

"Or course not!" he answered vehemently. "But I don't wish to be ordered away from her."

"Were you planning on seeing her again?"

He hesitated. She could tell he wanted to tell her that it was none of her business. Finally, he said, "Perhaps."

"Well, you can't," Lady Phoebe said. "And stop glancing at the door as though you're about to storm out before I can explain. I locked it when we came in."

"When has a lock ever stopped me, Aunt?"

She chuckled. "I hope one never does, my dear. Sit." The word was an order, and this time he obeyed, stretching out his long legs and folding his arms across his chest while he waited for her to take her seat.

Once settled into her comfortable favorite chair again, she said, "The only reason I was annoyed when I saw you dancing with the princess is that I do not like seeing *any* member of my family calling attention to themselves. We were not at the Bororavian Embassy to be conspicuous."

"Why were we at the embassy?" he asked. "You never told me why you wanted me to attend, but I didn't think it had anything to do with an assignment."

"Neither did I, until halfway through the ball— after you and the chit put on your little show."

"It was one short waltz."

"With two very close bodies. I do believe the temperature in the room went up a few degrees while everyone's attention was on the pair of you. I can think of another term for seeing two healthy young people moving in rhythm so closely together—but never mind the dance, it's over and done with." She did not like the dreamy look that came into his eyes. No doubt her words had conjured up carnal images that hadn't already occurred to him, which had not been her intention. "It was Sir Malcolm Meevers who asked me to attend the Bororavian's ball. He is representing the Crown in negotiating some delicate treaties with the Bororavians."

"We have treaties with Bororavia?" Kit questioned. "Until tonight I was barely aware of the place's existence. It's a backward little dictatorship somewhere in the Baltic region, isn't it?"

"We have treaties with everyone," Phoebe pointed out. "Especially trading treaties. That is why Britain is an empire. Bororavia's only interest to Britain until now has been that it boasts one of the finest ports in the Baltic Sea. Bororavia has always been important to our shipping interests. Russia has attempted to influence Bororavia's relationship with Britain. It is Russian interests that are currently behind the increase in port duties and shipping taxes that Sir Malcolm is attempting to negotiate down to reasonable rates."

Kit listened to her with increasing boredom, his posture growing more and more relaxed, until at last he could keep from yawning no longer. "And what does this have to do with us, Aunt?"

"I wondered that myself when the invitation to the ball arrived from Sir Malcolm. Since I'd heard you'd just escorted a few of your sisters down from Skye to visit Harriet, I found that I yearned for your company."

He gave a bark of laughter. "I think Lucy, Bea,

and Sara's main interest is more in shopping than visiting with a love-blind sister just back from her honeymoon. I've settled into my old rooms at Bristol House for some privacy. Of course you knew that already, or your message to meet you tonight wouldn't have been delivered there."

"I know everything that goes on in this city. Besides, Harriet told me. I thought you might enjoy a bit of entertainment after performing so worthy and thankless a task. So I invited you along."

He glared at her. "I already had an engagement for the evening when you summoned me."

"Did you?"

"Yes. You kept me from exploring several new dens of iniquity I've heard about."

"Really?" she asked, with feigned innocence.

"I've been out of the country for nearly two years, Aunt. I have a great deal of British-style debauchery to catch up on. So you took me to a boring ball held by an unimportant foreign power to save me from having a good time?"

She smiled. "Having seen you with Princess Lily, I fear my stratagem was a failure."

"Lily?" His expression softened. "So, that's the girl's name."

"The butler did mumble. She's King Gregory's cousin, I believe. There's an odd story going on there, but nothing to do with our assignment," she hastened to add. "Sir Malcolm approached me at the ball and asked for our aid."

Kit sat up straight. "This Sir Malcolm knows about the family business?"

Phoebe gave a fondly reminiscent smile. "Malcolm and I have been close friends for a very long time. Malcolm has begun to suspect that King Gregory of Bororavia is involved with a group of anarchists."

"Excuse me?" Kit sat forward. "He's a king. Isn't assassinating all monarchs one of the prime tenets of anarchist philosophy? I would think that the last thing this King Gregory would want is to associate with a rabid band of international fanatics who want him and all his monarchist kind dead."

"You would think so, wouldn't you? Still, I trust Malcolm's instincts. What he wants from us— you—is to find written proof that King Gregory is involved with an anarchist plot. One aimed at the British monarchy. Malcolm believes Gregory brought a pair of known anarchists into the country among his diplomatic entourage, but we have no proof of this."

"You want me to ransack the embassy in other words."

"Yes."

"You might have mentioned this while we were there."

"If I had known in time, I would have. Malcolm didn't get a chance to speak with me until late in the evening. He'd almost been locked in a room with the chief Bororavian negotiator all day and barely got away for a few minutes. The embassy ball was the only place he could talk to me."

Kit nodded at her explanation, but his mind was already on the assignment. "*He* was detained, so *I* miss the perfect chance to search the premises, without breaking and entering." He sighed. "What a wasted opportunity."

"You did get the chance to dance with a princess," she gently teased.

He was all business now, and waved her words away. "I'll dance later, Aunt. And not with an enemy of my country," he added. "No matter how fascinating this Princess Lily might be."

Chapter 4

*O*f course, Lily might not be involved in her cousin's schemes.

It occurred to Kit that if the princess was an innocent bystander, a pawn unaware of any wicked plots, rather than an active enemy of the state, then seeing her again might not be such a dangerous thing. For he wanted to see her again no matter what he'd told Aunt Phoebe, and not only because he'd been told it was forbidden. Of course, Lily might have forgotten him as soon as their dance was done, but he could make renewing the acquaintance extremely pleasurable for both of them.

Perhaps I can even make seducing her part of the job.

Of course, that would not be honorable.

And since when do I worry about the honor of anyone who isn't one of my sisters?

These odd and foolish thoughts came to Kit as

he stood on the tiny balcony outside his bedroom. They'd been coming to him for hours, interrupting more practical thoughts about how to go about finding documents secreted in a foreign embassy. They kept him from rest, and from focusing properly on the job.

The residential hotel overlooked Bristol Square, one of London's many pleasant fenced-in parks. His rooms were on the second floor, and he appreciated the balcony not only for the view, but also as an extra means of exiting and entering his quarters should the occasion warrant. It was always wise to be prepared for anything.

One thing he had not been prepared for was still having his mind on a beautiful girl so many hours after meeting her. It was not that long from dawn, and here he was leaning on a railing, staring across the city. Kit had a half-empty flask of brandy in one hand and an unlit cigarette in the other; as though he was still waltzing with her, his thoughts revolved around a princess named Lily. The brandy was there to help him relax. So far, it hadn't proved much help.

He'd rolled the cigarette out of habit but had no intention of lighting it, and was annoyed that he wanted it so badly, though a month had passed since he'd last smoked. He was trying to break the habit picked up while living in America, and not because both his parents had expressed the opinion that cigarette smoking was a nasty practice. He

was abstaining from it now because an odor from
the smoke clung to clothes and skin, and it was un-
wise to carry even the faintest recognizable trace
when going about his business. There was a great
deal that could not be left to chance to remain successful in a world full of life-and-death risks. He
liked taking risks, and he liked to win, which
meant every risk had to be carefully calculated,
whether it looked that way or not.

He smiled, and spoke to the night. "Then, sometimes, I like to take risks for the hell of it." He remembered how warm and good his hand felt
grasping Lily's willowy waist. He remembered her
voice, deep and rich as creamy chocolate. An un-
commonly beautiful, womanly voice. A bedroom
voice, he thought.

"Welcome to my bedroom," he had said. *She looked
up at him, wide-eyed and expectant. Her lips were
parted slightly, moist and inviting.* "Hardly fit for a
princess, but . . ." *He put the tip of a finger on the delicate point of her chin and tilted her face up. He breathed
in the fresh scent of her skin while he lowered his mouth
to hers.*

Kit shook his head to dispel the cloud of fancy,
though he couldn't help but glance wistfully back
into his bedroom with a faint smile. His body was
tight with wanting. "If I let my imagination run
away with me I'm never going to get any rest tonight."

He wondered what Princess Lily would think

about his fantasy. Or him, for that matter, for surely she was used to mixing with only the cream of the crop, the elite of the ton, with princes rather than paupers. He'd never had anything but a jaded, cynical view of the upper classes, despite his love and respect for the aristocratic ladies who'd first taken him in and the decent, dangerous man who'd married Mum and given Kit his name. Kit appreciated his family, and was proud of being a MacLeod, but MacLeods were different despite their aristocratic lineage. MacLeods worked for a living. MacLeods respected people for their worth, not their pedigrees.

Wonder what Her Highness would think of the MacLeods?

After a moment he tossed the unlit cigarette over the side of the balcony, straightened, and took a small sip of brandy. The view of the park across the way gave him an idea. He remembered noticing that there was a similar square across the street from the embassy. He had sisters visiting London. Surely the girls would like to accompany him on a walk. If the embassy was guarded—and *if* there was a conspiracy involving anarchists afoot—then one lone man spotted anywhere in the area would raise suspicions and security would be tightened. But place a gaggle of pretty girls giggling and cavorting—not that it was all that easy to get MacLeod girls to giggle and cavort—in the square, and the lone man accompanying them would not be noticed at all. He could use them as cover for a daylight reconnoiter of the embassy grounds. And not only as cover, for the MacLeod girls were trained espionage agents. Of course, Sara and Beatrice were a bit young yet for any dangerous activities, but he and Lucy could use the expedition to give them pointers.

And if he should happen to run into a princess in the park . . .

No. That wasn't likely. Nor was it to be wished for.

"Business, my lad," he reminded himself, in a fair imitation of Aunt Phoebe's crisp tones. "Never let your guard down on an assignment. Never get involved."

Right. If Mum and Da had listened to that, and Harriet for that matter, where would the rest of the clan be? Still, it was best to take Aunt Phoebe's advice. At least for now.

The dance was over, but the mysterious stranger did not let her go. The teasing look in his eyes deepened into an enticing summons, and she was powerless not to respond. The hand on her waist drew her into an imperious embrace, and suddenly she was whirled from the dance floor and onto a starlit balcony. They were alone and she was in his arms. She could not help but run her fingers through the silky thickness of his rich brown hair. Scintillating warmth swept through her as his thumb traced the outline of her collarbone, up her throat and slowly across her lips. Her mouth opened at this touch, while her heart raced and her head fell back against the strong support of his arm. He claimed a kiss with—

"Highness, did you hear me?"

Where am I, she thought? Oh, yes, she'd just walked out of the dressing room into her bedroom in the embassy, though she'd been too distracted to notice what her maid had chosen for her to wear this morning. Lily blinked, noticed her dress was cream and blue print, and focused on Lady Ornov's concerned face.

"Are you all right?" Lady Ornov asked. "You looked as though you were a thousand miles away."

Lily could not help but smile at her lady-in-waiting. She glanced briefly out the sunlit window. "Not nearly so far as that." Generally when she daydreamed her imagination took her home to the peaceful environs of Harelby House. Homesickness was not the subject of this morning's flight of fancy, though she was experiencing a yearning that was nearly as strong. She'd never been given to daydreaming at home, where she'd been happy and needed nothing to shield her from fear of the future. Of course, she'd never met anyone as fascinating as last night's mysterious waltzing partner. If she closed her eyes she could almost feel his hand still on her waist and—

She took a deep breath, fighting off fancy as she

gestured at the pile of envelopes resting on the writing desk. Except for letters from her mother, Lily wasn't used to receiving correspondence at the embassy. "What's all this?"

"The butler delivered them while you were dressing. It seems the ball given for Princess Lily last night was a success," Lady Ornov answered.

Puzzled by this smug answer, Lily went to pick up the first envelope on the pile. The paper was heavy and expensive, and had been sealed with a blot of deep red wax. Though the seal had been broken, Lily could make out that a crest had been stamped into the warm wax. "Impressive," she commented and turned the envelope over to see who had sent it. "Duchess of Pyneham . . . I've heard of her. Why would she be writing to me?"

Even as she spoke, Lily knew she'd made a silly comment. She knew she had to stop thinking of herself as Lily Bancroft.

"Well, *Highness*, I suggest you read what the duchess has written and find out," Lady Ornov replied.

Lady Ornov took the matter of rank very seriously. Her father had too, Lily had to admit, when her mother hadn't been looking. Lily's mother was something of a revolutionary, at least certainly a radical about some things, such as class and status. Mother consorted on an equal footing with sheep farmers, artists, poets, philosophers, craftsmen and the local gentry, and expected her husband and daughter to do the same. In fact, Lily thought that her mum was often slightly embarrassed at having married an exiled king, though she doted on him to distraction. Lily missed her wonderfully eccentric mother desperately, and worried about her welfare constantly.

Lily unfolded the paper and read. When she realized it was an invitation, her first thought was, Maybe he'll be there. She tried not to be excited.

It had nothing to do with her personally, Lily knew, for she'd hardly had the chance to get to know any of the people who were not eager to have her attend their functions. It was the title they wanted. None of these people would be interested in issuing invitations to a country bumpkin like Lily Bancroft, but the cousin of the king of Bororavia was an entirely different matter. And so what? Let them use her, she would use them right back, everyone would get what they wanted and no harm done. They wanted luster, she wanted a way out. No knight in shining armor was going to come riding to Lily Bancroft's aid. Or to the princess's for that matter.

Good lord, I never imagined I'd end up like a princess in a fairy story, locked up in a tower—or is it a dungeon?—in need of rescue.

"You look amused," Lady Ornov observed.

Lily glanced sharply at the other woman, saw

that Lady Ornov looked genuinely pleased for her, and managed a tight smile for the Bororavian noblewoman. She couldn't resent Lady Ornov's role. The woman was serving her king and country. Neither of the Ornovs were responsible for Gregory's actions; they did their duty at his command. In their own way they were quite honorable. She was stern, but not unkind, and she certainly had her own troubles, what with her constant concern about her daughter Irenia's gleeful and long-term fall from grace as the king's paramour.

"Not amused," Lily prevaricated. "Pleased. Gregory wanted to make a social splash, and has succeeded." She held out the invitation, then recalled that she did not read English as well as she spoke it. "We've been added to the guest list for the Duchess of Pyneham's ball tomorrow night."

Lily quickly glanced through the rest of the pile. "I have no idea who anyone else is, or which invitations to accept."

Lady Ornov came over and scooped up the papers. "The Pyneham affair is appropriate for you to attend, of course. As for the rest, it is enough for you to have seen them. The embassy's social secretary will attend these and present you with a schedule of activities later. No need to worry your head over anything, Highness."

Lily almost screamed in frustration. She *wanted* something to do, even if it was only writing polite notes to strangers. No need to worry her head, was there? Fine for Lady Ornov to say; her head wasn't about to be thrust into an unwanted matrimonial noose. Then again, Lady Ornov thought Lily should be delighted at her current circumstances. This thought softened Lily's reaction enough so that she actually managed to smile at her lady-in-waiting. "Then what shall I do today?" she asked. "More embroidery?"

Chapter 5

"**A** walk in the park would be an acceptable pastime, don't you think, my dear?" Lord Alexander Ornov declared as he stepped into the sitting room. "And good day to you, Highness," he added, along with a precise bow, when he saw Lily. He then concentrated his considerably charming attention on his wife.

Lily watched Lady Ornov's face light with joy at the sight of her husband, and bent her head in concentration over her embroidery hoop to give the pair as much privacy as possible.

Lord Ornov was a very busy man. Not only was he King Gregory's chancellor, he was also the country's chief diplomat. It was Lord Ornov who was in charge of the current treaty negotiations with Britain. Lily did not know what these negotiations entailed, as no one seemed to think it was any of her concern. She did know that Lord Ornov was very, very busy, and had very little time for his devoted wife.

"A walk in the park?" she heard Lady Ornov say. "I don't know. I've only just started the most complicated part of this design on your new vest."

"I would like to wear it to the meeting with the Prime Minister, my dear," Lord Ornov told his wife. "But I think you can spare a few minutes away from your stitching on such a lovely day."

"But—"

The heavy door banged open so hard it hit the wall, cutting off Lady Ornov's answer. Lily looked up anxiously, though the sound of rough laughter and wild giggling eased her anxiety even as she saw Gregory reel into the room. He grasped Irenia tightly around the waist, and her feet dangled off the floor. The king wore only a shirt and trousers, and his lover was working on unbuttoning the shirt. The front of Irenia's dress was unfastened far enough to show the lacy top of her chemise, and her thick dark hair tumbled in disheveled locks around her shoulders.

Lord Ornov stared at his daughter in shock.

Lady Ornov pushed over her embroidery stand as she shot to her feet, her hand covering her mouth.

Lily stared at this carnal tableau with a combination of revulsion and curiosity. She noted that the countess's full lips were bright red and swollen from kisses, her cheeks were pink, and her eyes bright with pleasure. She looked at Gregory and found him repulsive. He was burly and hairy and rough. She could not imagine his hands on her, touching her the way he touched his mistress. She couldn't bear the thought of having him look at her in the possessive, hungry way he was looking at Irenia. The thought made her go cold, and she had to put her hand over her mouth to fight off the urge to throw up.

Gregory put Irenia down. Rather he slid her down his body until she was on her feet, though she was still pressed tightly against him. Irenia threw back her head, and the king bent to kiss her throat.

"Sire!" Lord Ornov spoke up. Gregory spun away from Irenia with a surprised roar of fury. Lord Ornov put himself between Lily and the king. "Apologies, sire," he said hurriedly.

"Father!" Startled, Irenia put her hands over her mostly exposed bosom. Then, spotting Lily over Ornov's shoulder, she met her gaze and dropped her hands, as though daring Lily to compete with such magnificent cleavage.

"No contest," Lily murmured, her hand still covering her mouth.

"What are you people doing here?" the king demanded, glaring around the room. "Can't a man have any privacy?"

"Irenia, what are you doing here?" Lady Ornov demanded. "And in such a state?"

Irenia tossed back her hair. "Gregory and I were looking for somewhere private to—"

"Have a discussion," he interrupted, quickly buttoning his rumpled shirt.

"Our nuptials," Irenia purred.

"Don't be ridiculous," Gregory replied. He turned his look on Lily. "I'm marrying a virgin."

"I was a virgin when we met."

His gaze swung back to his mistress. "You were not. I found you in General Presisky's bed."

"Irenia!" her mother gasped.

"And I shall go back to it if you marry that—" she pointed at Lily—"skinny foreigner. I'll let him finish the deed he started."

"So many years ago," Gregory reminded her.

"Sire," Lord Ornov interrupted. "We were preparing to go for a walk in the park before your arrival. With your permission, the princess, my wife and myself will proceed with our plans." He gestured Lily and Lady Ornov toward the door.

"Fine," Gregory answered, even as they scurried to make their escape. "Go. Leave. And close the door behind you."

"I'm not letting you marry her!" was the last thing Lily heard as the door closed.

She couldn't help but wish Irenia well.

* * *

"Sara, I don't see how you can manage to walk and read at the same time," Kit heard Lucy say to their youngest sister. Kit was walking beside Beatrice on the tree-lined path ahead of Lucy, the oldest of the MacLeod girls, and Sara, the youngest.

"It is an acquired art," Sara answered.

"Well stop it," Kit said. "It makes you look conspicuous."

"Oh. I hadn't thought of that."

"Mum says Sara will take a book to her hanging," Beatrice spoke up.

"Well, it will give me something to do while waiting."

"Let's hope it doesn't get so far as that," Lucy said.

"Sara would never be hanged," Beatrice said.

"That's right," Kit agreed. "MacLeods never get caught."

"Then what about that scar on Da's neck?" Beatrice wondered. "I've always meant to ask him about that."

"Don't," Lucy advised. "It upsets Mum."

"I would attend a hanging, though," Sara told them. "If I could get the fresh cadaver to autopsy."

Kit felt Beatrice's shudder. "Euww! Sara!"

"How else am I supposed to study anatomy?"

Lucy laughed. "I'm sure Kit could explain a thing or two about male anat—"

"Euww!" Sara interrupted. "No thank you! I

don't want to know about gender relations. It's bad enough catching Mum and Da kissing in every nook and cranny of Skye Court. I'd rather be hanged than caught behaving like that."

"Besides, Mrs. Swift already had *that* discussion with us," said Beatrice.

"Mrs. Swift?" Kit asked, and shuddered. "I don't think I'd want to have been in on that conversation." While he was quite fond of the family's formidable housekeeper, there were some things he couldn't imagine her doing.

"Well her name is *Mrs.* Swift," Lucy spoke up.

He glanced back at her. "I think that's only a courtesy title. I shudder to think of what happened to *Mr.* Swift, if there ever was one."

"I do not think we should discuss Mrs. Swift's personal life," Sara said primly. "Or anything personal for that matter. Or I shall go back to reading while we walk."

They'd entered the park through the gate on the opposite side of the Bororavian Embassy. It was a pleasant park, larger than the square across from Kit's residence. The criss-crossing paths were lined with white gravel that crunched beneath their feet. The walks wound through a small stand of trees, past a pond and through a garden full of flowers. There were many benches scattered throughout the gentle landscape. Ducks argued in the pond, and fat pigeons strutted along the paths and perched on a fountain waiting for handouts. The morning fog had burned off, and it was shaping up to be a rare cloudless day in London. It was a perfect day for a gentleman to escort a group of young ladies on an outdoor jaunt.

"Sara, my love," Kit said as they approached the street entrance closest to the embassy. "I believe we might have a use for your book after all." He led his sisters to a pair of benches that faced each other in the shade of a huge old oak tree. "There now," he said once everyone was seated. "Sara can read to us—which gives us a perfectly sensible reason for lingering in one place for a while should anyone be watching from that large white building across the street. No. Don't look that way, Beatrice. My job is to lounge lazily against this tree and pretend to listen and gaze at you ladies admiringly while I am, in fact, making a study of the embassy grounds and the comings and goings of its inhabitants."

"So endeth today's lesson," Lucy added.

"Well, if the girls are going into the family business—"

"I am going to be a physician," Sara declared.

"I already am in the family business," Beatrice pointed out.

"You are not a field operative," Lucy told Beatrice. "But if you want to be one there's a great deal you have to learn. Read, Sara," she directed.

Sara looked around, blushing. "You won't find what I'm reading interesting."

"That doesn't matter," Lucy answered. "We'll act interested, no matter what boring medical tome you're studying. I might enjoy it."

"You are a botanist, Lucy," Beatrice said. "Of course you'll enjoy boring scientific writing."

"You're still blushing," Kit said to Sara, who held the book she'd brought with her tightly against her chest. "That's a novel, isn't it?"

"Novels can be educational," Sara answered. "But I—"

"Read," Lucy ordered.

Kit thought Lucy's tone sounded just like Mrs. Swift at that formidable woman's sternest. He wouldn't have argued further, and neither did the embarrassed Sara. She opened her book, and the family's outspoken critic of all things emotional began to read the opening page of a famously passionate novel.

Chapter 6

❧

The guard who'd accompanied them from the embassy held out a cautious hand, halting them from proceeding up the path. "There's someone up ahead."

Lily sighed, and felt compelled to point out, "This is a public park, Captain Cherminsky. People have a right to be here." The place had been remarkably quiet. They had made three circuits of the grounds so far without encountering anyone until now.

Lady Ornov clutched her husband's arm tighter. "I hear voices."

Lily might have laughed if everyone hadn't been so seriously worried. Bororavia was a dictatorship, she recalled, ruled by a usurper who relied on spies and threats to keep control. She suspected that there must be a continuous current of unrest bubbling below the surface, enough to keep people nervous even when they were visiting a place as peaceful as a London park.

"There's nothing to worry about," she declared, and slipped under their guard's outstretched arm to walk briskly forward. She was not going to have this outing spoiled by a bit of uncalled for anxiety.

She heard the crunch of gravel on the path behind her, and ignored Lady Ornov's call as she eluded the Bororavians. She soon rounded a gentle curve and spotted a tableau of three young women seated on benches in the sunlight. The voice they'd heard belonged to the youngest of the trio, and she was reading aloud from a book.

"*Wuthering Heights!*" Lily nearly shouted with delight, instantly recognizing the passage the girl was reading. She couldn't help but hurry closer as the reading stopped and the eyes of the strangers were all turned to her. "I grew up in Yorkshire," she explained. She came and sat down on one of the benches without asking leave or introducing herself. She hadn't realized she was so lonely that she'd start babbling to total strangers at the first sign of anything familiar. "In fact, when I was little I had a pair of Jacob's rams that I named Heathcliff and Cathy. Cathy's a ridiculous name for a ram, I know, but I was too young to know better at the time. They were wretched creatures that forever wandered off their pasture—which meant I had the ridiculous privilege of—"

"Running across the moors shouting Cathy and Heathcliff," an amused male voice finished for her.

She recognized that voice. She leapt up to face him. "You!"

"Me," Kit answered, for the moment frozen in place by the sight of her copper hair and smiling face in the bright sunlight. Did she have any notion how lovely she looked? And fresh? And vulnerable? A princess should not have so frank an expression, he was sure of that. Especially an expression that showed such open delight that he could not help but respond.

He knew he was grinning like a fool when he spoke to her, but managed to tame the rush of elation into a more acceptable smile when he stepped away from the shade of the oak. His sisters were on their feet and staring as he bowed.

"Delighted," he murmured, and found himself kissing Lily's palm before he knew what he was doing. Once his lips touched the soft skin of her hand, he couldn't help but move on to brush his lips across the inside of her wrist.

"Oh," she murmured, and the sound was more of pleasure than of shock.

He glanced up at her face and found her flushed and wide-eyed. So innocent, he thought, so delightfully ripe for the picking. His blood sang with the knowledge of how pleasurable it would be to teach this beauty the ways of the world. His thumb slowly caressed the spot on her wrist that his lips had touched.

"He never does that for us," he heard Sara complain as he straightened.

"Ahem," Lucy said.

He glanced over Lily's shoulder into the stern face of his eldest sister. He knew exactly what she suspected, that he'd lured them there as cover for an assignation with a pretty girl. He frowned at Lucy. As if he'd ever draw Bea and Sara into anything so improper. A bit of spying was acceptable for them, but witnessing one of their brothers flirting with a bit of crumpet was not.

"I don't kiss *your* hand because you are not a *real* princess, Serendipity," he informed the youngest. "Your father only *calls* you princess."

"He does no—" Sara managed to curb her indignation as she recognized the code word that warned them all that they should shield their identities.

"You are still holding my hand," Lily spoke up.

"I notice you are not trying to pull away," he whispered.

"I see," she whispered back. "So you don't intend to take full responsibility for such improper behavior."

"Why should I?"

"Perhaps I should slap your face for insolence." The words were stone, but she smiled as she spoke.

"You can't," he countered. "I'm holding your hand."

She smiled slowly. She had a rich, full mouth, and he very nearly kissed her then and there. "Why, indeed?"

Lily did not know what was the matter with her. Actually, she did. It was him. Or, more likely, it was the idea of him, she tried to tell herself. Someone who was handsome, witty, young, who looked at *her*, spoke to *her*—someone who was *not* King Gregory of Bororavia. She couldn't flirt and tease as though she were a free woman. Her fate was not in her hands. And until last night's dance with this impossibly attractive stranger she had inwardly railed against it, but not openly rebelled. She knew her behavior at the moment was improper at best, and perhaps completely mad. She knew that to get hold of her actions she must first detach herself from his strong and steady grasp. For the truth was, this man made her emotions fly off in a hundred different directions.

One of the stranger's companions stepped up and said, "Have we a real princess here or a shepherdess, for I would like to know whether we are supposed to bow or ask for advice on foot rot?"

The woman tried to make her tone light, but Lily heard the suspicion underneath. Lily looked at her and guessed she was the eldest of the three young women whose afternoon she'd so rudely interrupted. She could hardly blame the woman's attitude after she'd behaved so strangely. Besides, it belatedly occurred to Lily that her dancing partner was escorting a *trio* of young women. She was stung hard by a stab of jealousy when it hit her that perhaps one of the attractive women standing next to him might be more than his friend. Lily truly did not know anything about him, after all. Not even his name, she remembered.

"Excuse me, but who—" she started to ask.

"You should curtsy, my dear," Kit said to the oldest girl. This drew Lily's attention away from her jealous curiosity.

"Please don't," Lily said hastily.

"For this is indeed a princess. The lady is from Bororavia and—"

"My father was from Bororavia, I'm—"

"She is staying in that lovely, large building across the street. It is the Bororavian Embassy. Princess Lily and I met last evening."

"Briefly," Lily added.

"But memorably."

He smiled at her, and for an instant she thought she was going to melt.

He turned back to the oldest girl again. "And what do you know about foot rot?" he asked.

"You'd be surprised," the woman answered. "There's someone coming . . ."

Kit gave his sister an annoyed look, but heeded her warning and moved away from Princess Lily. He glanced up the path and saw a trio of people moving toward them. He recognized the woman who'd been Princess Lily's watchdog last night. She looked most unhappy now. With her was an elderly and rather official-looking gentleman. Leading the way was a burly fellow in a military uniform. It appeared that the princess required an escort and guard—yet seemed to be mischievous enough to slip away from supervision for at least a few moments if she wanted to.

And didn't that sound promising for the prospects of future assignations?

Hold on, lad, he reminded himself. She's off limits, remember? Don't even think about her while you've got a job to do. Emotions were distracting when there was a job to do. Yes, yes, he knew that lesson. It was a good one, a true one; a damnably irritating one if a man wanted to have a bit of fun with a fresh pink lily that was all ripe for the plucking.

Kit Fox, you should be ashamed of such thoughts in front of young Beatrice and Sara.

He scolded himself, but was ashamed of nothing in front of the eldest, of course. Lucy was a woman of the world—but *she would* scold him later if he didn't extract his family from what looked like a possible confrontation with an angry group coming from the place they'd been sent to reconnoiter. With that thought firmly before him, Kit forced his thoughts away from his "Pink Lily," and to the matter at hand.

"You are gracious to have taken the time to speak to us, Highness," he said quite formally as Lily's attendants came within hearing distance. "We will withdraw now, if you do not mind." He took a step back, and another, and gestured for his sisters to move away as well. He did not let himself feel any regret when Lily looked puzzled and a little hurt.

"But—"

"Highness!" The soldier was among them before she could finish. "Who are these people?" he demanded.

The soldier looked faintly ridiculous, Kit thought, with his hand on the hilt of a dress sword in a peaceful London park, especially surrounded by a gaggle of harmless young females. Harmless-looking, Kit amended, aware that Lucy at least would not have left the house without carrying something more lethal than a parasol.

Though the man looked foolish to Kit, Lily's reaction showed that she did not see his presence that way. "I am so sorry I hurried ahead, Captain Cherminsky. I meant no harm. I'm afraid I am the one who intruded on these people."

"We must go," Lily's chaperone declared. "You have a fitting for your gown for Duchess of Pyneham's ball."

"Come," Cherminsky ordered. "We have been out too long."

Lily flinched under their words, and cast a miserable glance toward the embassy building that loomed across the street. Kit had noticed the guards at the door, dogs in the yard, faces regularly appearing in windows as the inside of the house was patrolled. There was even someone on the roof. It would not be an easy house to enter. Nor to leave, he thought, and noticed the strain deep in the princess's eyes.

She's frightened of them, Kit realized. What did a princess have to fear from her own people?

He could not let it concern him. "You must go," he said. "Forgive us for intruding on your walk. We must be off as well." He gave a slight bow, stiff and formal, then turned to his sisters. Lucy had already hustled Sara and Bea toward the nearest gate. He followed after them without looking back.

I still don't know his name, Lily thought as she followed Lord and Lady Ornov through the embassy's front door. *He broke his promise to tell me his name when we met again.*

He didn't introduce her to any of his friends, either. There was something peculiar about that. What was she missing? What had she done wrong—other than babbling like a fool and behaving so familiarly with someone who wouldn't even tell her his name. He hadn't seemed disappointed to see her. The look in his eyes made her feel alive, and *so* aware—of her body. And his. For a few moments she'd soared, but now she'd crashed back to earth, and everything about the incident was confusing and awful.

She did not know why she was so disappointed, but still not knowing the identity of her dancing partner after a second meeting hurt her far more than it should. Seeing him had been an unexpected delight, but now she felt let down and confused. She felt as though she'd somehow been made a fool of, while she was also embarrassed at having behaved foolishly. She fought the impulse to look back before the door was shut on her prison again. It would do no good anyway, for Captain Cherminsky followed close behind her, and his height and width would block out any view of the outside world.

So Lily marched determinedly into the wide front hall of the embassy, and was surprised to find the king and Bishop Arkady standing face-to-face in front of the staircase. Michael was there as well, but standing well away from Gregory and the bishop. Gregory looked furious, and the bishop stern. Michael looked like he'd rather be anywhere else.

A moment later, Lily wished so as well, when Arkady stated, "It is my duty to point out that you have not fathered any children. Not with your late wife, nor with your mistress of many years. It is your duty to your kingdom, sire, if you truly wish the continuation of your dynasty, to reconsider marrying Princess Lily yourself."

The king's lips curled back over his teeth in a terrible snarl of rage. "If you were not a priest you'd be dead right now for speaking like that to me."

"It is my duty as a priest to always tell the truth, sire, no matter that you do not want to hear it. If you love your people, you must consider Prince Michael as—"

"Never!" Gregory shouted. "I would never let that filthy maggot into a princess's bed." He laughed, and it was a very ugly sound. "I'd only throw the girl at my Gypsy brother as punishment if she'd already proved herself a whore."

Lily wanted to cover her ears or, better, die and sink into the ground. She couldn't help but look toward Michael, and to her surprise it was pity she saw in his gaze. Not for himself, but for her. She couldn't bear that. She couldn't bear being around any of her so-called family anymore.

"Come, Lady Ornov," she declared. "We have a dress fitting to attend to."

Gregory's head swung around at the sound of her voice, becoming aware of her for the first time. She did not glance at him at all, but marched purposefully toward the stairs. Much to her relief, both the king and the bishop stepped aside to let her pass, and no one said a word.

Chapter 7

"**A**ren't you supposed to be cracking a safe about now?" Lucy asked, without turning away from her mirror.

She did not comment on his expertise at silently entering her locked bedroom at Kestrel House, where she and the girls were the guests of their sister Harriet. Instead, she calmly continued finishing her toilette for this evening's party. Perhaps she did not want to spoil him with praise.

Kit glanced at the clock on the mantel, then their gazes met in the mirror. "It's far too early for housebreaking," he told his sister. "Though my plans for the evening do not necessarily include it."

He had spent last night and all day today considering options and methods for successfully pilfering the Bororavian Embassy, but his plans were not yet set. So, he'd put the operation in the back of his mind to simmer.

"I've come to bother my sister while waiting for a brilliant idea for getting past dogs and guards to pop up, fully formed like Athena out of Zeus's brow. You smell good," he added, catching a whiff of her delicate, spicy scent. "Did you brew your perfume yourself?"

"Of course." Her tone was serious, for Lucy took great pride in her abilities as botanist and chemist. She could brew a potion to kill you, cure you, or make you fall in love.

"In another era you would have been burned as a witch."

"I suppose I would have."

"You look lovely," he offered, when not even the faintest flicker of amusement softened her expression.

"I look acceptable for accompanying Bea to her first ball," she countered. "And that is enough."

He didn't try to argue the point. Lucy considered herself to be quite plain, even took a perverse pride in it, but she was wrong. "Is Beatrice attending the duchess's ball?"

"She's seventeen, Kit."

"Really? I hadn't realized." He shrugged off a pang of sadness. "I go away for a couple of years and my sisters grow up without a by your leave. I ask you, is that fair?"

She sighed, and ignored the question. "Anna

was supposed to do this, but hared off to the continent instead."

He came up behind her and put a hand on her bare shoulder. Her fashionable emerald-green ball gown showed a bit more sisterly skin than he approved of, but he fought down the prudery MacLeod men tended to show toward their womenfolk. He'd meant it when he said she looked lovely. "You are left to perform social duties you despise," he commiserated. "Poor dear. It's a good thing I'm here," he added. "To keep you company and save you from boredom. I thought you might need my arm to lean on tonight."

Lucy finally looked away from the mirror and up at him. "I had noticed that you are dressed for a ball."

He touched the lapel of his black tailcoat. "My tailoring, as usual, is exquisite." He stepped back. "The coat sets off the width of my shoulders, don't you think?"

She did not look impressed. She stood and turned to face him. "No," she said.

"No what?"

"No, you may not come with us to the ball. No, you may not use me as a pretext to attend the ball. No, you may not use attending the ball as a flimsy excuse to see the princess again. *No*," she added for emphasis.

Kit looked surprised, and he was a very good

actor. "Sister!" he protested. "How could you think—"

"I had tea with Aunt Phoebe this afternoon," she interrupted. "She warned me you might try to see the girl again at the Pyneham ball, despite your promise not to have any more contact. Our aunt is a spy mistress, after all. Don't think she doesn't keep tabs on all of us. Of course, after yesterday's incident in the park I didn't need the warning."

"Incident?"

"You ogled her like a love-struck fool. Even Sara noticed."

He was outraged, and this time he wasn't acting. "I had no idea she would be there. She was completely surprised to see me—though, I could tell she was pleased."

"Kit, your vanity is beyond measure."

"So it is. But Lily wouldn't know how to plan an assignation if her life depended on it," he added. "She's as pure as the driven—"

"Sheep?"

He'd been working up to a good tirade, but Lucy's comment brought him up short. He peered at her curiously. "I beg your pardon?"

"Your princess seems to be fond of sheep. Don't you find that odd? There is a great deal odd about the Bororavians. You need to bear that in mind, Brother. You need to be careful."

"I am always careful on an assignment."

"I know. Your assignment is not altogether what I'm talking about." She sat back down on the dressing table chair, and he took a seat on the damask-covered bed. The colors in the room were all creams and rose, an incongruously soft setting for someone with Lucy's flinty disposition. "You have a reckless nature," Lucy went on. "A reckless heart. Don't let it rush you heedlessly on to any involvement with this princess. That sort of thing . . ." Lucy made a small, futile gesture. "It's not for the likes of you and me, my lad."

"My lad?" he asked, taken aback by her vehemence. "What do you mean by the likes of you and me?"

"You know exactly what I mean, Kit. We're a pair of street urchins, nameless charity cases Mum took in out of the goodness of her heart."

Her bitterness burned like acid. Her words also stung deeply because they were so close to the insecurities that had been bubbling inside him ever since he returned to Britain. "Good Lord, Lucy, have those poisons you brew gone to your head? You sound as if you expect me to tug on my forelock and be grateful for what crumbs I'm given."

"Exactly. Precisely. If you don't know your place, lad, you'll be put in it, and hard."

"I do not believe I am hearing this. There you sit, dressed in satin for a duchess's ball, and you tell me that you and I have no place—"

"Among our betters," she cut him off.

"We're MacLeods."

"Adopted. Mum and Da don't care. We're loved at home, and sometimes I resent that love. It didn't prepare me for the cold truth out here in the real world."

"And that truth is?"

"That the MacLeod name they let us wear is good enough entrée to the toffs' parties, but we dare step no further in. We have nice clothes, soft hands, and the right accent, but no breeding."

"Breeding?" he scoffed. "What about Harriet? She's happily wed to a lord. Mum and Da weren't exactly married when she came along."

"Aye. But remember that she is their flesh and blood. Mum's granddaughter to an earl, Da's from old Scots nobility, and knighted by the Queen besides. Harriet's birth records might cause a faint stir, but ours, if there were any, would cause a major scandal. We couldn't trace our ancestry without a police report. The mere fact that we're adopted makes us no better than trained monkeys in the eyes of the nobility. They might be amused enough at our presumptions to let us into their beds, brother dear. But they won't let us into their hearts, not once they know the truth about who you and I really are."

"I'd be content with the girl's bed." The words came out thoughtlessly.

Before he could take them back, Lucy said, "No you wouldn't. I saw how you looked at her."

"Must have been a trick of the light," he scoffed. "For I know better than to fall in love with anyone—especially a princess."

"Do you? You were raised a MacLeod. Mum and Da turned out to be the marrying sort, and now Harry's followed their example. MacLeods fall in love hard."

"As you've pointed out, you and I are not MacLeods."

"She'll use you if you give her the chance, lad. Just you wait and see."

"You can tell that from just one meeting with Lily, can you?" he asked, dangerously angry in defense of his own personal princess. For a moment he actually saw red.

It was the bleakness in Lucy's voice when she said "I know that type" that brought Kit back to his senses.

He found that he was standing before his sister, tense with outrage. He slowly relaxed, and some of his anger turned into concern. "Who was he, this bastard who left you feeling so unworthy and hurt? And does Da know his name yet? Or would you like me to cut his heart out for you?"

She smiled a little, and it was the saddest thing he'd ever seen. She made a small gesture. "Leave Da out of this. It's my business, and I deal with it in my own way."

"By nursing a secret heartbreak? No one knows, do they? Not even Mum?" He quite carefully did

not allow any indication of pity in his manner;
Lucy would not stand for that.

"There is nothing for anyone to know," she insisted. "Leave it, Kit, but learn from my lesson.
Don't pursue this impossible flirtation."

"Nothing is impossible, love."

She shook her head. "I think you really believe
that—and I suppose you must be considering what
it is you do as a profession. Don't attend this ball
tonight. Contact with the princess is dangerous."

"Did Aunt Phoebe tell you to deliver that message?"

"She shouldn't have had to."

Kit opened his mouth to say something
scathing, then closed it again as he could think of
no defense. Other than *I want her*! "I *am* spoiled," he
admitted. "I lack discipline."

He did not admit to his sister that he'd told himself at least a hundred times since he first held Lily
in his arms that she had no place in his bed, let
alone his life. Contact with her endangered his assignment . . . but he *wanted*. Wanted to see her, talk
to her, touch her. Simply because he couldn't have
her? Probably. The forbidden was always so much
more attractive.

"Then you will stay away from the ball?" Lucy
questioned.

He frowned. He wanted to pout. It left a taste of
bile in his mouth, but he started to say, "I wil—"

The door swung open before Kit could finish.

Harriet came striding in. She looked vividly beautiful in a blue and gold gown. "Good thing you left the door open, Luce," she stated. "For I might have broken it down when I went to knock." She stopped when she saw Kit, and said, "So, she didn't leave the door unlocked. You have very bad habits, Christopher Fox MacLeod."

"Would you have me mend my ways, Harry?" he asked as he leaned back on Lucy's bed.

"No." She turned back to Lucy. "Do you know what that man has done? Do you?"

"Which man?" Kit asked.

"Your husband?" Lucy guessed. "Women only get that sort of hellfire in their eyes when speaking of the men they truly love," Lucy explained to Kit. Addressing Harriet again, she asked, "What did Lord Martin Kestrel do to deserve your ire, Harry?"

Harriet gave a bark of laughter. "What hasn't he done? But most recently—this very evening— when he and I are to be the guests of honor at a ball held by his godparents in honor of our marriage, Lord Martin Kestrel, who is not even an *official* ambassador of her majesty's government, has been sequestered in some *delicate* negotiations with the Turkish ambassador. He sent a note," she added after she took a breath. "And his apologies."

"The swine," Lucy agreed.

"If he thinks I'm walking into a ball given for the both of us alone he has another think coming."

"You're terrified," Kit concluded.

"Petrified," Harriet agreed. She suddenly looked at Kit as though really seeing him for the first time. "You!"

He sprang to his feet. "Me?"

"You. Lend me your arm this evening."

He waggled his right arm like a duck. "Only my arm?"

"The rest of you looks presentable enough as well. I don't intend to attend my first London society ball unescorted."

"But Kit is engaged elsewhere."

Lucy sounded desperate, but Kit was not one who could resist temptation when more than one opportunity to fall from grace presented itself. "It is fate," he told Lucy. "Can you doubt I am meant to attend the duchess's ball? Harry, my love, I'll gladly break my engagement to escort my darling sisters. Anything else would be improper."

Lucy shook her head, but didn't try to argue.

Harriet said, "Then what are we waiting for? Let's collect Beatrice and be off. I, for one, do not approve of being fashionably late."

Chapter 8

Lily climbed into the coach with the last words of the latest scene ringing in her ears and unshed tears burning her eyes. It had started with Countess Irenia's confronting Gregory as they were leaving for the ball. Irenia was furious at not being included in the party—she was a countess! She was a lady of the Bororavian royal court! This was an outrage! An insult! How dare she be left behind? There were tears along with the tirade, and it all devolved into accusations that this slight, this affront was all Lily's fault. There had been abusive language directed at Lily. Worst of all, Gregory found the whole distasteful scene amusing, and eventually dragged Irenia off after telling them he'd join them later.

The last thing Lily had heard from Irenia was, "Play the princess all you like, but I'll see to it you'll never be queen!"

Lily had had to bite her tongue to keep from shouting back that she didn't want to be queen!

It was all so sordid. So very humiliating. She prayed that this would be her last sight of the Bororavian Embassy as the coach pulled into the street. Of course it would not be. Tonight she'd be displayed like a dressed up doll before the British nobility, then she'd be bundled back into the coach and returned to prison to endure yet more dread and humiliation.

It had to stop. Somehow *she* had to make it stop. Lily wasn't used to being helpless, she wasn't used to being a puppet, and she didn't like it. Much of the time she felt like she'd been thrown into deep water and was in danger of drowning. Every time there was a tiny bit of bright light, like the two encounters with her mysterious stranger, she only seemed afterward to sink farther into the depths.

She took a deep breath. The carriage swayed as it rumbled down the rutted cobbled streets. She had an instant of pleasure at the sight of passing buildings. She held on to the hope that maybe a few hours away from the embassy would do her some good. She needed to restore her balance, somehow.

I need to learn to swim.

Because she had no intention of drowning. She wished she could learn to fly, but since there was no escaping from Bororavian waters, she found a sudden determination growing in her to learn to navigate them. She made a vow to herself.

I will not be overwhelmed. And I will not be marrying Gregory.

Just because she was not sophisticated did not mean she had to be naïve. Trapped in this situation she might be, but surely she could find a better alternative than marriage to the man who must be the most disagreeable monarch in Europe. She almost smiled at this thought, knowing that most women would jump at the chance to marry *any* monarch. That was the object of fairy tale dreams, wasn't it? Pity that in King Gregory's case kissing the frog could not do any good. The man was already a pig.

"Turning into a frog would only be an improvement," she murmured.

"What's that, Highness?" Lord Ornov asked.

Lily glanced from the window to the couple seated on the opposite seat of the carriage. In the intermittent glow of gaslights on street corners she could easily see how pale and stricken Lady Ornov looked.

Lily leaned forward, concerned. "Are you all right?"

"She was a good girl, once, my little Irenia." Lady Ornov sniffed. Her shoulders shook with the effort to control her distress. Her voice shook as well when she said, "Before he corrupted her. I should never have brought her to court."

"Do not speak of such things," Lord Ornov cautioned his wife. He put his arm around her shoulders. "I'll speak to the king, try to persuade him to send her away. All will be well."

"And what will that change?"

Lord Ornov gave Lily a pleading look, and Lily realized the diplomat was imploring her to distract his wife from her misery. What came to mind was something Lily was curious about.

"Tell me, Lord Ornov," she ventured, "why is it that Gregory, a king of an independent nation, is so anxious for acceptance by British nobility? Why go out of the way to take part in the English social season?"

Ornov chuckled softly. "Why should a king be delighted to be invited to an old duchess's boring, silly party, you mean?"

"Well, I wouldn't put it that way, Lord Ornov, but . . . yes."

"For many reasons, Highness. When dealing with the games of kings you must learn to consider all the possibilities, all the ramifications, every favorable objective of each action. You must plot out moves and countermoves. You must learn how to make one move have more than one result."

"I'm not sure I understand."

"As the future queen of Bororavia, you must learn that everyone is your opponent, my dear, and how to keep them off balance. It is to your advantage to make everyone think you are doing what they want, and achieve your objectives before anyone realizes what those objectives truly are. You must learn the facts of political life, if you wish to aid your king in the service of your country."

But Gregory was not Bororavia's rightful king, and she did not think of herself as Bororavian. She did have sympathy for the people of that far-off land and wished them no harm, but she did not want to be their queen. She had been raised to be honest, to be nice, but not always to do as she was told. Gregory counted on her compliance, her passivity. He knew he had her were he wanted her. But—if she could find a way to make him think he was the one who didn't want her . . .

Her heart began to race. There was something he'd said . . . if she could but grasp what it was dancing about in the back of her mind. "Go on, Lord Ornov," she urged while she tried to remember. "Please tell me what you mean? How does going to parties achieve the king's goals?"

"The simplest reason is that being cooped up in the embassy during treaty negotiations, and clearing the way for your wedding, is boring. No reason not to be entertained while one waits. Another reason is to appear friendly and open to all things British. The British like to feel superior and important. Socializing with them will lull them into thinking that we will give them more favorable terms. Another reason is to gather information. But the most important reason for appearing to favor the British is to make the Russians nervous. Bororavia is in the shadow of the Russian Empire. The British Empire is their great rival. If the Russians think we have the British as an ally, they will woo us with gifts and favors to keep us loyal to their interests."

"So, we're visiting a duchess half a world away to trick the Czar."

"That is how the Great Game is played, Highness. The British and the Russians move countries around like chess pieces as they jockey to rule the world. Bororavia is but a small piece on the board, but there is no reason not to take what advantage we can from both the empires that use us."

Lily thought some more, only to conclude that this was all too much for her. "I see." She decided it was best for her to concentrate on her own problems. She said, "You've set my head spinning, but thank you, Lord Ornov."

"No need for you to worry about such matters, Highness," he answered. "It is not your place as a woman to play any active part in the games of kings. But it is best you be aware of the larger designs. Ah," he said as the coach came to a stop. "We're here."

"She reminds me a great deal of me at that age," the Duchess of Pyneham remarked.

"Except that she's a foot shorter," answered the duke.

"Not quite. She's a tall girl. Like I was. And with hair like mine."

"Silver?"

"Red, James. You do recall that my hair was once red?"

Kit knew about whom they were speaking. No names needed to be mentioned. He paused behind the old couple standing near the garden doorway as he came back into the reception room. He hadn't caught sight of Lily yet, and was making no effort to do so. She'd obviously made her greeting to the hosts or the ducal couple would not be discussing her. Just because she was here didn't mean he was going to go looking for her. Lucy was right: business and professionalism did come first. Never mind the other nonsense about the girl being too good for him. It was true, of course, but what respectable woman wasn't too good for him? He'd still made a private vow to listen to his sister's advice while Lucy glared at him through the coach ride. He swore that he would make no overt effort to approach the princess. But should fate bring them together . . .

Always hedge your bets was Kit's philosophy.

He shrugged, and shamelessly listened in on the Pynehams' private conversation, fascinated by what others thought of Princess Lily.

Besides, the spot where they stood next to the open French windows was probably the coolest place in the crowded room. Kit had spent the last few minutes having a vigorous walk up and down the garden paths, where the sounds of the city and the party were muffled and distant. He spent the time watching clouds fly across the moon, drinking in the rose-scented night air, and trying to rid himself of the urge to smoke a cigarette as he tried to keep his mind off the lovely Lily. He had no tobacco or papers with him, but every great house contained a smoking room for the gentlemen. He knew he could procure the makings of a cigarette at the merest suggestion to a servant. He chose to fight off the urge instead. Music beckoned in the distance as the orchestra began to play in the ballroom on the floor upstairs. Kit loved to dance, but he paused behind the elderly couple out of curiosity to eavesdrop on his hosts' conversation.

The Duchess of Pyneham was indeed tall, nearly equal in height to her husband. There were a few streaks of red left in her upswept hair. When she turned her head slightly, Kit caught sight of a sapphire and diamond tiara of such magnificence it made his fingers itch. Once a thief . . . he thought, as the couple continued to talk.

"*You* had red hair, Honoria" the duke answered his wife. "That girl's hair is copper. Not at all like yours."

"She has magnificent skin."

"You have freckles."

"I had a fine figure at that age. *You* said so."

"You were a strapping lass. That girl could eat more."

"She has lovely blue eyes."

"Without the need of spectacles as far as I can tell."

"All right, we aren't as alike as I'd thought. I'm a duchess, she's a princess."

"And she's never been kidnapped by pirates," the duke added.

"Pity," the duchess answered. "More girls should be kidnapped by pirates in these dull, straight-laced times. Would do them good."

"Honoria, I am shocked at such a scandalous suggestion."

"James, you are no fun."

"Then how did we come to have five children?"

The duchess was no more embarrassed at this comment than Kit's parents would have been. She laughed, and Kit could not help but smile as he moved off. The old woman's earthy good humor lightened his mood and he was unable to resist the call of the music swelling overhead any longer.

She was not going to look for him.

She wasn't.

Lily had made that promise as she entered the Pyneham mansion what seemed like hours ago. There had been so many introductions and brief conversations that it had taken her a long time to get from the front door, through the reception room, and finally find herself at the bottom of a very grand staircase indeed.

She made her promise again now as the crowd

on the staircase parted long enough to let a princess enter the ballroom. She was hot, she was starving, she had a headache, she wanted to go home, but she was going to dance. Lord Ornov had told her it was expected of her. She'd like to think she'd agreed to grace the ballroom with her royal presence so readily out of a sense of duty, but didn't lie to herself. She wanted to see *him*.

She moved slowly, mostly because her own pride wouldn't permit her to hike up her skirts and dash off in search of the only person she wanted to meet at this gathering. Perhaps those around her thought she moved with royal dignity, but in truth, she was only trying to curb her eagerness.

It was not right, or fair, or proper. What if she saw him, and he smiled at her? What would she do then? Her heart would break with longing even if she were to only see him across the room—

Well, perhaps that was a bit dramatic.

Perhaps.

She sighed, rather than give in to equally strong urges to laugh and cry.

Princesses do not do either, she told herself. Not in public, certainly. She was a representative of Bororavia. She'd use that as a shield against acting like a fool. Lord Ornov would be disappointed in her if she were to show anything other than a regal poise. And Gregory would be furious.

That thought alone very nearly stopped her in her tracks. But she couldn't turn and run with so many people watching, so she continued on, and found Lord Ornov waiting for her at the entrance of the ballroom.

"May I have the honor?" he asked, holding out a gloved hand to her.

She looked at him with relief, accepted the request to dance with a gracious nod, and did not search the crowd for a tall, graceful man with dark brown hair that had a hint of red in it.

"Time to make yourself useful as well as ornamental, as Mum would say."

Kit was not surprised that Harriet had managed to appear silently at his side, but he was surprised to see her alone in the ballroom. He had planted himself in the shadow of a potted lemon tree in a silver urn, and was watching the dancing while leaning with his arms crossed against the wall. He'd been trying to decide which one of the fiercely chaperoned young women standing across the dance floor he was going to cut out of the herd and ask to dance. Some of them were quite pretty, but he hadn't found anything appealing in any of them so far. Now, here was Harriet.

He turned to his sister, more glad of the diversion than irritated by it, not that he let that show with a sister. "Where's your husband? I last saw you clinging to Martin's side."

"Don't get me started on the subject of Martin Kestrel," she answered. "First he arrives late to his own ball, and seems to think I should be thankful he arrived at all." For all her outward show of irritation, Kit saw the gleam of fondness in her eye. It was his impression that the Kestrels took a certain amount of pleasure in irritating each other. "Now he's instructed me to find a subtle way for him have a word in private with a certain Lord Ornov," Harriet went on. "It seems he thinks I'm a mistress of intrigue."

"I can't imagine where Lord Kestrel got that idea." Kit straightened from his elegant slouch. "And how are you going to deliver this Lord Ornov to your husband?" he inquired.

Harriet gave a bright smile. "Why, dance him over to my darling, of course."

"And how do I fit into this plan?"

Harriet pointed with her fan to a spot where Kit had been trying not to look. "First I have to detach the elderly gentleman in question from that stunning redhead in yellow. I'm sure you're capable of distracting the young lady while I hustle away her dancing partner. Come along," she said, and pulled Kit onto the dance floor.

The music was a waltz. Gaslight and candlelight lit the room in a golden glow, and there, pale and perfect in the center of it all, was a copper-crowned Lily ripe for the plucking.

Within moments they were whirling purposefully in the direction of Harriet's objective. Kit went along with his sister on a breathless rush of elation. He didn't know if it was fate—a perverse one—or luck, or possibly a curse, but he took a moment to kiss Harriet on the forehead. "You are my angel or my demon," he told her. "And I don't care which."

Chapter 9

"We meet again."

Lily wasn't sure how it happened, but she slid into his embrace without missing a step, especially since the sound of his voice sent a shiver through her, took her breath away, and curled her toes. One moment Lord Ornov was pretending that she wasn't treading on his feet, the next a hand came around her waist and turned her completely around. And suddenly there he was. It was as if their dance had never ended.

"Am I dreaming?" she asked him.

"Have you dreamed of me?" he countered.

Would she dare admit it if she had? She knew that she could not be dreaming now, because the arm circling her waist had the weight and warmth of flesh and muscle. As much as she'd tried, her memory had not been able to conjure the exact amount of deviltry in the way his lips curved in that wicked smile. She still could not figure out how such dark eyes could be so bright with wicked merriment when they looked into hers. Something in his eyes beckoned—no, tempted. And something in her could not help but respond.

"You are a very dangerous man." She supposed she sounded inane, ridiculous, but—

"You speak nothing less than the truth, Highness."

As he whirled her around in a great arc that led them closer to the edge of the dance floor, she asked, "Will we ever have a coherent conversation, do you think?"

Her body was suddenly pressed much closer to his. She'd never in her life been as aware of anything as she was of the ways they touched and fitted like the pieces of a perfectly matched puzzle. The air around them was charged with a vibrant, brilliant energy. Colors were brighter, the music more beautiful, and it played only for them. They moved as one in the pattern of the dance.

"Do you think we really need to use words?" he asked.

"I'm dizzy," she answered. "You make me dizzy."

He knew it wasn't from the dancing. He was not modest about his gifts at all. "I have that effect on women. Like champagne."

"I've never had champagne before."

The look of wonder on her face struck Kit to the heart. She looked like a girl who had never been kissed, and he badly wanted to be the first man to kiss her. Kit had never found naiveté charming before. It was the lure of the forbidden that fueled the attraction. It had to be. He found himself wanting to give her the world.

He said, "I can promise you champagne."

Even that was not his to give, if truth be told, but he was certain the duchess served only the finest wines. He promised himself that before the night was done, he would liberate a bottle of the old lady's finest vintage and a pair of crystal glasses. Perhaps they could even toast the dawn. He'd found a perfect place for a tryst on his earlier walk. At the very end of the garden was a secluded little arbor where boughs heavy with blossoming roses grew all around and arched overhead. The heady scent and dappled shadows there were intoxicating enough by themselves. He'd steal her away to this perfectly private spot. Then he and his Lily would share her first sip of champagne, and her first kiss.

His Lily? Good Lord, what a mad thought.

"I must already be drunk or I wouldn't be feeling this way."

"I think I must be as well," he answered her.

"Actually, I feel more like I've stepped through

the looking glass," she told him. "I feel like that all the time, but the effect multiplies in your presence."

"Through the looking glass?" Kit gave a softly mocking laugh. "Highness, I am a fox, not a rabbit. It would not be wise to follow me down any holes in the ground."

"Fox, is it?"

He nodded.

"Is that really your name?"

"It's a name I'm known by."

It was the sort of answer she expected from her illusive dancing partner. "I'm under the impression that it would not be safe to follow you anywhere, Mr. Fox."

"A wise impression." His lips lifted in an irrepressible, irresistible smile that set her heart pounding. "But following me would always be fun."

"Promise?" Lily couldn't keep from asking.

"Promise." He managed to look utterly sincere, while his eyes laughed at her. "And I'd never break a promise to a princess," he added.

"Why? Do you think the princess might have your head cut off?"

"I'm sure that would be the lightest punishment you could inflict."

"Really? What's worse than having your head cut off?"

"Why, having your heart broken, of course."

Lily considered this grandiose statement for a

moment, then concluded, "No. Having your head cut off is worse."

"And you're a practical princess, besides."

Lily really wished he'd stop bringing up the matter of her being a princess. True, from him she took the use of the title as teasing for some reason. He made it seem light rather than the heavy burden of obligation so recently and unwillingly thrust upon her by virtue of her father's ancestry.

The music came to an end and the illusion of the magical circle of privacy they shared disappeared as the dancing stopped. Lily tried hard to come back to her senses as polite applause for the orchestra moved in a sedate wave across the ballroom. She managed to take her gaze from her partner's and became aware that other couples were moving away from the dance floor. She took a step backward as Mr. Fox's hand dropped from her waist. His other hand slipped to grasp her wrist. She stared down at his hand, grateful that a connection still existed between them.

"Hungry?" he asked.

Hungry? Dear Lord, yes. Unfamiliar hunger shuddered through her at the sound of his voice, was fueled by his touch. Her gaze rose slowly to meet his. A fever rose from deep inside her, flaming her throat and cheeks. That same fire burned in his eyes. "Ravenous," she answered, voice ragged and barely a whisper.

So this is what Cathy felt with Heathcliff?

She finally understood what *Wuthering Heights* was all about. *So this is passion.* And a very peculiar form of madness it was. She gave her head a hard shake. It loosened hairpins, but helped bring a bit of sanity back to her thoughts. Rather than continuing to make sheep's eyes at the man standing far too close for propriety's sake, she took a look around the ballroom and saw that the crowd was thinning.

"We've been called in to supper," Lily concluded, and suffered momentary embarrassment at realizing that his question had been a prosaic enquiry about whether or not she wanted to eat.

He released her wrist, but then offered his arm. Aware once more of the outside world, Lily moved a step away, delicately placed her hand on his coat sleeve, and walked sedately at his side into the dining room.

As they waited their turn at the buffet table, she couldn't help but ask, "Fox what?"

He tilted his head curiously. "What fox?" He looked around. "Is there a fox in the room?"

"At least one, apparently. I'm standing beside him . . . if Fox is indeed your name." They had never been formerly introduced, which was really quite shocking, almost scandalous. They shouldn't be talking to each other, let alone dancing, joking and, at least on her part, entertaining improper thoughts.

He stepped back, brought the tips of her fingers

to his lips and gave her a formal bow. "Kit Fox at your service, Highness."

"Lily Bancroft at yours," she answered, before remembering that she wasn't here as herself, but as Princess Lily Victoria of Bororavia. Gregory wanted her to drop Lily and be known by the grander Victoria, but that was the one thing she'd refused him. She was not going to completely bury her identity in the role she must play. She saw the question in his eyes, and put a finger to his lips before he could speak. "Shhh . . . I've never mentioned that name to you. Or Yorkshire. Or sheep. It's a long, rather torturous story with revolutions and exiled kings and much melodrama, but I really am technically a Bororavian princess. Are you *really* named Kit Fox?" Surely Kit had to be a nickname, for a kit was a young fox.

"Technically," he answered, a little stiffly. The expression in his eyes went a bit hard and distant when he echoed her, "It's a long story."

"Melodramatic and torturous?"

"Definitely torturous. My governess was an escaped convict, after all."

Lily was not impressed. "I thought the same about my governess. Everyone does."

"Ah, but mine really was."

"Of course," she replied.

He put a hand over his heart. "Your skepticism wounds me. I'd swear that I'd never lie to you—but, alas, I'm too honest to swear that to anyone."

"Your honesty is very . . ." Lily struggled for the proper word.

"Dubious?" Kit tried to help.

"Inventive?" she tried.

Her smile was very inviting. He took a step closer to her. "I can be infinitely inventive."

He watched as her expression changed, first to puzzlement, then his meaning sank in, and a blush warmed her alabaster skin. He realized that he'd gone a step too far. The girl was naïve. She was innocent—and she was offended. Kit could almost feel a swat on the back of the head from his father's large hand, and Court MacLeod's deep, righteous burr asking how he'd react if someone spoke to one of his sisters like that.

"But, Da . . ." he muttered. Lily wasn't a sister, but a beautiful, vibrant woman with an unexplored sensuality bubbling just under the surface. Seduction was an art he thought he understood. It wasn't like Kit to move too quickly, to make a misstep, but despite all the lovers in his past, with Lily he was in dangerous new territory.

"What?"

"Nothing," Kit replied. He gestured toward the buffet tables. "Here we are."

Lily firmly took this opportunity to turn her attention to something besides the man beside her. His comment had rattled her to the core. He'd shocked her with his boldness, but worse, she'd shocked herself by very nearly responding with

equal boldness. That it took her a moment to realize that he'd uttered a sexual innuendo embarrassed her. She could not afford to be innocent. You
are not at some country-house dance, my girl, she
reminded herself.

She was especially aware of the splendor of her
surroundings as she got her first look at a vast expanse of tables draped in pale peach linen cloths
and an array of overflowing silver and porcelain
dishes, enough to feed five or six villages of party-
goers. Not only was there an abundance of food,
but each dish was a work of art. Pink shrimp and
salmon contrasted with something in a fragrant
green sauce. There were wedges of cold pies lay-
ered in stripes of pale white meat, green vegeta-
bles, and bright berries. A rich gold-colored curry
warming in a huge silver chafing dish sent exotic
fragrance into the air. She didn't know the names
or ingredients of half the food, but her stomach informed her it was willing to taste it all. With a
growing sense of awe, she took in the sight of ice
sculpted into statues, tall arrangements of flowers,
and liveried servants waiting to serve her. Her
senses feasted on colors and scents and shapes, and
she almost clapped her hands like a delighted
child.

"What would you like?" her companion asked.

Lily looked at him, at the feast, and back again.
"Good Lord," she said. "Everything!"

Kit loved her honest enthusiasm. She obviously

did not hold with the philosophy that a lady should eat like a bird for propriety's sake. He looked her over. "Where will a little thing like you put it all?"

"What?" she asked, gazing down at the tightly fitted yellow silk bodice of her ball gown, artfully made to show off her long, elegant waist. "Do you think I'm skinny?"

"Slender as a willow," he corrected.

"As to where I shall put it all," she went on, "I think on a plate is probably the best answer."

"Well spoken," he agreed. "Let's have a bit of everything for the princess," he instructed the waiting servers. "Where shall we eat?" He looked around while they waited. Instead of formal place settings, small tables had been set up that would hold no more than four people. "The arrangement's meant to encourage an informal atmosphere," Kit explained to the wide-eyed Princess Lily who turned to regard the noisy crowd with a far too open expression of wonder and trepidation. "Pretend you are one of the duchess's five hundred best friends."

"I will." She leaned her head close to his. "Which one is the duchess?"

"If you see a very tall old lady wearing spectacles, that's her. How about over there?" he suggested, pointing toward an empty table set between a pair of potted trees in huge blue-and-white porcelain urns. It was out of the way enough to calm her nervousness about the crowd, and secluded enough for him to resume serious flirtation.

"Will you have champagne?" one of the servers asked.

"Yes," Kit replied, remembering his plans for a rose-arbor tryst. "A bottle of your best."

Prepared for the thrill of contact this time, Lily delicately put her hand on Kit's arm. "Lead on," she said, glad that her voice did not shake at all, though her knees did when he smiled at her. For a moment she was quite lost in Kit's smile, but then she heard a stirring in the crowd and the sound of an ominously familiar heavy tread behind her. "Oh, dear," she murmured.

Then her wrist was roughly grasped and she was whirled to face the large and very angry Gregory. "What are you doing?" he demanded. "Who's he? Where's Lady Ornov?"

Though her pleasure had turned to fear, Lily managed to make a passable curtsy, and say, "Good evening, Highness. So good to see you could join me at last." She made a sweeping gesture with her free hand, hoping that Gregory would notice that they were in the midst of a crowd. "Will you have something to eat. It all looks wonderful."

She noticed with disappointment that Kit Fox had moved away. She couldn't expect him to stand up for her to a king, especially an angry bull like Gregory who was flanked by Captain Cherminsky and another officer in a gold braided dress uniform. But the reminder that knights in shining armor were not in her future still left her feeling hollow and sad and far too vulnerable.

Gregory looked anything but mollified by her mild words and silent warning, but he didn't shout at her again. His grip tightened painfully on her wrist. "Come."

Kit recognized the king and remembered himself just in time to keep from doing anything stupid. He retreated into the crowd to watch in anonymity, as a good secret agent should. All eyes turned to the scene, and stillness reigned while the Bororavian monarch snarled at the princess. Kit wondered if he imagined the fear in her eyes. He watched the royal bully's treatment of Lily, and fought hard against the impulse to interfere. It was over quickly, though, with the king striding out of the room, pulling the girl behind him like a well-dressed rag doll.

"Well, that went well," he murmured once she was gone, and dug into his coat pocket. Kit deeply regretted that now there would be no tryst with an innocent princess in the rose garden, but he was anything but disappointed in the outcome of the evening. He pulled out the amber bracelet he'd removed from Lily's wrist sometime earlier and held it in his palm. "This will come in handy later."

He was feeling fairly satisfied with himself, then he glanced up and found himself looking into the spectacularly angry eyes of his sister Lucy.

Chapter 10

"**A**ren't you ashamed?"

"For what?"

"You got that girl in trouble."

He shrugged. "It was her choice to be with me."

The look his sister gave him was so blistering it stung. He reacted with anger.

"Did you appoint yourself to be my conscience, Lucy?"

"I suppose I'll have to take the job as conscience. You don't seem to have an internal one, Kit. So I suppose an external one will have to do."

"You needn't bother."

"Grow up."

Sisters.

First she told him to stay away from the girl, then she got annoyed because . . . he didn't stay away from the girl? Or he stayed away from the girl when he shouldn't have? He shook his head. Lucy would have been the first person to point out that princesses don't need rescuing if he'd made the chivalrous attempt to the possible ruination of his cover. He frankly admitted that he should not have been with the girl in the first place.

It was fate. And a distinct lack of willpower on my part.

And he had taken the opportunity to use pleasure for business. Even Aunt Phoebe could not fault him for the flirtation since it yielded him a key into the Bororavian Embassy. The sooner the assignment was completed the better, for, frankly, his head was spinning with desires, urges, and downright impossible possibilities.

"Lily." He whispered the name aloud, and felt like a fool doing so. But her name was like a perfume on the air, a scent light as a lily of the valley, but deceptively intoxicating all the same. He stood now beneath the tree across from the embassy where he and Lily had spoken the day before. No, the day before the day before, for it was a little past midnight. The ball was over for him, and though other late-night pleasures of the city could still accommodate his restlessness, he had a professional appointment to see to first.

Kit held a carved cinnabar box in his palm. The deep red of the exotic wood complemented the deep gold of the oval drops of the Baltic amber and filigree bracelet he'd placed inside. Upon reflection and study of the simple piece of jewelry, he'd come to the conclusion that the bracelet meant something to Lily. It was not a valuable object, but it did have the look of something old that had been well cared for. Perhaps it was a family heirloom, or a present from someone Lily loved.

Not a lover, he thought, the words practically a growl in his head, to banish the nonsensical, jealous notion that *he* should be the only man she'd ever desired. Not that why she cared for the bracelet should matter to him. It wasn't as if he'd stolen it permanently. She'd get her bauble back, and with the added gift of a very pretty box worth more than the jewelry it contained . . . To remember him by?

Kit stepped out of the shadow of the tree. The time for daydreaming while studying his objective was past. He wanted more than anything to get this job over with. After that, he didn't know. Right now it was time to set his plan for getting inside the embassy into motion. He would have preferred procuring a floorplan for the inside of the building instead of going in blind. He might be reckless in his personal life, but he was a consummate professional when it came to being a thief.

"But not beyond improvisation," he said, and deftly tossed and caught the box as he crossed the brick pavement between the park and the embassy gate with a casual, confident stride.

There was no traffic in the street to impede his progress, no one was out for a casual stroll in the neighborhood. A thin layer of cloud stretched over the sickle moon riding high in the sky. Most of the lights in the nearby buildings were long out. The windows in the front part of the embassy were not entirely dark, but that was all to the good.

"Good evening," Kit spoke to a deeper shadow behind one of the brick pillars flanking the embassy gate. He came to a halt before the wrought iron gate, and waited for the guard to reply. "I saw the lights and decided to stop. I'm delighted to see that you're all still up at this hour. Hello," he called out, and waved. "Hello?"

After a few seconds hesitation, a Bororavian soldier stepped from the darkness to stand before the barred gate. Heavy brows furrowed over small eyes, and after a painful hesitation, the guard asked, "What you want?" in heavily accented English.

"Why, to come inside, of course, my good fellow. That's why I'm at the gate." Acting the dandified fool was not particularly hard, and Kit liked to present a front that seemed harmless and faintly hilarious. People liked fools; it made them feel better about themselves. "Do they make you stand out here all night? Of course, it is an honor, isn't it? Being the doorman at a king's residence. Could you please tell them I'm here? It's only a small errand, but she's such a nice girl. It's the least I can do. I meant to send it back in the morning, with a note. But here I am, and I have it with me. Only I haven't written the note yet. So, of course I must come in. Just for a moment. To leave the note, and my card. One must observe the proprieties. You understand."

After another long silence, the guard asked again, "What you want?"

Kit sighed, dramatically. "Ah. I see. I don't speak Bororavian—but then who does? You do, of course, you *are* Bororavian, but I'm afraid no one of any consequence is. So of course *I* don't speak your barbaric, unrefined, *foreign* language. So you'll simply have to fetch someone who does." Kit waved toward the embassy door. He smiled in an inane, friendly, but utterly superior way as he added, "Be a good lad. Bring me someone I can *speak* to."

It was likely the hand gestures that finally got through to the guard. He did respond to Kit's smile with a slight one of his own. He was probably thinking *stupid English git*, but he said, "You. Stay." He turned away to do as he was bid.

"Noblesse oblige works every time," Kit murmured, and jumped lightly over the iron gate to follow the guard silently up the walkway. Other guards appeared as he got closer to the building. But because Kit seemed to be with the man he followed, they watched rather than challenged him. Kit's walk was a relaxed gait, and he kept an inane smile on his face. There was nothing dangerous about him, nothing in the least bit threatening to the security of their beloved Bororavia.

From what I hear the real threat to your motherland is from the man you work for. Good kings and honorable men don't have dealings with international terrorists, or act like bullying pigs toward women, for that matter. The memory of King Gregory's treatment of Lily at the ball sent a stab of white hot anger through him that nearly stopped him in his tracks.

By the time Kit's sharp reaction passed, the guard was knocking on the door. He fixed his smile in place and stepped up behind the surprised sentry as the door opened.

"Good evening!" he announced loudly, in the manner of a man who assumed foreigners would understand English if he only spoke loudly enough to them.

The guard jumped and whirled around at the sound of Kit's voice. Kit pretended not to notice that the man's hand now hovered at his waist, near the grip of a concealed weapon. Kit just kept on smiling.

The man who'd opened the door was in his shirt-sleeves and a worn red silk vest, there was ink on his frayed cuffs. He blinked from behind thick glasses, and said in Oxford-accented English, "Good evening, sir." He gestured imperiously at the Boro-ravian soldier, who instantly moved back toward his post.

Kit strode quickly up to the open door. "I know it's late, my dear fellow," he said to the man at the door. "I'll only be a moment."

The man looked sleepy, and his face showed confusion. "Sir—who are you?"

"Indeed," Kit answered, projecting inane harm-lessness for all he was worth. "And who are you?"

"Constantine Verkovari. The embassy's social secretary," the man answered. "I am the only one up. I heard the knock. No one else bothered to an-swer," he added, with weary bitterness.

Kit edged closer to the man, and the entrance to the building. "And what keeps you up so late, Con-stantine. May I call you Constantine? Hard to wrap my English tongue around Verko-Verkowhatever. You look tired," he empathized. "Does the king make you work at this hour? Where's the door-man?"

Constantine gave a tired laugh. "Asleep in a re-ception room, no doubt. Captain Cherminsky has altogether lost interest in discipline."

"That's too bad. And that leaves you to do other's work when you've too much of your own, doesn't it?"

"Indeed," the social secretary heaved a deep sigh. "I'll be up all night as it is making out the invitations now that His Highness has decided to hold a dinner party at the end of the week. He seems to think all of England's nobility are going to drop what they're doing at short notice and come running here at his whim." Constantine cleared his throat and looked around nervously, as if afraid of being overheard in the empty entrance hall. "Of course, kings have a way of drawing attention."

"I'd certainly give up any previous engagement at the opportunity to dine with a king," Kit told the other man. "But I suppose your king wants the invitations to go out first thing in the morning, leaving you no choice but to work all night. It must be hard on you."

Constantine nodded dismally, and yawned. Kit patted him on the shoulder, and slipped inside past the secretary. It was amazing what one could do by lending a sympathetic ear.

"And here I am wasting your time," Kit went on now that he was inside. He showed Constantine the box. "I won't keep you long. I'm returning an item your princess lost."

Constantine perked up and smiled at the mention of Lily. "How kind."

It pleased Kit that the embassy secretary thought well of the princess he served. "It's nothing," Kit said modestly. "As luck would have it you are the best possible person for me to have met this evening. I wouldn't presume to try to deliver the lost item to the princess herself, but I would like to leave her a note, if that's possible." He looked imploringly at the secretary.

"I suppose that would be—"

"You would understand the correct protocol, I'm sure. Is that your office?" Kit started toward the faint light that showed from an open door in a corridor off the entrance hall. "I'm sure you have pen and paper in there."

"Pounds of it," Constantine said, following at Kit's heels.

"Good." It was Kit who stood aside and ushered the embassy social secretary into his own office. An oil lamp and candle on the desk provided what little light there was in the shadowy room. Kit approached the desk piled high with creamy vellum sheets, envelopes, ink bottles, pens, seals, and sticks of red sealing wax. He pushed aside a stack of already sealed invitations and placed a blank sheet of paper in the cleared space as he said, "Do sit down, Constantine. You have much to do. I've kept you long enough. This will take but a moment, and I'll be on my way. You'll have the honor of restoring the princess's lost treasure to her." *Yes, return to you work. Let me lull you into forgetting about me when I've gone . . . don't even notice that you didn't see me out.*

Constantine did as he was directed, and Kit took up a pen and wrote a few words to Lily. That done, he folded the paper and placed the cinnabar box on top of it before backing away from the desk. By this time the secretary was deeply immersed in his own tedious task. He paid no attention as Kit moved silently toward the door.

The whole plan almost went to hell when a man stepped through the doorway before Kit could leave. Fortunately, there was a chair in the darkest shadows of the crowded room with a coat draped over it, and Kit ducked behind it before the newcomer caught sight of him. Kit recognized the man as Captain Cherminsky. He growled a question in Bororavian to Constantine, who jumped to his feet and stuttered out an answer. It was obvious to Kit that the social secretary both loathed and feared the captain. When Constantine picked up the box, it was also obvious that he was informing the man in charge of security about Kit's visit. Kit held his breath, hoping that explanations were enough, and that Cherminsky would not take a look around.

After a long, tense moment for Kit, Cherminsky proceeded to snatch the box away from Constantine, gave the secretary a short, sharp lecture, then wheeled around and marched from the office. Kit took this as a sign that Cherminsky was satisfied that the stupid English intruder had run his errand and left the embassy. Kit hoped that Cherminsky took Constantine's word about his leaving and didn't bother to question any guards. There was nothing he could do now but wait, which he did, painfully crouched behind the chair, until Constantine had forgotten about him once more. Long minutes passed, no alarm was raised, and Kit was finally able to go about the business of searching the building for secret papers.

Chapter 11

"You should be ashamed!"

"*For what?*" Lily had never raised her voice to Gregory before, but this time she couldn't help herself. She was only glad that the confrontation took place in the library of the Pyneham mansion after Gregory had dragged her downstairs.

"*For being alone with a man,*" Gregory had told her.

"*In the middle of a room full of people? How was I alone with anyone?*"

"*Such wanton behavior will not be tolerated from the woman I am to marry!*"

Lily had managed—just barely—not to snap back that if promiscuous behavior was allowed for him, why shouldn't it be allowed for her. She did mutter something about sauce for the goose being fine for the gander, but his English was not good enough for him to understand the reference.

Then he looked at Captain Cherminsky and Lady Ornov, who had been hastily summoned from the cardroom—*"Get her out of my sight!"*

So, she was brought back to the embassy long before the ball was over. Cinderella hadn't even had a chance to drop her shoe at midnight. But she did manage to drop her bracelet, a gift from her father. She refused to let herself mourn the loss right now, when she had so much else weighing on her mind. And here she was, alone in the sitting room of her bedroom suite, staring into the fireplace where an overconscientious maid had decided to make up a fire on a warm night, and too aware that she hadn't gotten to eat her supper.

Forced to go to bed hungry, like a naughty child.

All things considered, it had been a hellish evening. A debacle. A dark, stormy night with one brief moment full of starlight, moonlight, and music. Actually, Lily recognized that her interlude with Kit Fox had been more of a lightning strike than an interlude, and it was very much the cause of the storm that came after.

If she was going to be punished anyway, Lily almost wished she'd done more than mere flirting with the man. Irenia certainly did far more than flirt with Gregory.

"I'll wager bad girls don't go to bed hungry." If Irenia's lifestyle was any indication of the wages of sin, it appeared that girls who were really naughty ended up with diamonds and dresses from Worth of Paris. "Mother would be shocked at such thoughts," Lily said, then she gave a snort of laughter. "Not likely."

She was well aware that her mother was not likely to be shocked at worldly virtue or vice. Her mother was a very free-thinking sort. No, Father had been the innocent in the family, always thinking the best of everyone. He'd lost his throne, and very nearly his life, by being trusting, kindly, and gentle. Now Lily feared she was going to end up on a throne she didn't want if she continued taking after that good, innocent man.

I keep thinking I have to do something to get myself out of this. Well, it's time to stop thinking and start doing. She started to pace from one end to the other of the flowered rug before her bedroom hearth. The fact that she was talking to herself disturbed her, but her growing sense of purpose heartened her. She wanted desperately to escape. Even with thoughts of flight on her mind, Lily only went into the dark bedroom to open the French window because her quarters were stiflingly hot.

"Escape is not possible, my girl," she reminded herself in a barely audible whisper. She did not look longingly at the moon or out across the expanse of the greatest city in the world. There was nowhere for her to run.

Except . . . she couldn't get a vision of herself running into the arms of Kit Fox out of her mind. If she closed her eyes, she feared she'd find herself lost in a very pleasant hallucination, where his embrace surrounded her with warmth and strength and he whispered in her ear, "Don't worry, my love, I'll protect you." It was a very seductive fancy indeed, and one she dare not allow herself. Her dilemma involved dynastic politics that no ballroom flirtation could hope to—

"Wait a moment." She stopped dead in her tracks and stared into the hearth, where the evening's fire had burned down to barely glowing ashes. The idea that came to her was such a staggering revelation that it left her shaken. As she sat down again, her mind, heart, and blood started to race.

With desire. All right, she admitted it to herself. Desire for the one man that she could not have and desperately wanted. "Desperately?" she asked herself, trying for irony, but her voice shook instead. They had had but three meetings, yet her memory of each encounter was fresh, vivid, tactile. The places where he'd touched her with long-fingered, supple hands warmed at even the slightest thought of him. She remembered the feel of muscular thighs brushing against hers even through layers of cloth. Her heart and breath caught as he smiled at *her.* The twinkle in his dark eyes held a hint of promise. Some places he hadn't touched warmed with these memories as well, but this burning was a perfectly natural reaction from what she'd been given to believe about the physical aspects of—

lovemaking. She'd never expected the burning to be so intense.

"Lovemaking." The sound came out so raw that she wasn't sure what she'd spoken was words. Perhaps love was of the mind, but she was discovering that desire was very much of the flesh. She found that her arms were crossed tightly over her aching breasts. She'd never been so aware of her own body. She wanted to be touched! And, good Lord, how she longed to touch Kit Fox in ways that had nothing to do with following him in a dance.

"I want to see him with his shirt off," she admitted quietly to the empty room. "Yes—and his trousers, too." *Calm down. Think.* She covered her burning cheeks as she whispered to herself, but she didn't take the words back . . . and once she saw him, touching him would not be far behind.

But Her own future and her mother's life were in jeopardy: she had to be clear headed. And ruthless. She had to play a dangerous game if she was going to have any control at all over her future. She'd been living in fear since the day Gregory's thugs appeared at the door of Harelby House and dragged her and her mother into separate carriages. Lily had ended up in London, under threat of marriage to the wretched Gregory. And her mother was held somewhere, under threat of death if Lily didn't submit to her usurping cousin's dynastic ambitions for an heir. Lily and her mother had been allowed to write each other letters, but not to see each other.

Maybe I should have demanded to see her instead of humbly asking like that boy in the Dickens novel. Lily sighed. Then she straightened her spine and told herself to stop feeling so blasted sorry for herself. The boy's name was Oliver Twist, she reminded herself, and he managed to do quite well for himself after first escaping the poorhouse and then spending numerous chapters learning the tricks of the trade in a den of thieves.

"Well, I've been living in a thieves' den for some time now," she murmured. "I must have absorbed some tricks by now."

For example, she'd learned that the only thing standing in the way of her wedding to Gregory was the objections constantly raised by Bishop Arkady. She'd been thinking of him as a nice elderly cleric with moral and ethical qualms about the union. Perhaps he was, but it was likely that his genuine concern masked another agenda. Agendas seemed to be an important part of politics, all of them focusing on gaining power, whether personal or for a cause. One had to learn to maneuver people and situations to get what one wanted.

As Lord Ornov had said earlier tonight, *"It is to your advantage to make everyone think you are doing what they want, and achieve your objectives before anyone realizes what those objectives truly are."*

It had been a valuable lesson. His words had

been mulling around in her head since she heard them; now it was time to put them into effect.

Which was where Kit Fox came into it.

She really hated the thought of using anyone, but she had no choice. The elusive, mysterious Mr. Fox was the only weapon she had. If she could have her way she might plead with Kit to run off with her to some unknown exotic shore and be her lover forever and ever. Pleasant as that fantasy might be, she could not have her way. She could only have, perhaps, a bit of contentment in a life that was doomed to be controlled by her bloodline and the history of her father's country. If Gregory had his way, she would be his wife, his queen, his broodmare.

She tried to accept that she was doomed to be a broodmare. Her ancestry fated her to produce the heir to the Bororavian throne. But . . . What if she convinced Gregory to marry her to Michael instead? Of course, that didn't take into account what Michael wanted. But from what she could tell, Michael seemed to want most another drink. Perhaps if she was his wife she could help Michael find some other purpose for his life. Perhaps, but first she had to get the man to the altar, and Gregory's combination of overpowering pride, temper, and ambition was a formidable obstacle standing squarely in the way of any march down that aisle.

Lily knew her one sure ally was Arkady, and she

was sure that Irenia would do all that was within her power to keep Lily from marrying Gregory. But in the final outcome, it must be Gregory who irrevocably made the decision that he didn't want to marry her himself.

"I'd only throw the girl at my Gypsy brother as punishment if she'd already proved herself a whore."

Gregory's words resounded through her memory. Lily should have shrunk in shame, but she sat up straight and smiled. Gregory's attitude was hideous, but it could lead to her salvation. Or at least to an accommodation she could live with, and that would win her mother's freedom. All she had to do was sacrifice her self-respect.

"Nonsense," she told her conscience. "I've already done that. I've let them bully me and threaten and treat me like a thing. Letting oneself be used in any way is a type of whoredom, isn't it?" Well, perhaps that statement was a bit too strong, but she was so angry with herself for the weeks of meekly existing, she couldn't help but be harsh. Perhaps she'd had no choice, but until tonight she hadn't actively tried to make any opportunities for herself, had she? That she was going to have to use someone to gain her ends also bothered her. It bothered her even more than the knowledge that she was going to have to behave as brazenly as Irenia in front of the world at large to stand any chance at all of achieving her ends.

Gregory had a great deal to pay for having

usurped a throne and driven the rightful king into exile—and now he held Lily and her mother against their wills. But her father had not been interested in revenge, and neither was she. Lily wanted—

"Kit Fox," she whispered to the empty shadows, and another wave of longing went through her. He was attractive. No, more than attractive. Was *erotic* the word she wanted? The way he had approached her . . . with a swagger in his step, a charm that would not be denied, a knowing spark in his eyes. Then there was the way he looked, lean of hip and broad of shoulder, tall and wiry, with chiseled cheekbones and the rakish fall of dark hair across his forehead. *Yes, yes.*

But Lily had to chide herself. *This is no time to fantasize about the man. I can't think straight.* After all, she was going to have to ruthlessly use Kit Fox's attraction to her to get Gregory to let her marry Michael. She was going to have to behave in a sordid and dishonorable manner toward a man who had no ambition to use her. Well . . . she thought he wanted to seduce her, and that was rather dishonorable on his part, but at least his intent was for personal pleasure rather than political gain. Frankly, she wanted to be seduced. She wasn't exactly sure what the sex act entailed, but the heated yearning that came over her when she thought of Kit excited as well as frightened her. The thought of lying with Gregory sickened her. Michael was hardly repulsive, but she doubted he could ever rouse anything more than a sense of conjugal duty in her. With Kit she knew she could share a forbidden, wild passion, if only for the briefest time.

"Long enough," she murmured. Long enough to be labeled—quite rightly—a whore.

It was a matter of having one's cake and eating it too, she supposed. For, matters of state aside, she desperately wanted to see Kit Fox again. Her heart raced at the thought of being held close to him, flesh to flesh. She imagined the heat of his mouth on hers. She wanted to be kissed by him, to feel his hands on her, and hers on him, in ways other than being swept across a ballroom in the stylized seduction of the waltz.

She sighed, well aware and almost amused that for a country girl who'd never been kissed she was having some fairly decadent imaginings about what to do with a naked man.

What a shame every statue she'd ever seen of a nude male had been covered with a plaster fig leaf in the most interesting area. It left a great deal to the imagination. Now, the reproductive equipment of rams she understood, but she was no sheep, and certain aspects of her own species were a mystery to her, but not for much longer, she thought. One way or another.

Then Lily jumped to her feet. She thought she heard something in the bedroom.

"Who's there?" she called.

Chapter 12

It was the dogs' fault that Kit found himself standing as still as possible on the narrow balcony, with his back pressed against the brick wall. Not so much the dogs prowling in the back garden below, for the pair of hounds that roamed the embassy grounds had yet to lift their heads and notice his presence. They were not, perhaps, the best of guard dogs, which was a good thing to know now that he had spotted them. But the sight of them—rangy, sharp-nosed forms silhouetted by moonlight—sent a memory through him that belonged to a boy of five or six who'd been chased, bitten, and mauled by creatures very like them a long time ago.

His mum had explained that it wasn't the dogs' fault, when she'd discovered how terrified he was of dogs. They were only doing their duty, trying to keep him out of somewhere he wasn't supposed to be.

He'd thought the woman was punishing him when she got him a puppy and made him raise and care for it and keep it in his room. He'd come to love that dog, and many a dog since. But sometimes, when the moon glimmered just the right way on sleek fur and he spotted a flash of fang in a dark muzzle, the fear returned for an instant.

Kit considered this momentary paralysis a ludicrous end to an unproductive evening. He hadn't managed to kiss Lily, been fussed at by his sister not once, but twice, and so far his search of the Bororavian Embassy had proved fruitless. He suspected that at any moment the dogs were going to start barking. Or a sudden storm cloud was going to blow up and he was going to be hit by lightning. The damned thing was, he couldn't simply give up and go away. Aunt Phoebe wanted secret documents, and he needed to get the job done so he could go on with his seduction of Lily without anyone complaining that his emotions were interfering with his work.

He was amazed with himself, for he normally had absolute self-control in his relations with women. A few days ago he'd vowed that, attracted as he was to the copper-haired princess, he would have nothing to do with her. He'd broken that vow at every turn. In fact, his current vow was that they'd share at least one night before she was whisked away to her castle in a far off northern kingdom. Lucy didn't have to tell him he was being a fool; he knew it. But fool or not, he went about his assignment as efficiently as he could, if only the Bororavians would be more cooperative.

He knew that somewhere in this large, rambling old house there had to be a safe, a strongbox, a secret compartment, a locked desk or trunk or even a lady's hatbox that contained documents. The better hidden the papers, the more secret and sensitive to the security of Bororavia they would be. If Gregory were consorting with anarchists, there would be some sort of paper trail, no matter how quiet the king kept his dealings, especially if money had changed hands. Clerks were tidy fellows. There were always records of where money from royal treasuries went, no matter how coded the entries in the ledger books. Besides, where there were diplomats, bureaucrats and royal courts there were always documents, diaries and records. This was an embassy, it had to contain secrets. So far he hadn't found any of the usual hiding places of this sort of establishment.

So far, he was the only one hiding, and from a pair of not particularly nosy hounds, at that. It was not that he hadn't seen, found and heard things, it was only that nothing useful had so far turned up in a room-to-room search. Other complications were that the place was big, and it was busier than he'd thought it possible to be at this time of night.

In a proper English household, everyone would either be sleeping or out carousing, but not the Bororavians. He'd had to dodge servants, and soldiers in the halls, and he'd been driven out the window of the last room he'd been searching when a trio of angry people marched in and proceeded to have a heated argument. He'd lingered on a ledge outside the window only long enough to get a look at the noisy scene. He'd recognized Lord Ornov, and the woman who was Lily's companion. The one doing most of the shouting was a stunningly beautiful young woman that the other two seemed to be pleading with. Since he hadn't been able to learn anything from eavesdropping—the conversation was in Bororavian—he'd moved stealthily along the third floor ledge until coming to this tiny balcony, and spotting the dogs—

Kit forced his muscles to relax. He eased inside the open door and found himself in a dark bedroom. He normally enjoyed sneaking into bedrooms, but he preferred it to be at the invitation of a willing young lady. He stood very still, slowly turning his head to look carefully at these new surroundings. He listened just as carefully. He realized the bed was empty when he could not hear the sound of breathing or make out a shape in the darkness.

"Good," he murmured.

He didn't realize he'd spoken aloud until a voice called, "Who's there?" from the next room.

The beautiful, familiar voice of the woman he craved.

Kit swore and turned back toward the balcony door, but she was there in the doorway between the bedroom and a sitting room before he could make a clean escape. He caught the glow of the lamp she held from the corner of his eye, and caught his breath at the way it lit the burnished copper of her unbound hair. To flee was impossible. To turn back to face her was an undeniable compulsion, for all that the sane, professional part of him raged silently as the fool enthralled with the princess held out his arms. He was trapped. He was lost. His reckless nature took full control, and the words came out of their own will.

"Lily, my love!"

Her eyes went round as saucers. "Your—*what?*"

Her hand wavered even more than her voice. Kit moved swiftly to take the lamp before she dropped it. The flame flickered, casting odd shadows, but he set it down on a bureau before it went out, and it soon shed a steady light that illuminated the shocked young woman still standing framed in the doorway.

She put a hand to her cheek, and said, "How did you know I—"

Kit grasped her hands and pulled her forward. "I couldn't stop thinking about you. I had to see you again. I—"

"Broke into my room."

She blushed as she spoke, and something sparked in her aquamarine eyes. Guilt? Hope? Desire flared through him.

"Did you wish me here?" he asked, tugging her closer. Her mouth rounded in surprise, but she spoke no denial. "I think you did."

She wore only an embroidered white nightgown fastened with a blue ribbon at the throat. The lamplight tinted the cloth gold, and illuminated shadowed hints of the shape of her breasts, hips, and long, slender legs. She might have been made of porcelain, so perfect was her skin. Kit could not resist trailing his fingers across her warm cheek, and then slowly down her throat until they grasped one end of the satin ribbon. This was no china doll, but a live woman who trembled ever so slightly beneath his touch. Nerves? Desire?

"May I?" he asked, and tugged gently on the blue satin string before she had the chance to answer.

Lily thought it was a little too late to scream for help. She was so nearly paralyzed by the sensations running through her that she couldn't think. Despite the fact the very air around her sizzled, that her gaze was locked on Kit's dark eyes, her ears tuned to the seductive murmur of his voice, and her skin vibrantly aware of his touch, she was also well aware that he lied when he claimed he was there to see her again.

She knew full well that he had not been so desperate for an assignation with her that he'd climbed up to her balcony and into her room. In the first place, how could he possibly have known where her room was? In the second, he'd been in the process of leaving when she'd walked in. In the third, she'd seen the angry surprise at being caught for the briefest instant, when he'd first turned to face her. So, he was not here specifically for the purpose of seducing her, though his touch was expert and his attention fully attuned to the task that he now set himself to. He wanted her all right. Virgin she might be, but she understood the hunger radiating from him. An equal response of hunger flared deep inside her. She shuddered when the back of his hand brushed across the base of her throat, pushing aside the top of her nightgown.

The hunger was fierce in Lily, but not fierce enough to drown the pain of knowing that Kit Fox was using her. Just like everyone else. She did not know what he was or why he'd broken into the embassy, but surely he meant no good toward Bororavia. Was he a simple thief? Or was he a British spy out to discover information the English could use against Bororavia during the treaty negotiations? Not that who or why mattered. What hurt was the dark, wounding knowledge that there was no one in the world she could take at face value. No one who did not want something from her. No one she could trust.

The knowledge should leave her as coldly repulsed by Kit Fox as she was by King Gregory. It did leave her heart empty, but it didn't stop her body from wanting.

Whatever Fox wanted it wasn't her. Oh, he'd boldly approached her, courted her—no doubt planning the whole time to make her fall in love with him so that she would gladly betray her father's country for him. Or was his aim to persuade her to hand over jewels, gold or whatever riches from the royal treasury? His courtship might have been a back-up plan, for she was certain he had not broken into the embassy searching for her. Right now, he didn't want her to reveal his presence, so he made love to her as a distraction. He simply knew how to take advantage of the moment with the seductive touch and words any besotted maiden would long to hear.

She wondered if his actions would work on her if she didn't already have plans of her own?

Well, let him think she was a fool, and one totally susceptible to his charms. She *was* susceptible to his charms. She simply wasn't going to be the one who was used.

And to think she'd been aching with guilt over the necessity of using him only a few minutes ago! The man was a cad, a rake, and far worse. He was fair of face and form. His touch sent shivers of heat and thrills of anticipation through her, but all the outward beauty and charm masked whatever he really was. He had no heart to break. She had none to give. So they were well matched in that, she supposed.

"Let the games begin," she murmured, just before his mouth covered hers.

Kit was confused about what she meant, but the touch of Lily's soft sweet lips drove the momentary curiosity away. Her sigh caressed his mouth, and she relaxed against him, her arms coming around his neck. As she leaned into the kiss her thighs brushed his and her unbound breasts pressed against his chest, bringing him to instant arousal.

He'd meant for this first kiss to be gentle, a taste, a lingering moment of promised passion, but frankly, he was no saint. And the way her lips parted at the merest touch of his tongue told him she wasn't interested in sainthood, either. Her hands moved down his back as she responded. She grasped handfuls of his coat and gave a soft, sighing moan.

When their lips finally parted, Lily leaned her head back and looked into his eyes. Her breath caught once before she could speak. "We still haven't had a proper introduction."

He leaned forward, brushed a strand of hair away from her ear, and whispered, "Why be proper, when improper works so much better?" He then kissed the spot on her throat just below her ear. When she jumped slightly in his embrace, he asked, "Ticklish?"

"No." The word came out on a sigh. "It felt so— have you ever had a shock go through you?"

"Yes," he answered. "The first time I saw you." She stiffened slightly, and he sensed that what he'd said somehow displeased her. "Christopher," he said, trying to soothe whatever upset her. "I am Christopher . . . and you are my own Tiger Lily. With clever fingers," he added as she fumbled to undo his tie.

"Neither a tiger nor clever. Nor yours," she added after a moment of stark tension.

Kit heard nothing imperious in her words, but there was honest regret. He kissed her again, this time with a possessiveness he could not help but feel. "Mine," he told her. He left soft kisses on her throat and cheeks before whispering against her lips, "For this moment, at least."

Her laugh was barely audible. "Live for the moment, Lily," she whispered. "That's me." Then she kissed him with such hunger that it left him quite breathless.

Before he quite realized what he was doing, Kit picked her up and turned toward the bed.

For a moment Lily felt like she was flying—out of her senses, out of control, out into the unknown. She was held tightly in the arms of a stranger, yet she felt free, and so very aware. The sheets had never felt so smooth and sensual before. The pillows that were suddenly beneath her head were soft and deep as a summer cloud over the moors. She had not noticed before how the breeze that blew in from the garden smelled of sweet herbs and roses. The curtains stirred slowly, like drifts of smoke. The golden lamplight added auburn tints to Kit's thick, ruffled hair. She watched with pleasure but no thought, her senses as languid as if she floated under warm, sweet water as he sat on the side of the bed and took off his tie, his jacket, and black brocade vest. Because everything else he wore was black, it was almost a shock to see that his shirt was a bright, crisp white stretched across lean, hard muscles. A pleasant shock, for the sight of this broad-shouldered man wearing a well-tailored white linen shirt was a sensual delight to behold. If she was an artist she would have painted him this way. If she was a poet, she'd praise him with words. She thought she could look at him forever—if only the hunger for something more wasn't raging in her blood.

Then she experienced a sudden flash of guilt. She didn't know about princesses, but nice girls from Yorkshire didn't go to bed with men they weren't married to, no matter what the circumstances.

When Kit had his shirt unbuttoned, she tried to avert her eyes, but, frankly, the sight of a beautifully proportioned bare chest and muscular, flat stomach was not an easy thing to look away from. She did sit up and draw her legs away from him.

"Don't be afraid," he murmured, tilting his head to one side. "I understand that this is your first time."

"You *don't* understand."

She wished now she'd had another half hour to think through her decision to become dishonored. It had seemed a logical, practical, if not desperate reaction to her situation. She had intellectually understood the moral and ethical sides of the issue. What hadn't sunk in before Kit Fox showed up in all his glorious erotic masculinity like the answer to a girl's feverish carnal dreams was just how much she was going to hate herself in the morning if she went through with her plan.

Now I have to rethink the whole blasted thing. Lily scooted away as he reached for her. She held her hands up before her. "We can't," she said, while her body proclaimed that *oh yes* she could. "It would be wrong."

"Of course it's wrong." He smiled. It was a smile made to melt resistance. Made to melt a girl's insides. Made to coax a girl's nightgown right off. "That's why it's so much fun," he added.

She couldn't help but smile back. It was a very naughty smile, and she knew it. She ached for him to touch her. She wanted to be kissed again. She wanted to see what he looked like without a fig leaf. She wanted—she wasn't sure exactly what she wanted, but she knew it was something that went far beyond this ache of freshly awakened desire. She wanted completion. She wanted passion. She wanted to run across the moors shouting "Heathcliff!" and not be calling out for a stupid runaway ram.

She was not going to give herself to Kit Fox, no matter how much she wanted to. Maybe that had been the original plan, but she knew now that she simply could not go to her husband's bed anything but a virgin. Michael might be able to accept his bride as a soiled dove, but she couldn't accept herself that way. Nor did she expect him to. He was weak, but he was nice, and she could not treat him with less than honor and respect.

For which her heightened physical senses cursed her roundly at the moment.

So the trick was to make Gregory think she was sullied without actually being sullied. That could be tricky, considering that she currently had a half-dressed man with a wicked, persuasive, gleam in his eye sitting on the side of her bed.

And she wanted him!

Lily rolled to the opposite side of the bed and got to her feet. She retied the top of her nightgown and slipped on a shawl. "You must go," she said, though both her voice and knees were shaking. She might have pointed dramatically toward the balcony door, but thought he might take her hand if she held it out. She'd be lost if he touched her, or kissed her palm, possibly her wrist and . . . She clasped her hands behind her back. "Go."

He crossed his arms across his bared chest, and tilted his head at just that—adorable—angle again. "You really want me to, sweetheart?" His voice was intoxicating, like honeyed spiced wine.

"No."

He chuckled. The sound was low, masculine.

Lily closed her eyes and tried again. "Please leave."

"The dogs are out there, you know," he said. "And guards."

"You got past them the first time."

"I could be hurt. Would you want that on your conscience?"

She opened her eyes to give him a stern look. "Better that on my conscience than something else."

He pulled her hand from behind her and brushed his lips across her wrist. She made a small, piteous noise. He looked up at her, through thick lashes. His eyes were hot and sultry. "You want me."

Of course she did. That was not the point! She made herself glare when what she really wanted was to melt into his arms. *No melting,* she ordered herself, and she managed to make herself stand up straight and speak without her voice shaking. "You do know how to take no for an answer, don't you?"

"I do," he answered. "But I'd rather not."

"I could threaten to call the guards—but that would only get us both in trouble. And I am the one who put my own virtue at risk." She shook her head. "This cannot be. We both know it." She tugged her hand from his grasp and turned her back to him. "Please get dressed and go."

"Well . . ."

The word trailed off into a long, long silence. The silence grew heavy and cold, and so did Lily's heart. Sparks of fire still sizzled in her blood, though after a while even those turned into aching ashes. She felt both heavy and empty when she finally turned around. He had gone without a sound, taking all the light with him, leaving her in a silence so deep she thought she might drown.

Chapter 13

"**W**omen did not use to confuse me, Aunt." Aunt Phoebe continued patiently stitching. "With all your sisters, dear, I should hope you know something about dealing with the fairer sex."

"Sisters are not women, Aunt. Sisters are . . . paragons of virtue." Aunt Phoebe gave him a very skeptical look from over the top of her embroidery hoop, but Kit chose to ignore the sarcasm in the tilt of her raised eyebrows and went on. "Women are—"

"Defined by you as whatever bit of skirt you can manage to seduce."

He'd been stretched out in one of the chairs in her floral-decorated sitting room. Now he pulled in his long legs and sat up straight. "Such crudeness, Aunt." He glanced toward the door. "And the girls due for tea any minute."

She glanced at the mantel clock. "They're late. Women who travel in packs tend to be."

He smiled at her disapproving tone. "And you are ever the lone wolf, eh, Aunt Phoebe?"

The elderly lady tucked a strand of soft silver that had come loose from her tightly bound hair behind her ear. "Let's say that I've never had much interest in spending time with members of my own gender."

"Who are not relatives," he added.

"Even then, I prefer them in small doses. One of the reasons I sent your mother looking for her long lost love was to get her and her three children out of the house."

"So you said at the wedding, I recall."

Phoebe sighed and shook her head. "But my miscalculation was in not realizing the pair of them would start breeding like rabbits when they finally got back together. I don't believe your father's ever heard of a French Envelope, do you?"

Kit covered his eyes with his hand for a moment. "There are some images I really don't want in my mind, Aunt."

"Children can be so prudish where their parents are concerned." She went back to her stitching and ignored him.

Kit grew restless and began to pace the room. The place was almost frighteningly feminine, strewn with needlework pillows, and lace anti-macassars on all the furniture. The chairs and settees were all upholstered in floral tapestry, yards of lace curtains draped the windows. The pastel walls were hung with paintings and prints of flowers in gilded frames. Tables, the writing desk, and the mantel were positively littered with china figurines, painted porcelain boxes, and vases of all sorts filled with dried and fresh flowers.

"A man would confess to anything after being trapped in here for a few hours," he muttered.

"The carpet is Aubusson," Aunt Phoebe told him. "Kindly stop pacing a hole in it."

He looked down at the rug. "It has flowers on it. I want a cigarette," he added.

"You want a princess," she said. "Both are bad for you."

He whirled to face her. "You don't know that!"

She looked at him with cold sternness that was frightening, even for her. "You seem to be fighting an addiction to both. That makes you distracted. Distraction is bad for you. I thought you said you were going to stay away from that girl?"

He shrugged. "I tried."

Gentlemen did not talk about their sexual escapades. Men should be discreet, protective of their paramour's privacy, and certainly of a lady's reputation and place in society. Kit had liaisons with married ladies, so he knew how that game was played. An affair with an unmarried woman of such high rank would certainly be disastrous for the young woman if it was discovered. Of course, he should have thought about that already where Lily was concerned. Instead he'd followed his own selfish hunger, and now, instead of being able to rouse any self-recrimination, he suffered from the thought that if he didn't have her he would surely die. Still, he had an urge to protect her . . . as if she was his own fragile Lily. How could he be both seducer and knight? When had he come to care for the person inside the princess's willowy form? Why should he? He was so confused. And frustrated.

Addicted, as his all-knowing great-aunt had said.

"Lily said no," he admitted.

"Wise girl," Aunt Phoebe commented. She put down her embroidery and folded her hands in her lap. "You were strong enough to take no for an answer, I trust."

It hurt that she even thought to make the comment. "Of course! But"—he couldn't help but add—"I wish I hadn't."

Her hands clenched together. "Oh, dear." Her expression softened somewhat. "Christopher, lad, this is not like you. I know you hate to be thwarted, and take great glee in acquiring what does not belong to you, but—" She closed her mouth abruptly, then gave him a hard, hostile stare. "When . . . *Where* did she say no, young man?"

"Last night. In her bedroom."

Aunt Phoebe rose to her feet. "Do you mean to

tell me you've been in the embassy and all you did was attempt to get into this girl's—"

At that instant the sitting room door opened and a quartet of MacLeod sisters entered, all talking at once. For a few moments, all Kit could make out was the scent of perfume, glossy hair and fresh skin, the colors of bright summer dresses and hats, and the sound of equally bright chatter. There were greetings and kisses on cheeks all round, and eventually Harriet, Lucy, Beatrice, and Sara settled onto couch and chairs.

Aunt Phoebe rang for tea and settled back into her chair. She picked up her embroidery hoop, and no one but Kit knew how angry she'd been moments before. She smiled benignly now, though her smile was turned on her nieces rather than the nephew standing by the fireplace. Kit was quite content not to have Aunt Phoebe's attention. They talked about fashions, shopping, home, parties, and other innocuous female pastimes until after tea and cakes had been brought in and passed around. Kit stayed out of the way, and was generally ignored.

It was finally Lucy who turned his way and asked, "Finished up your business with the Bororavians, Christopher?"

Kit decided to take Lucy's question at face value. "Very soon, I hope." He smiled at Beatrice. "With the help of a clever sister." He reached into his coat pocket and brought out a cream-colored envelope.

Beatrice stood as he held the paper toward her. "What's this?"

"Invitation to a dinner party tomorrow night. I liberated it from the Bororavian Embassy last night. Think you can fix it up to look like I'm on the guest list?" he asked the family's adolescent expert in codes and forgery.

Beatrice took the invitation over to the writing desk and looked it over in the light from the window behind the desk. "Simple copperplate style," she said. Then she sat, opened a drawer and brought out a selection of ink bottles and several pens, pushed back her sleeve cuffs. "Piece of cake."

"I still have a headache," Lily complained.

She had not wanted to leave her bedroom. She certainly didn't want to go down to dinner, but almost welcomed the upcoming social event to this pre-party gathering of her "family" in the upstairs sitting room that Gregory had insisted upon. She and Lady Ornov had been the first to arrive, and now that everyone was present, Lady Ornov was standing before her, looking like she was about to give Lily a lecture.

"My head really does hurt, Lady Ornov."

Her companion was not in the least bit moved. "You used that excuse not to go out yesterday,"

Lady Ornov pointed out. She gestured for a servant who carried over a tray of drinks. She handed Lily a glass of wine. "This will help. You *must* attend tonight's state dinner. Rank has its obligations, Highness."

Lily's father used to say that. Then her mother would ask why, and they'd get into long, philosophical discussions that they seemed to enjoy, but left Lily bored to tears. The fact that her parents talked so much was one of the factors that led Lily out to the barns and pastures and sparked her interest in animal husbandry. Sheep, she'd long ago concluded, were more interesting than people, and her involvement with present company did nothing to change her mind. Kit Fox was likely an exception to this conclusion—but, Kit wasn't here, was he?

Lily took a sip of her drink. It went straight to her head, and did not help her self-pity. Kit wouldn't be and shouldn't be in her life, and, good Lord, she was miserable. And maybe she should have made love to him at least once, because the misery she suffered the last day and half had weighed more on the side of regret for the path to hell not taken than for the righteous misery of knowing she was keeping herself pure for one of two men she didn't want.

Lady Ornov must have thought she'd fallen into a coma, for Lily had to take a physical as well as mental deep breath when the other woman passed a hand in front of her face to get her attention.

"Are you all right, Highness?"

"Yes, Lady Ornov," she answered. "Except for the headache." Lily was tempted to point out that having a headache was no less valid an excuse today, but she was well aware that her lady-in-waiting was not really annoyed with her. Not with Irenia in the same room with them. Lily found the fact that Lady Ornov was standing in front of her, shielding the princess's view of the notorious mistress who'd marched in on Gregory's arm, both touching and pathetic.

Lily didn't mind their relationship, as long as neither the king nor his mistress paid any attention to her. Of course, after what she'd almost done with Kit Fox, Lily would have felt like a hypocrite to condemn Gregory and Irenia's illicit affair too strongly. In fact, had they been nicer people she might have sympathized with them. The couple was in love—of a sort. Not like her parents had been, and not in the way she would like to be—with Kit for example, if he were not out to use her for his own gain, the way Irenia used Gregory.

Kit. Handsome, treacherous, dishonest, sensual, magnificent-with-his-shirt-off Kit!

Lily finished the wine and let the servant take the empty glass away. Her head really did hurt, and her stomach was still tight with the ache of need that would not go away. She suffered from a bit of shame, but mostly because she could not stop thinking about the man she'd let come as far as her bed. Though he'd come no farther, she could still feel his hands on her, his lips, the caress of his gaze and his smile, and it was all maddening even though it was only memory. Lust was not a safe, sane thing for the senses; she'd figured that out quickly enough. What she hadn't realized was that it could be so physically daunting as well. So much so that nearly two days later she still wasn't prepared to face the world where he would not be.

Lily had taken to her bed after the departure of Kit Fox and would not have gotten up if Gregory had not ordered Lady Ornov to make her. He wanted a princess in attendance to add luster to his dinner party. Irenia did not. Apparently there had been a great deal of shouting and tears between Gregory, Irenia, and Irenia's family while Lily hid in her room. She was glad to have missed out on a fracas in which no one would have asked her opinion anyway. The upshot was that they were all going to the party together, but first they'd been called to the sitting room for a bit of Bororavian togetherness before consorting with the cream of foreign devil English society.

"Hooray for the home team," Lily murmured.

"What?" Lady Ornov asked.

"I was remembering a game played on village

greens here in England," Lily replied hastily. "It is called cricket."

"Perhaps you are feverish, Highness," Lady Ornov suggested after she scrutinized Lily for some time. "Your cheeks are flushed, but that could be the wine. Well, even if you are, your duty is to head the banquet table tonight. You must persevere."

"Yes, Lady Ornov," she said meekly, then stepped out of the corner of the sitting room where her lady-in-waiting had protectively herded her. The woman could give lessons to a border collie, Lily thought.

Once she had a clear view of the room, she saw that Michael, Bishop Arkady, and Lord Ornov were standing in a close group near a window, drinking and talking quietly. Captain Cherminsky stood by the door. His attention was centered on Irenia, and why not? For Gregory's mistress stood resplendent at the king's side in the very center of the room. Her dark hair and ripe red lips glistened, her eyes flashed. A pearl choker circled her lovely throat, and diamonds flashed in the delicate lobes of her ears. Her scarlet dress was cut to show off the flare of her hips, the trimness of her waist and a great deal of the high, round globes of her bosom. She was a woman who knew how to be noticed. Lily did not blame Captain Cherminsky for noticing, though she hoped Gregory did not catch sight of the open hunger in the guard commander's eyes.

Lily wondered if Kit would notice if she dressed

like Irenia, and wore her sexuality so blatantly for everyone to see. Stop thinking about Kit, she ordered herself, just as Irenia raised her hand, and Lily noticed the bracelet fastened at Irenia's wrist.

Lily gasped, loud enough for Gregory and Irenia to look her way. The Ornovs, Michael, and Arkady looked where the king looked. Lily was aware of everyone's attention on her, but all she had eyes for was the amber bracelet fastened around the wrist of the other woman.

This was too much. She'd already put up with quite enough from these people. This was the last straw. She was not going to put up with any more.

Lily had never been more angry in her life than when she marched up to Gregory's mistress. "That bracelet is mine," Lily informed Irenia. She held out her hand. "Give it to me."

Everyone continued to stare at her in stunned silence. She didn't think anyone was breathing. Servants exited the room. Cherminsky stiffened to attention. She understood their reaction. The Bororavians were not used to her being emphatic and less than polite about anything. Lily ignored the way they stared. She concentrated on Irenia.

"Give it to me," she said again.

Irenia drew herself up, her magnificent chest heaving with great indignation. "What are you talking about, you silly girl? Are you calling me a thief?"

"I could call you a great many things," Lily

snapped back, letting her temper get the best of her tongue. "But I have not yet accused you of anything. I lost my bracelet. Apparently you found it, now please give it back."

Irenia's response was what Lily expected. She lifted her chin proudly. "I will give you nothing, silly girl." She was looking triumphantly at Gregory when she added. "What is mine, I keep."

Oh, good lord! "I am not in competition with you."

"You have nothing to compete with."

"I don't need to compete."

"Of course she doesn't," Gregory spoke up. He seemed quite amused to see the two women fighting. "Lily will be my wife," he egged Irenia on. "You are my mistress. Everything is settled. Let us go down to dinner."

"Nothing is settled!" Irenia exclaimed.

"Give me my bracelet," Lily insisted. She turned to Gregory, something she thought she'd never do. "My father gave that amber bracelet to me. It belonged to his mother."

"It is mine," Irenia countered. "It was given to me. The silly girl is lying."

"I am not a silly girl!" Lily had been trying not to come down to Irenia's level, but she was tired of being insulted. And she was not leaving this room without what was hers.

"Who gave it to you?" Gregory demanded of his lover.

He bristled with jealousy. Irenia saw it and laughed. "An admirer," she told him. "You are not my husband. Why should you care if I look out for my interests if you are going to abandon me for that silly girl."

"I am not abandoning you!"

"Nor will you have the silly girl," Irenia shot back. "I will see to that! There will be no marriage."

"Try to stop it!"

"I can. I will. You think I don't know how to arrange things to my advantage? I am as ruthless as you are Gregory."

"Both of you stop it!" Lily added her own raised voice to the shouting. "Give me what is mine," she demanded. "The bracelet," she clarified. "That's all I want at the moment."

"And dinner," Michael interjected, his only comment so far. "Guests are starting to arrive. You should be there to greet them, Highness," he urged Gregory.

"Dinner." Gregory nodded. "I'm starving. Irenia, give the girl her bauble. I'll give you diamonds."

"I'd rather see her gone. I *will* see her gone," Irenia threatened.

Gregory laughed. "Enough of your drama." He held out his hand. His attitude brooked no nonsense when he said, "The bracelet. Or you will not come down to dinner with me."

Irenia evidently knew when to back down. She went pale, and pressed her lips angrily together to keep any retort inside. She hesitated, but she did lift her arm and let Gregory take the bracelet from her wrist. He nodded, then tossed the bracelet toward Lily with a casual gesture.

She thought he meant for it to land at her feet so that she would have to scramble to pick it up off the floor. Lily thwarted the insult by easily snatching the bracelet out of the air. What nonsense, she thought, and fastened the bracelet around her own wrist where it belonged without asking anyone's aid. Were all Bororavians so melodramatic?

"There," she said when she was done, and made herself smile brightly at everyone in the room. "Now that I'm properly dressed we can all go down to greet our guests.

"Bishop Arkady," she added. "I'd be honored if you'd escort me downstairs."

Chapter 14

"**S**poiled for choice," Kit murmured. "Or so I would say normally."

"Excuse me, young man?" his dinner partner questioned.

"There are two very beautiful women seated at either end of this table," Kit informed the elderly baroness to his left. "It's hard for a man to know which way to look." Kit was seated closer to the magnificent raven-haired creature in the revealing scarlet dress. He studied her profile as he spoke.

"It is considered polite to pay attention to the person seated next to you," the baroness said, but she did not sound offended. In fact, she chuckled, and informed him, "In case you're thinking of approaching the woman in red, be warned that she is Countess Irenia Ornov"—and added with a sniff—"a title she earned for service to King Gregory."

"As I suspected," Kit said softly.

The countess was seated to the right of the king at the head of the table. King Gregory's attention was centered on the woman in red and her glorious bosom. While Kit certainly appreciated the view, his personal preference was for the less blatant beauty that reigned at the other end of the long table. Lily looked as fair as a flower, and as regal as a princess should. Her dress was of cream lace, her copper-tinted hair arranged in high-piled curls. While the countess was earthy, Lily was elegant without being ethereal. An approachable princess, he thought.

"And the lady at the other end of the table?" he inquired of the baroness. He knew he should not let curiosity get the better of him. The less he knew about Lily the better. The less he thought about her the better. He could not stop himself, though he kept his gaze fixed on the king's end of the table. "Do you know anything about the princess?"

"I should hope so," the woman answered. "Her mother and I have been friends for years. In fact, I'm surprised Eleanor allowed her daughter to take part in this nonsense. I'm sure the rumors about Princess Lily being engaged to King Gregory are mistaken. I know for a fact that she never wanted the girl to set foot in Bororavia. I wrote to her at Harelby House asking her if I should support her daughter socially in these rather odd circum-stances, but I've received no answer. I still don't approve, but I came tonight because of my friendship with her mother."

Kit didn't like what he heard. He remembered how overbearing the king had been to Lily at the ball. Even now His Highness was carousing with his mistress at the opposite end of the table from Lily. It was best that he not think about the princess's future. He decided it would be wise not to ask for explanations, but he found that his gaze had drifted to the other end of the table. His view of Lily was obscured, but even at a distance she was a joy to watch. He was charmed by the way she tilted her head to listen when someone spoke. There was graciousness and grace in her every movement, whether nodding to a server to set the next course, or making a small gesture as she answered some question from the person seated to her right. He noticed that she wore the bracelet he'd returned and was pleased, glad for her even though he was the one who'd stolen the bracelet.

Kit was in awe of Lily's slender, long neck. The neckline of her gown was modest, but the way the lace bodice outlined her breasts and long waist was exciting. Her pale skin took on a positive glow in the warm candlelight. He had touched that skin, and knew how warm and soft it was.

Worshipping from afar, he scoffed at himself, like some medieval knight who'd taken a vow to chastely love his lady fair. What was next, he wondered? Should he offer to slay a dragon for her?

Fetch home the holy grail? How far he'd fallen, and how fast.

You're not in love, he told himself sternly. It's only frustrated lust. She's the one who wants to be chaste, not you. Let her stay in her virgin's tower; you have more important things to do than continue a seduction. He knew it wasn't going to be easy, but tonight he was not going to give in to impulse. He wasn't going to approach her. He was going to stick to his plan, do the job, and get out.

Piece of cake, as Beatrice would say. A dry, hard to swallow one, he added sulkily.

He had come into the party quietly, mingled with the crowd, entered the dining room early to make sure the placecard Beatrice had also forged for him was placed shielded by flower arrangements and silver display pieces. He had done everything possible to be a nondescript fellow who drew no attention to himself. That he was in the same room with Lily turned out to be an utter confusion to his senses, but this time he could not let it interfere with his job.

"Fruit cake," he murmured. And all the air went out of the room as their gazes suddenly met.

"Good Lord, he's here!"

"What, Your Highness?" The admiral at her side asked. He held a hand to his ear. "I'm a bit deaf, you know."

What was Kit Fox doing here? Was he here to

see her? Had he just come for the meal? She could read nothing in his eyes or his expression. What did that mean?

It meant that the man was nearly half the distance of the room away from her, which made details of expression a little vague, and also that he knew how to keep his composure in a crowd. She should strive for some of the same social poise. In fact, she'd been managing to fake a certain amount of self-possession up until a moment ago. Though it wasn't easy, Lily broke her gaze from Kit's. At least she hadn't shouted. Oddly, no one was looking at her. She forced herself to turn her head and smile at the admiral, and continue a conversation. She had no idea what she said.

Until she found herself gazing into a pair of dark and inscrutable eyes, her evening had been going well enough.

Lily had decided early on that whatever Gregory and Irenia were doing at their end of the table was none of her business. She'd rather hoped that Irenia was exerting all her wiles to convince Gregory that Lily was not the bride he wanted. While the courses came and went and she made vapid conversation, she'd prayed for the night to be over soon. Fortunately, she was hungry, and there were several large flower arrangements obscuring her view of the other end of the table. So she didn't have to think about how someday she could easily be involved in the same sort of scene: heading

Gregory's table as his wife while his mistress held court at Gregory's side. She knew that such a scenario was but one of the humiliations that loomed in her future if Gregory got his way.

Lily had her meal to concentrate on, as well as her duties as hostess to direct the conversation at this end of the table. Her duty was to be gracious and accessible while the time passed. After all, it was not every day that the guests at the Bororavian Embassy had the chance to socialize with an exotic foreign princess.

She was about as exotic as a Border Liecester ewe in a Yorkshire pasture, but she was under explicit orders not to bring up her English roots or loyalties. She supposed sheep were off-limits as well. Pity, since wool and mutton production were far more interesting than anything else she'd spoken of this evening. Oh, the weather was a fascinating subject. As was fashion, the latest art exhibits, operas, the doings of people she didn't know, and the history of the Battle of Trafalgar as recounted by Admiral MacReady, who certainly looked old enough to have been there.

She had managed not to yawn through the dull period before she noticed Kit's presence. Now she had to manage not to scream from the hysterics mounting with her awareness of him. Not that she was prone to screaming fits, of course. After several weeks of emotional pressure building to the point of hopelessness she didn't see why she shouldn't have a fit. Irenia had fits all the time, and didn't seem to be any the worse for them. No one locked her up, or threatened her parents.

Perhaps I think hysterics are out of place because I'm three quarters English, Lily thought. Maybe I should give in to my Bororavian side. We are a passionate people. Probably because passion serves to keep the blood warm during the long, cold winters on the coast of the Baltic Sea.

And you have given in to the irrational side of your nature, she reminded herself. Remember your mad plan to get yourself dishonored?

It might have been a mad plan, she countered her own critical voice, but it would have worked.

It doesn't have to be true, but he has to think it's true.

"Why didn't I think of that before?" She exclaimed as she looked at the admiral. "And I have just the man to do it."

Before the poor man could respond, she turned her attention to the middle of the table, and the magnificent, broad-shouldered figure of Kit Fox. His head swiveled toward her as if she'd called his name, and when she had his attention, she waved.

Kit did not linger long at the dinner table with the other men when the ladies exited at the end of the meal. He stayed long enough to shake his head when the cigar box was being passed around. He was one of several men who used a declared aversion to smoking as an excuse to leave the table. Frankly, he would have liked a smoke, but this was too useful a diversion to pass up. So Kit rose, bowed in the direction of the king, who was too drunk to notice or acknowledge anything but his brandy glass, and made his exit.

Once in the wide reception hall outside the dining room, Kit congratulated himself for escaping his craving for tobacco. But now that he was free of the formality imposed at a state dinner, he had to fight an even stronger craving to find Lily. If she had not noticed him it might have been easier for him to put her out of his mind. In fact, he thought he might even have been able to continue worshiping from afar—if she hadn't actively flirted with him through the last two courses and the dessert.

And he'd flirted back, of course. How could he help himself? He stood and stared at the wide black and white squares of the polished marble floor and recalled how she behaved. She smiled, she waved, she made big, suggestive eyes at him over the top of her posey holder while pretending to sniff the rose in the delicate gold filigree container. She'd eaten her dessert in the most provocative manner he'd ever seen. The performance had left him feverish.

There had been nothing subtle about her obvious interest in him. People had even begun to quietly murmur about it. Kit had been embarrassed for her. But, to his shame—or it would be to his shame if he had any—embarrassment had not stopped him from reacting with smiles and suggestive glances of his own. The elderly baroness beside him had whispered to him to mind his manners and his place, which only annoyed him. What good sense he had flew out the window around his Lily Princess.

Kit glanced at the front stairway with a pang of lust. Maybe he should hide in her bedroom and wait for her after he was finished with his search of the rest of the embassy. No doubt she regretted her fit of maidenly modesty, and has decided that tonight she would not say no. That was surely the message she'd been sending from the head of the table.

It was a pleasant thought, but meeting her for a midnight tryst was something he would not follow through on should he find what he was looking for. It must always be business before pleasure—or Aunt Phoebe would box his ears for sure.

He tried hard to keep the image of his stern aunt in his head as he once more went about the business of searching the Bororavian Embassy for evidence of collusion with international revolutionaries out to overthrow the world's governments. This being an embassy, there were no doubt many interesting documents to be found. What he looked for was the most secret of secret documents, therefore they would be the most cleverly hidden. His search two nights ago had been brief, interrupted, and but for the interlude in Lily's bedroom, fruitless. Even that had turned out to be ultimately frustrating. The memories of taste and touch and scent were vivid and maddening. *Tantalizing*. He frowned at the word, being too well-educated in the classics not to recall that the word originated in the Greek myth of Tantalus, whose punishment in Hades consisted of having a goal set out of his reach for all eternity. Kit loathed the idea of ending up like that poor Greek fellow. *Then put her out of your mind. Let it go.*

If only the memory of how she caressed her dessert spoon wasn't branded into his mind.

Branded or not, he must concentrate on the job at hand. He decided to start with the formal rooms on this side of the ground floor even though they were occupied with servants and guests at the moment. It was an art form to conduct a burglary in plain sight, an art he practiced with ease. Someone was playing piano in the music room, so he strolled through that doorway first.

Only to find Lily standing just inside the doorway, as though she'd been waiting in ambush. He was trapped, and she didn't hesitate to pounce.

"There you are!"

"Here I am," he agreed, powerless to do anything but step close to her and gaze into her magnificent aquamarine eyes. She reached up to touch his cheek. She was not wearing gloves, and the warmth from her touch seared through him. Distantly, he heard the sound of piano music, and a susurrus of shocked whispering. The room was full of women, wasn't it? Yes, out of the corner of his eye he could make out the colors of many dresses. They reminded him of a flock of brightly-colored exotic birds set against the dull background of dark furniture and green wallpaper.

A few moments before Kit entered the room, Lily told herself that she could not go through with this seduction game. Now that he was here, she forgot that it was a game. Touching him was a compulsion, an action as natural and necessary as breathing. It didn't help that she'd gotten herself all worked up trying to play the coquette over dinner.

"Young woman," Kit admonished, putting his hand over hers, urging her to cup his cheek. "You were flirting with me."

She grinned with pleasure. "You noticed?"

"It was impossible not to."

"Good. There was a girl named Pansy I used to see at house parties back home. Everyone used to talk about what a terrible flirt she was. I modeled myself after her. She used to shock the old ladies something terrible, but Pansy never lacked for beaus. In fact, she married a baronet. Sometimes I'd get a bit jealous that everyone courted her while I stood there growing older by the minute."

He took her hand and raised it to his lips, and lingered for a few lovely, tingling moments, while his eyes laughed into hers. "You, lack for suitors? I can't believe it. No one as beautiful as you, and a princess beside, could ever be ignored."

Her insides fluttered at Kit Fox calling her beautiful, but Lily hastened to explain, "Don't you believe it. No one courts princesses."

No one until you. The fire that rushed through Lily wiped out any awareness that they were not alone. "No one in Yorkshire," she told him.

"Perhaps you should have come to London sooner." He turned her hand over and kissed her palm.

"Perhaps I should have."

"There's another journey you need to take," Kit told her.

"There is?"

Kit nodded. His voice lowered to a seductive whisper. "One we started together."

"Ah." She nodded. Her breath caught, and she flushed. Her eyes were bright as stars, and he saw his own hunger reflected in them. "I think it would be a pleasant journey."

His hands sought her waist, drawing her closer. "I can promise you that."

Kit was aware that he was spouting the worst sort of romantic rubbish, but the words came of their own accord. He never had any trouble talking this way to the ladies, but this time he meant it, God help him. He was aware that he hadn't yet said anything that might commit him to any kind of actual pledge to the lovely Lily, but he knew he was in danger of making an emotional attachment. Love was an emotion he reserved for members of his family. He must not let his heart go unguarded: it was the first lesson a secret agent must learn.

Grab hold of your cynicism man! he told himself. Use it. It's the only thing that's going to save you. You didn't start this, Lily did. The girl who sent you from her room before you could make love has for some reason decided to change her mind. Don't automatically believe that it's because she'd been pining for you since she made that regrettable decision. Don't let your overinflated opinion of your charms waltz you into a trap. Don't presume the girl is an innocent in anything but the arts of love. A pretty face and charming air may well be hiding a shrewd schemer out to use you for some reason. Please try to think of her as a foreigner, and that duty to your own country comes first.

"This has to stop," Kit decided.

"Does it?"

"Don't tease."

Kit stepped away, his hands dropping to his sides. Lily heard someone cough at the same time, and this brought her back to the real world. A room full of English and Bororavian nobles stared at her. A cold shiver went through her, but she wasn't sure if it was because she had succeeded in behaving scandalously, or because Kit was no longer touching her.

Please remember that you are acting, Lily reminded herself. She forced herself to take a hard, objective look at the handsome stranger. This man did not break into the house because he wanted to make love to you. He is here for purposes beyond having you as an after-dinner sweet, and whatever they are, they're opposed to Bororavian interests.

No matter how distasteful using someone is, if you must do it, Lily, he deserves it. Kit Fox is a thief, or why else would he be a housebreaker? And he's possibly worse than a thief. He's a secret agent most likely. Never mind that you cannot help but be attracted to him. You cannot allow the attraction to be real. Oh, he wants you, all right, but it certainly doesn't mean anything to him. He'll steal your heart and not even notice he's pocketed it.

It was all so confusing. And to add to her confusion, Lady Ornov came up to her and said, "Highness, the display cases are ready."

Lily looked at the woman in complete puzzlement. "The what?"

"The viewing," Lady Ornov said, as though Lily knew perfectly well what she was talking about. "The entire royal family must be there."

Memory finally stirred while Lady Ornov grilled her with the sternest of stares. "The viewing. Of course!" How could she forget the ostensible excuse for holding this party in the first place? And the whole family would be there. That included Gregory, who would be all puffed up with pride, and probably too much drink, to show off before the British nobility.

Lily looked around as Kit headed toward the door. He stiffened in surprise when she grabbed him by the back of his finely tailored black coat. "Come along"—Lily put her arm through his—"let me show you something you might find interesting."

Chapter 15

Kit found it frustrating, as well as interesting, that Lily was once more standing so close to him. Her voice had been a purr; there was a sparkle in her eyes . . .

He couldn't get away from her. Even when he tried, there she was. He laughed. "I thought I was the one offering to show you."

Her cheeks flushed bright pink. "Not that." She tapped him on the tip of his nose with the pink rose in her posey-holder. The scent of the flower was almost as intoxicating as being near her. "Come along, rascal."

With her arm in his, she led the way, and everyone who'd been in the music room followed. Lily brought them to a large reception room where the rest of the dinner guests were waiting. The crowd was gathered around a table, but they parted in deference as he and Lily approached.

She stopped before a table set in the center of the room. "These are Bororavia's national treasures."

Kit gazed into a small glass case set on the table. Inside, on a bed of blue velvet sat a small silver ring set with an orange-yellow citrine that looked to be of no great value, and a magnificent ruby brooch that any kingdom would be proud to call a crown jewel. "Lovely," he said of the ruby. "The ring is—"

"It doesn't look like much, does it?" Lily leaned against him, her gaze fixed on Kit rather than the jewels.

"You are certainly more beautiful than rubies," he told her. He was doing it again. He couldn't seem to stop. Had they been alone, he would have leaned forward to kiss her. As it was, he could barely turn his attention back to the jewels. "They have an historical significance?"

"Oh, yes," Lily answered. "I've heard the stories about the ring and brooch all my life. They were like fairy tales for me when I was growing up. They have been in adventures for hundreds of years."

"Jewels do not have adventures," he pointed out.

"This pair does. They're always getting stolen, then retrieved. It was nice to finally get a chance to see them."

"Finally?"

"They're usually kept in a vault in the royal treasury."

"Then what are they doing in England?"

She blushed, and then sighed dramatically. She touched a finger to the glass. It seemed to Kit that she would have pushed the case away if she could. "They have a symbolic function."

"What?"

"They must be worn by the king's bride on her wedding day."

Kit turned his head to look at the man who had spoken. "Good evening, Bishop Arkady. Duke Michael," he added to the dark man standing beside the Bororavian clergyman.

Arkady did not give Kit even the briefest of nods. His attention was on Lily. "It will be a great privilege for you to wear these jewels on your wedding day, Highness. How much of the jewels' history do you really know?" He gave Duke Michael a look that was both proud and fatherly before continuing to speak to Lily. "The jewels date back to the Middle Ages, and legends say they have magical properties."

"Yes. I was telling—"

"You know all this," Arkady interrupted her. "But do you know, Princess, how the jewels were stolen during the Napoleonic wars?"

"Yes. My father—"

"Your father was a boy still in the nursery then. Your grandfather was quite mad—"

"We don't talk about that." It was Lily who interrupted this time.

Arkady ignored what she said, while still intensely concentrating on her. "One of the jewels ended up in England, Highness, the other in France. It was Duke Michael's Romany grandparents who took it upon themselves to find the ring and brooch and restore them to the royal family. They were great patriots, and their son the greatest defender of our country. Your aunt believed it a great honor to marry the son of this brave couple. The blood of heroes as well as the blood of the royal family flows in Michael's veins."

"I blush at your commendation," Duke Michael said, and then took a sip from his wineglass. "But I think we all know what flows in my blood most of the time."

"If you had a purpose in life, you would not feel the need for drink," the bishop stated with fervent conviction. Michael shrugged.

All this praise for Michael was not lost on Kit, and a glance at Lily told him that she understood what the bishop was getting at as well. Arkady was offering her Duke Michael as a matrimonial alternative to her other cousin, King Gregory. Did she have a choice? Would any woman of intelligence and ambition choose a duke over a king? Would any woman of intelligence and breeding choose a foundling thief over any respectable man?

For all that he knew Lily couldn't and

shouldn't marry him, Kit didn't like the thought of her marrying either the Bororavian prince or king, for all their royal blood. She deserved better than a king.

The two other men still took no notice that Kit was there. Arkady's attention was intently on Lily. The duke did not seem to really be interested in anything. Kit should have appreciated that he was a nonentity to these people; anonymity served the purposes of a secret agent. Instead it roused a streak of defiance in him, causing him to slip his arm around the princess's waist. He actually smiled with cold triumph at Prince Michael when Lily leaned against him.

Standing hip to hip, awareness of her was a pulse pounding in his blood. He had never felt so right with anyone. And she was clearly attracted to him rather than to either of her royal cousins.

Michael took no notice of the pair of them. Arkady looked ready to deliver a lecture, but he did not get the chance.

"You have your arm around my fiancée's waist, foreigner. Take it away or lose it," demanded the king of Bororavia as he marched up to them. The king slurred the words, but Kit did not mistake the harsh tone as anything but dangerous. "What's the meaning of acting the slut with this vermin again?" Gregory demanded of Lily

Kit bristled at the insult to Lily, but she spoke up for herself before he could respond. "Don't be a pest, Gregory. Kit and I are old friends, and I am enjoying his company."

"How dare you!" the king snarled at his cousin.

Lily stood her ground, and leaned closer into Kit's embrace. "We are not officially betrothed, Gregory."

The man loomed over Lily like an angry, dark shadow. Fury boiled in his eyes, and clenched his fists. "How dare you speak to me that way?"

"Very well—we are not officially betrothed, Your Highness."

The king's mouth hung open for a moment. Then he continued to upbraid Lily in his native language. She blanched at his words, but she held her head up proudly, and still didn't move away from Kit.

Finally, Gregory gave the girl a glare that threatened retribution, but for now he concentrated on Kit.

"Cherminsky." The king waved the man forward. "Escort this interloper from my house."

Lily gasped, and clung to him, but Kit considered it the better part of valor to pry himself away from her. "It's all right," he told her. He did take her hands and squeeze them gently for a moment. He felt her trembling and realized she was terrified of the overbearing king. These last few minutes had been an act of rebellion.

His Lily hated her circumscribed life, and he

hated that there was nothing he could do about it. He had wanted a simple affair but he had come to want more. Lily belonged to the brutish king and Christopher Fox MacLeod belonged to the service of the Crown, and there was nothing either of them could do to change it. He had a brief, mad notion of challenging the king to a duel—and if it was only for himself and Lily perhaps he would.

Instead, he let her hands go and said to King Gregory. "Of course I'll go."

Kit knew things were ominous when Cherminsky did not escort him to the front entrance. Oh, no, the guard captain sneered at him, and took Kit in the opposite direction of the entry hall. He was not being allowed to leave as a guest, but thrown out like a piece of scum that had dared to look above his station.

"Ah, the cut direct," Kit murmured as he was marched along.

He was led to the servants' entrance at the back of the building, into the darkness between the kitchen and the stables. Kit made himself relax when he walked through the door. That way he was prepared for the fall when Cherminsky shoved him hard in the base of the spine. Fortunately, he didn't hit any of the steps and it wasn't a long distance to the ground, and Kit had the reflexes and training of an acrobat. He waited on the rough brick paving beneath the stairs, pretending

to be stunned while he waited to see if the Bororavian had any further unpleasantness in mind for
the English interloper. He could feel Cherminsky
hovering above him, thinking about it. It was probably less than a minute, but seemed like an hour
before the door slammed and Kit let out a sigh and
got to his feet.

Things actually could not have worked out better for him if he'd planned this outcome himself.
He smiled and whispered, "Thank you, Lily my
love."

He now had more freedom to roam at will. Getting back in the building was no problem for him,
and no one would think he was there. With large
numbers of guests in the embassy, the guards were
out of sight and the dogs locked away in their ken-
nel. It would make his actual exit from the embassy
so much easier than it had been two nights before.

Kit had a quick look around the outside. The
only thing he found that seemed vaguely out of
place was an unattended hitched carriage waiting
outside the stables. It looked like someone in residence was planning on leaving after dinner. It was
puzzling, but Kit noted it and put it out of his
mind. The comings and goings of the Bororavians
were not his business, finding incriminating documents was.

Kit approached the back of the embassy and
studied the row of unlit windows on the ground

floor. He rubbed his hands briskly together in anticipation, and chose the window on the left corner of the building as his insertion point. He smiled, the joy of the daredevil boy housebreaker bursting through the surface of the civilized, sophisticated, mostly ethical man. The dark and the danger suited this part of him. These days he usually took more pride in his work than he did pleasure, but he was going to enjoy stealing everything he could from King Gregory of Bororavia.

Gregory dragged her into the library, which was the closest empty room, and pushed her so hard that she had to catch herself on the edge of the desk to keep from falling. Then he slammed the door, but it didn't catch and bounced open a few inches instead.

Lily thought about running out that barely open door, but all she managed was to turn to face him before he roared, "Make no mistake, girl. You are in trouble. Deep, desperate trouble."

She made herself stand straight, and tried to keep her voice from shaking. She had gotten Gregory where she wanted him; she dared not back down now. "Is this new trouble somehow different than the trouble I am already in?"

The only light in the room was moonlight that came through the window. She could hear the sounds of carriages being loaded and leaving on the street in front of the embassy. The king had declared the party over, and now everyone who was anyone among the British aristocracy was going to be gossiping about the princess's wild behavior. Lily knew that social disgrace was the least of her problems. Gregory lunged at her like a monster out of the darkness. She jumped back and grasped the edge of the desktop at her back. She gasped, and he laughed. The sound twisted her stomach. Gregory was very much her problem.

Meaty hands settled on her shoulders, fingers squeezed into her flesh hard enough to leave bruises. "What have you done with the foreigner? Has he touched you?"

All the air seemed to go out of the room. Her head grew light, then she realized she was holding her breath. The impulse born of fear was to deny everything. She made herself say, "Of course he's touched me. You've seen him."

"He's had you."

The flat statement was rife with filth. It sent images through her, of naked bodies shining with sweat and writhing with unbridled lust.

He shook her. "Tell me."

Lily flinched and squeezed her eyes shut. She knew she needed to stand up to the man, but he terrified her. His breath stank with wine; it made her stomach turn.

"I own you," Gregory reminded her when she remained silent. "If he's had you I'll kill him."

This was not going at all the way she'd planned. She needed to be bold, brazen, and fearless. Shrink from him now, she told herself, and you'll be doing it the rest of your life.

"Perhaps Kit and I have—been together." She opened her eyes and met Gregory's accusing gaze. "It's a trifling affair. What does it matter? Among the British upper class, it is discretion that matters, not what one actually does."

"We are not English."

"I am."

"You were not being discreet."

"Why should I be? You and Irenia are not."

"I am a man."

"Really? I haven't seen any evidence of manliness from you."

He obviously mistook her meaning, or he wouldn't have slapped her. The blow knocked her back across the desk. She was so shocked at having been struck that she didn't feel any pain. She hastened to roll all the way over the desk and land on her feet on the other side. Her heavy skirts swept objects to the floor. A glass bottle shattered. Trim on her ball gown ripped, and lace was torn, but she ignored such small obstacles in her haste to put space between herself and her cousin.

It was too late to point out that she meant she'd thought he'd acted like a coward, a cad, and a bully since the day they'd met, but his taking it as a sexual insult was better for her cause anyway. She kept the desk between them as Gregory came toward her again. "Don't you touch me." She barely whispered the words.

He sneered, but he didn't shout. His voice remained low and menacing. "A *man* touches what he wants. If I want you I will take you."

"You don't want me. You want Irenia."

He stopped. "Is that what this nonsense is about? Are you trying to get my attention? Flaunting yourself with another man because you are jealous?"

His self-satisfied laughter mocked her. "Play the whore, girl, but the game belongs to me. You'll have a visit from my physician in the morning. I'll have the truth. If you prove to be less than a virgin, your mother will be dead within the week. And your lover will be dead much sooner. Now get out of my sight."

Totally defeated and feeling like the world's worst fool, Lily did not hesitate to pick up her skirts and run from the room.

It looked like his incident with the king had caused the party to break up early. Kit didn't mind having the place to himself, especially since the king's outrage seemed to have sent the household into hiding. The evening kept getting better and better. He felt lucky. Nothing could go wrong now. Easy in. Easy out.

"Piece of cake," he whispered. He even vaguely considered stopping off by the jewel case and liberating the ruby as a memento on his way out. But he decided against that instantly, for considering his mad behavior of late it was likely he'd send the brooch back to Lily gift wrapped as a love token. Or possibly he should take the ring. It was smaller, of far less value, and might look pretty on her finger. "It's the royal wedding ring, you idiot. Of course it will look good on the princess's finger." She was going to be queen. He was going to complete his mission. They would never meet again. Too bad, but there were plenty of other women in the world—even if none of them were anything like his Lily.

Kit shook his head, which he decided had gone distinctly soft. Fortunately while his thoughts rambled, he moved with practiced skill from room to room conducting a thorough search.

It came to him in a flash of insight. Kit came to a sudden halt in the center of the fifth room he searched, and slapped his palm against his forehead. He knew exactly where Gregory hid his documents. It was so obvious Kit felt like a fool. Served him right for letting himself get involved with a woman.

Where was the best place to hide something? In plain sight, of course.

Fool, he mouthed silently, and made his way swiftly and cautiously toward the social secretary's office. He remembered piles and piles of papers stacked in bins and boxes, on chairs and tables and the desk itself. It was going to take hours to search the place.

The hallway remained empty, but Kit slowed when he heard voices from behind a door that was slightly ajar. One angry man shouting, and a woman's less distinct responses. He hesitated, not sure whether to find another route or go on. With all the intensity of the argument, Kit worried that the door could burst open at any second and the couple would spill into the hall.

He'd decided to simply go on when he heard the sound of a blow, the thud of fallen objects, and the tinkle of broken glass.

It was Lily. She was in trouble.

Kit's hand was on the doorknob before cold, professional logic and years of training took over. If he ran to her aid, his mission was compromised and his country might well be in serious danger from an anarchist threat. The British Empire must now, and always, come first. Otherwise, he was nothing but a thief in the night and his whole life a sham.

She would have to fend for herself.

He took his hand from the knob, and turned away. For the sake of his country, he moved on.

Chapter 16

"**W**ell, that didn't go exactly according to plan." Lily sighed, and sat down on her bed. At least she was alone, in her nightgown and out of that corset and all those wretched petticoats. Being comfortable was certainly no compensation for all the awfulness that came before. Even memories of the brief moments with Kit brought her no comfort. She knew that she would never see him again, and the knowledge hurt more than she could say. Certainly far more than the throbbing bruise on her cheek. Worse, her actions may have put him in danger. He might be up to no good, but he didn't deserve to be the object of Gregory's revenge for having dishonored her.

Which he hadn't. And Gregory would learn that soon enough.

"Oh, Lord." She dropped her head in her hands

as thoughts of the impending medical examination filled her with dread. Why hadn't she considered that possibility when she formed her scheme to escape Gregory's bed?

She ran a hand along the cool smooth linen sheets of her turned-down bed. She remembered lying back, eyes half-closed, the breath catching in her throat, and avidly watching while Kit sat in this very spot, undoing his clothing. Anticipation boiled in her then. It still simmered just below the surface, a longing for pleasure she would never know. How was she supposed to get through the rest of her life with only memories of a few kisses, touches, and furtive short minutes in this bed that had come to nothing?

"Blast!" she muttered, and slapped the mattress with her fists. "I should have gone through with it."

Too late. And poor Kit might end up getting beaten, or worse. It was all so futile.

"And all my fault." She sighed again, and was wiping away tears when her head came up suddenly. A mix of elation and fear brought Lily to her feet. "Who's there?"

While she hoped it was Kit back for another midnight tryst, she still grabbed a tall silver candlestick off the bedside table for protection before she inched toward the doorway of her sitting room. Good Lord, what if it was Gregory come to find out if she was a virgin? The thought of being raped by her cousin set her stomach roiling in revulsion.

She'd barely made it to the doorway, when a tall man loomed out of the darkness in front of her.

She stepped back in shock. "Captain Cherminsky."

"Be quiet." He snatched the candlestick away from her. Cherminsky grabbed her left wrist and pulled her to him, lifting a folded piece of cloth toward her face.

Lily caught a whiff of sickly sweet scent permeating the material. It made her dizzy even as she ducked her head away.

"Very well," she heard Cherminsky say while the room spun around her. "Better you walk for now. Come along."

He led her forward, out of her rooms, down the hall and the stairs. Lily went with him, wanting to hold back, break away, protest, but the dizziness took away all her will.

She wasn't able to fight the drug until they were at the bottom of the stairs.

What was he doing? Where was he taking her? Gregory's apartment was on the second floor, wasn't it?

She asked the questions, but she thought she knew the answers. "Irenia," she said, though she found it hard to form the word.

"Yes," he answered.

Even though the word came out a rough whisper, she heard the devotion in it. So the king's mistress had seduced the captain of the king's guards to abduct the princess. Amazing. It was all very melodramatic. The British royal family certainly didn't behave this way.

He hurried her along, down a hallway on the ground floor. She didn't know what time it was, but no light shone from any doorway they passed. All the guests were long gone. It was as though she and Cherminsky were alone in the world.

What was Cherminsky going to do with her? Kill her? Irenia might have talked him into going that far.

She could not let this happen. She didn't dare leave. "No! You don't understand."

"Quiet." He pulled her into a tight embrace. She struggled, but the big man took no notice. He thrust the drugged cloth toward her face again.

Lily held her breath, and went completely limp. This took him by surprise, and his grip loosened for a fraction of a moment. It was long enough for Lily to drop to the floor. She scrambled away, jumped to her feet, and ran. Her bare feet slapped along the hardwood floor and she heard his boots behind her.

It occurred to her that she should be screaming for help, but before she could do that a door to her right opened. A man carrying a bundle of papers stepped into her path. She slammed into him, knocking the air out of her and the papers out of his hands. She went down, and the papers floated down on top of her.

She looked up and saw Kit staring down on her. Then Cherminsky was there.

Lily heard Kit say, "What the—" And then the two men rushed toward each other.

The fight between the two men was fast. Lily heard more than she saw. She might have made more sense of it if the cloth hadn't been knocked out of Cherminsky's hand and she got a good sniff of it in passing. She gagged and fought dizziness, and managed to make it to her feet. Shadows moved while grunts and blows sounded out of the wavering world around her.

Kit had not hesitated when he saw Cherminsky bearing down on the girl. He didn't know what was going on, but his first thought was that Lily was in trouble and he needed to defend her. He took great satisfaction in every blow he landed. Cherminsky was a big, hard man, dangerous, but slower than Kit, and far less agile. Kit moved fast and struck hard. The last thing he wanted was to give the other man time to call for help. He took a few blows himself in order to get in close under the man's guard, then he used the proximity to make two quick strikes—a blow to Cherminsky's throat, then a punch in the jaw. This combination sent the Bororavian down for the count.

Kit made a quick check to see that the man was indeed unconscious. Kit heard Cherminsky groan and reasoned the man wouldn't be out for long. He considered making a more thorough job of it, but he turned to Lily instead. She'd gotten to her feet during the fracas, and was now staggering around the hallway gathering up the documents he'd dropped.

The impulse to hold and comfort her was forced to take a backseat to the necessity of completing his mission. He reached out. He spoke softly, reassuringly, but with command, for the girl looked quite dazed. "Give me those, Lily."

She backed away. "No."

He quickly gathered up the documents she'd missed, then followed after her. "Please, Lily?" *Are you all right, Lily? How can I help you? Did he hurt you? Why were you being chased by that bastard while wearing only your nightgown? Why are you drugged?* He didn't ask the questions, but concentrated on retrieving what he'd come for.

"You're a thief, aren't you?" she asked. "A spy."

"Yes."

"You should be ashamed."

"Sometimes I am." As they talked she backed down the hall toward the servants' entrance. He followed her. "Lily my love," he told her. "I need what you have."

Lily caught the gleam of his white teeth when he smiled. She shook her head. "You don't want me. Only the documents."

"I do want you," he answered. "But I need those papers right now."

She fought off dizziness, confusion, and heartache. Nothing went right. Nothing was sane or sure or good or true. Kit was a thief—well, she'd suspected that, but it hurt to witness his perfidy. "Perfidy," she mouthed the word. "Does that sound like a town in Wales to you?"

"Very like one, yes," he agreed. "You're out of your head, my love."

"Nobody loves me," she countered. "I'm feeling sorry for myself, aren't I?"

"It does sound that way. You have good reasons," he soothed.

She shook her head wildly. That only made the dizziness worse. Her head hurt and her heart hurt and everybody was so mean to her! "You have no idea."

"Don't I?" He kept edging closer.

"No. I'm going to tell on you." She backed up against a heavy wooden door. "I'm going to scream for help any moment now. I'm going to tell everyone that Kit Fox is a British spy who used me to steal from Bororavia . . . and then you'll be sorry."

"I'm sure I will be. Why would you call for help, Lily?"

She raised her head proudly, and that made her dizzy too. Her brain felt like it was getting bigger and bigger and was going to explode. "Because I have to look out for the interests of Bororavia. Because my father—"

Kit pounced. She hadn't expected him to, and she screamed.

He grabbed the papers, then he grabbed her, and pressed his mouth over hers to stop the sound from going any further than between them. It was too late, of course. Her screaming was going to bring slamming doors and shouted questions, and guards were going to be called out. Finding Cherminsky's unconscious body was only a matter of time. He had to get away now, and he had no choice but to take the screaming princess with him. She did know who he was. She could give information that would expose British spying on her country. She could put his family in danger, and that he would not have. Cherminsky posed a similar threat, but Kit's instinct told him that the captain had nefarious plans of his own. That carriage waiting outside was there for Cherminsky's getaway.

How convenient.

Since it was meant for an escape vehicle, Kit had no qualms about using it.

This stolen kiss was sweet but it had to stop. Much as he loathed to do it, Kit was prepared to knock Lily out to keep her silent and cooperative, but he didn't have to worry about it. When he lifted his head, hers fell gently backward against his supporting arm. She was quite unconscious. This was not the way he normally liked his women, but right now it was fine with him.

He quickly tucked the documents into his coat, then lifted the sleeping princess in his arms, flung open the back door, and sprinted toward the stables and the waiting carriage.

Chapter 17

"Where am I?"

Lily had always heard that was the first thing anyone who had fainted wanted to know. Now she understood how disturbing the disorientation was. She'd emerged from deep darkness a moment ago aware that something awful had happened.

She was lying down on something very soft, and there was light behind her closed eyes. Daylight? She was still dizzy, but certain that nothing but her sense of reality was twirling around in a circle.

Fingers brushed gently across her forehead, brushing back hair. She wasn't alone.

"Have I been kidnapped again?" she whispered.

"You're safe."

The voice was deep, yet soft as satin, reassuring. Enticing. Anything but safe.

She was with Kit. Joy suffused her, from the tip of her toes to the top of her aching head. Why was her head aching? She doubted that delight was the proper reaction. She was on a bed, wasn't she? Beds and Kit seemed to go together.

"Am I in bed?"

"You could open your eyes and find out."

She supposed she could. "I'm not ready yet."

"I see."

The amusement in Kit's voice made her want to smile. She felt the mattress shift slightly as he sat down beside her, moving her body closer to him. Her hip had rolled up against what felt like a muscular thigh.

"Am I still wearing my nightgown?" she asked suddenly.

Kit gave a soft, wicked chuckle. "For the moment."

Implications and temptations flittered through her already fuddled mind, and desire pooled inside her.

"I could help you off with it if you like."

"Good Lord!"

Her eyes flew open as she bolted up. Pillows scattered from behind her, landing with soft thuds onto the floor. A wave of dizziness might have sent her headfirst after the pillows, but firm hands grasped her shoulders, steadied her and—

Meaty hands settled on her shoulders, fingers squeezed into her flesh hard enough to leave bruises.

"What have you done with the foreigner? Has he touched you? He has, hasn't he?"

"Don't touch me!"

Kit knew he shouldn't have teased her like that. He was also certain she wasn't seeing him, though her eyes looked straight at him. Guilt twisted through him, knowing that she must be reliving the scene with the king he'd overheard last night.

He *should* have come to the rescue, he realized now, instead of walking away. She'd have been spared anymore bullying. In the end they'd ended up here at the MacLeod family safehouse outside London anyway.

The fear he saw in her wide open eyes was bad enough, but Lily's sudden scream rattled Kit to the core. He pulled her into a tight embrace, not to stop the sound, but wanting only to comfort her. With one hand he caressed her back, settling into a slow, soothing, rhythmic pattern. At first she remained stiff as steel in his embrace, but gradually, as sobs gave way to weaker tears, she began to relax against him. Kit became aware of soft breasts pressed against his chest. The skin beneath the thin linen was warm and supple. He breathed in the scent of her hair and for a moment was lost in her.

It took Lily some time to realize that her wet face was pressed against Kit's solid, broad chest. It seemed wide as a wall. Then again, walls were not as intriguing and didn't have such decidedly male shape and texture. Walls didn't have warmth and a heartbeat. Not like a man. This man.

She lifted her head, not at all surprised when his mouth settled over hers in a soft, tender kiss. She sighed against his lips as desire curled through her, replacing both fear and the cobweb veils behind which memory hid.

Gradually, the kiss deepened, and his hands caressed her. Her own fingers traced down his back to his waist and down to his buttocks when he leaned her back against the bed. She felt his fingers undoing the ribbon fastening her nightgown. She remembered that happening before, but this time he pushed back the fabric. A touch so soft it might have been a summer breeze brushing across her breasts. Sparks shot through her when this same soft breeze brushed her nipples. His hand settled over her naked breast. Her body rose to meet this intimate touch.

"Oh, my . . ." She breathed the words like a prayer.

"My sentiment exactly," he whispered, lips close to her ear.

Lily opened her eyes and tried to concentrate her attention on his face. The first thing that came into focus was his lips. Lovely lips. His mouth was wide, expressive, mobile. She traced a finger around the outline of those wonderful lips, following his smile even as it widened at her touch.

"You have lovely teeth," she told him.

"Thank you." He stuck out his tongue. "Wha abo dis?"

"It looks healthy."

"Thank you, doctor." He touched his tongue to the tip of her nose. It made her giggle. "What a lovely sound," he said. "We'll have more of that later. But first . . ."

Then he kissed her again, and his hands boldly roamed over her in ways that shocked Lily with the indescribable sensations he drew from her.

Not indescribable at all, actually, she decided after a wonderful while. It was a hunger, a craving that flowed through all her senses, turning the desire and the need to satisfy it into all there was in the world.

She wanted to be touched, and was being touched. Kit knew all the right places, all the right ways—softly, lingeringly, playfully, and so many more. His long fingers were skillful, practiced, so very knowing. Her need to touch him was part of the growing hunger as well. The warmth and texture of his skin fascinated her, enthralled her. She liked the sounds he made when she touched him in a way that pleased him. Gradually, her eyes closed again, allowing the rest of her perceptions to be drenched in sensation.

Sound was definitely a part of it. That she kept her eyes closed heightened Lily's sense of hearing.

The sounds of breathing, of cloth on skin and skin on skin. It was all quite amazing. Then there was taste. And smell. The only way she could define these things about Kit was "male." Keeping her eyes closed made the experience of every other sense all the more erotic.

Keeping your eyes closed also allows you to pretend that it isn't real, now doesn't it?

Lily hated that this thought intruded on all the wonderful flood of passion. She really wished reason would stop rearing its ugly head whenever she started to have a good time. Why, oh why, had her parents raised her right? Or, possibly, the drugs had finally worn off.

Lily eventually dragged herself out of the sweet beginnings of bliss, opened her eyes, and firmly pushed against Kit's broad shoulders.

"I'm starting to hate being a good girl."

Kit moaned loudly, and lifted his head from the spot he'd been kissing between her breasts. He was flushed, and there was wildness in his eyes. He licked his lips, blinked, met her gaze, and ground out, "You're saying no again."

"Yes."

He grinned, "Good."

She grabbed the thick veil of hair that had fallen across his forehead and pried his head up with it before he dived into her bosom once more. "Yes means no!"

"Ouch!" When she let go of his hair, he plied her with a wicked grin and coaxed, "No usually means yes."

She shook her head. "No."

"Are you sure?"

"No. I mean—"

"Good."

"Kit!"

He rolled off of her and rose reluctantly to his feet. "Why do you keep saying no?"

Lily sat up, pulled the nightgown down around her legs and fastened the ribbon at her throat in a double knot. She looked up at Kit. "Because it's the right thing to say," she answered.

He held his hands out toward her. "You want me. I want you. What's the harm in making love?"

"We aren't married. And we aren't going to be," she added unhappily.

"We've wanted each other since the moment we met."

"That's very likely true."

"Well, at least you don't shy away and protest your maidenly modesty."

"I'm not modest. But . . . I have to stay a maiden." She glanced at the bed, then up at him from under her lashes. He wore nothing but snugly fitting dark trousers. She had a fine view of his wide, lean, muscular chest and arms in the sunlight streaming in the window. And there was a bulge evident beneath the dark cloth covering his groin that awakened her imagination. He was handsome, virile, bold. She had no doubt of the kind of pleasure they could bring each other. She'd had two small tastes. Another taste would surely find her addicted. How could she bear anyone else but Kit in her bed then?

"I must marry royalty," she pointed out.

"Fine. Understood." He bit the words off angrily. "You don't have to be married to make love."

"But I'll only make love to the man I'll marry."

He looked her up and down. The heat in his gaze sent fire through her. "Girl, you want me."

"You've said that before." Her shoulders slumped and she gave a despondent nod. "It's the truth. But I must say no."

He threw back his head and howled. Lily would have scrambled for the door if she hadn't been certain it was locked. Then again, why should she take anything for granted? She got up and strode to the door. It was locked. She went back and sat on the bed. Kit continued to make frustrated noises. He turned around and struck a fist against a wall. This only caused him to jump around for a bit, wincing.

When he was done making a fuss he flexed his fingers as he said, "There's only so much a man can take, don't you know that? If not, you best learn. Men are not honorable when pushed beyond certain limits." He shook a finger at her. "If you don't want to get into trouble, you have to stop getting into situations where you are alone with randy dastards—"

"Such as yourself."

"Such as myself."

Lily listened to this lecture with growing dismay and annoyance. She rose to her feet and advanced toward the man by the window. It was her turn to shake a finger at him. "Getting myself into compromising situations? What are you talking about? I didn't show up in your room the other night, now did I? I'm not the one who dragged me off screaming and shouting—there was screaming and shouting, wasn't there?"

"A bit."

"To God knows where." She stopped her tirade to look around the room. It was sparely furnished with clean floors, and there wasn't a sign of dust or clutter anywhere. There was a bed, a chair, a wardrobe, and a nightstand with a flowered porcelain basin and pitcher. She found it curious that there were no curtains on the small window or a rug on the polished floor. No pictures hung on the white walls. This was a prison, she decided. She was no better off than she had been before. Considerably less, she knew, and this prison was nowhere near as nicely decorated as her rooms at the embassy. Fear curdled in her stomach, and panic threatened. This state of sudden anxiety helped open up the wall of drugged disorientation and lust that had separated her from reality since she'd woken.

"Where am I?" she demanded.

"It's a safe house." He held his hands out before him. "I can't tell you where we are."

"Why have you brought me here?"

"For your own good."

"Is it for ransom? Gregory will pay to get me back."

"I can't take you back there. You don't want to go back," he added.

"Yes I do."

Kit was a secret agent of some sort, a thief at the very least. He'd tried to steal something from the embassy. She vaguely remembered that. And she had tried to stop him.

"And what has Captain Cherminsky to do with all this? Was he in on it with you?"

He sneered with disdain. "I do not work with amateurs. He was—"

"He was the one who drugged me," she remembered suddenly. "He and Irenia—"

"The king's mistress?" Kit interrupted her.

"She was trying to get me out of the way so Gregory would marry her."

"They make a lovely couple."

"I think so too. But Gregory has other plans."

"Plans you agree with."

Why did he sound bitter? She was the one with reason for bitterness. "I have no choice in the matter."

"You could say no."

"I can't. I must marry one of the royal family. I tried to influence which one I married, but that didn't work out." She discovered that her hand covered the bruise on her jaw. "I tried to be clever. I think I deserve this."

Kit was suddenly before her. He took her wrist and gently pried her hand from her face. "No woman deserves to be struck. Ever. For anything."

Their gazes met, dark brown and blue-green, matched in fire and intensity. She could not breathe or think, and for a few endless seconds she could not look away.

It was Kit who blinked, and his expression changed. He was smiling, but there was something cold about him when he asked, "How was it I figured in your trying to be clever?"

"I used you," she admitted. She had no intention of explaining Gregory's fixation on taking a virgin bride. It was simply too humiliating. "I realized you were using me, so it seemed only fair to return the favor. I didn't think you'd mind," she added when Kit continued to smile while his expression grew more and more distant.

"You didn't think I'd find out."

"I didn't think I'd ever see you again once you stole whatever it was you were after."

"You knew what I was doing, and said nothing?"

She noticed that he didn't deny her assessment of his involvement with her. She nodded. "I needed you."

"But you tried to stop me last night."

"Did I?" He nodded. "Yes—I remember. There were documents. You stole them. Then you abducted me. You should be ashamed."

"I'm not. Your king is up to something that could harm the Empire."

"Nonsense. Bororavia could not possibly do anything to harm the greatest empire on earth. On the other hand, Britain can do a great deal of damage to Bororavia."

She didn't particularly want to argue international politics right now. She had to worry about her own crisis. But she would try to help her father's country if she could. She didn't want to rule Bororavia, but she owed something to the people her father's family had ruled for generations.

Wait a moment—he had said "last night." They had been talking about events from only a few hours ago, hadn't they? Was it only last night? She'd wondered how long the drug kept her under. It wasn't only the drug. Kit was the most distracting person she'd ever known.

She glanced out the window at the morning light. They couldn't be too far from London, could they? Perhaps she could get back to the embassy before any damage was done. Before Gregory sent someone to harm her mother.

Lily would not let herself think about her mother and what might happen. If she gave in to the worry she might spend her time dithering and pacing and get nothing productive done. What she must do was concentrate on preventing anything from happening by returning to Gregory as swiftly as possible.

She hated to do it, but desperation made her say, "If I make love with you will you let me go?"

"No!" The word was an outraged shout. Kit drew himself up in indignation, and snatched up his shirt, as if he was the one who had to defend his honor. Then he laughed, and shook his head. "That shows what sort of fool I am. I should have lied and said yes."

She should not find this bald statement endearing. She should be offended, possibly even frightened that a man could entertain and admit to such a thought. He didn't pretend to be a saint. She liked that about him, but she still needed to get away.

She said, "I doubt you'd get much pleasure out of the act of lovemaking if you let me buy my freedom with my body."

He chuckled. "You don't know much about men, do you?"

She recalled her debacle with Gregory. "Apparently not. Let me go," she pleaded.

"Can't do it, Lily my love."

She didn't suppose this was any time to insist on being addressed by her title. "Then at least tell me you've sent a ransom demand."

"No."

"Oh." She paced in her bare feet on the bare floor for a few moments, agitation growing in her. "What are you going to do with me?" she finally asked.

He turned his back to her, and looked out the window with his fingers laced together behind his back. "I have no idea."

She didn't know whether to believe anything he said. He was a man of charm and flash, with an ability to keep her off balance and diverted.

The worst thing was she didn't feel like he even *tried* to bamboozle her. Being with him was as exhilarating as breathing clean mountain air, from the very top of the highest mountain in the world. It was refreshing, and dangerous. She could fall off a cliff at any moment with him, and knew that if they were holding hands she'd be laughing all the way down. Looking into his eyes was like staring into the sun. And yet—when she was with Kit she felt more like herself than she ever had in her life. She didn't understand this reaction—the feeling that she could say anything to him, tell him anything and he'd be interested, that she could listen to anything he said and be totally fascinated. Maybe it was because he had such a nice voice, deep and smooth, like strong coffee laced with fresh, thick cream.

Nice voices do not make nice people. She didn't know where that particular aphorism came from, but it popped into her head to chide the flight of fancy about Kit Fox's effect on her. He'd probably been trained to be a good listener, that same stern voice went on. And to make his victims feel somehow both at ease *and* disoriented. A spy's job is to do whatever was necessary to find out information. Whatever he told her would likely be a lie, even swearing undying love—a subject he hadn't brought up, thank goodness—and whatever she told him would be reported to his superiors in the Foreign Office.

"I am not going to tell you any Bororavian state secrets," she announced.

"Do you know any?"

Why did he have to sound so amused? "Wouldn't *you* like to know?" Good Lord, she sounded like a petty eight-year-old!

"Interrogation isn't my department. Now my Mum"—he continued, turning back to face her—"You'd be terrified to know what that woman can do with a pair of pinking sheers and a bit of knitting yarn. You've no idea how dangerous a sewing basket can be until you meet up with Mum and Mrs. Swift in a dark alley."

"I see."

Of course she didn't, but she accepted his statements and refused to give in to the urge to ask more about Mum and Mrs. Swift. He was only trying to divert her again. She had to escape.

"Would you let me have a few minutes of privacy?" she asked.

He immediately looked suspicious. "Why?"

She glanced toward cabinet doors on the bottom of the washstand. "I assume there's a . . ." She cleared her throat. "A chamberpot in there."

"Oh." It was his turn to clear his throat. "Of course." He snatched up his vest, took a key from the pocket, and crossed to the door. "I'll wait outside."

"Thank you." She turned her back so that he wouldn't think she intended to dart out the door once it was open. She waited until the door closed and she heard the key turn in the lock once more before rushing to the window.

The square of glass was not very large, but she was slender. If she could get the window open she might have a chance of squeezing out. The main problem, she discovered as she peered out, was that her prison cell was on the third floor of the house. All she could see was a fine view of a large walled garden and wooded countryside stretching away into the distance. She had no clue as to where the building was located, but she'd worry about finding her way back to London once she was free. Escape was the first priority.

Take one thing at a time, she thought, and found to her delight that the window latch worked perfectly when she tried it. Once the window was open she stuck her head out as far as she could, searching for any possible way to reach the ground without falling. There was a tiny ornamental windowsill forming the narrowest of ledges. She saw that the window to the next room had a similar ledge, and beyond that ledge, a rainspout ran down the corner of the wall. The house was made of painted brick, so perhaps she could cross the two ledges and then use the bricks as hand and footholds and the rainspout to steady her going down the side of the house. It was a dangerous plan, but she had no choice. She didn't have much time. Besides, if she thought about this mad, dangerous scheme she wouldn't go through with it. So she took a deep breath and began to wriggle out the window.

Kit paced the hallway and fumed. He wrote his mood off as a mix of sexual frustration and the knowledge that snatching Lily away from the embassy might not have been the smartest move he'd ever made. Not that he could have let Cherminsky harm her, but . . .

I must marry royalty. And you're not a prince. And not a word of thank you for saving her pretty hide. "Women," he grumbled. "Princesses. Virgins."

Virgins were the worst.

"I need a cigarette."

Why is she taking so long?

And why was he indulging her maidenly modesty by lurking outside like a lowly chambermaid?

All right, he knew the answer to that one. He had many sisters. Men with sisters learned young never to disturb a woman while she was involved in any sort of personal matter.

Still, it had been a while. He could at least knock and ask Lily if she was all right. Taking a deep breath, he tried to put on his usual insouciant demeanor, and went to the door.

He heard the distant scream before he could knock. He was heading down the stairs even as the muffled crash that followed rang in his ears. He cursed himself as he ran. He knew exactly what the damned fool girl had done.

He only hoped the fall hadn't killed her.

Chapter 18

"**C**hristopher Fox MacLeod, you look like something the cat dragged in."

"Thank you for that assessment, Harry," Kit answered. His sister Harriet was leaning against the doorway of the family dining room of the Kestrels' townhouse. He tried to appear his usual relaxed, casual self, despite the fact that his nerves were drawn tight as violin strings. While his hair was mussed, and his clothes wrinkled, he really didn't think he looked that bad. True, it had taken him a few moments to convince the butler to let him inside the house, but butlers were the worst snobs in the world.

The scene in the breakfast room was one of domestic bliss, and Kit hated to disturb it. A large assortment of food was laid out on the sideboard, buffet style. Harriet sat at one end of the table, her husband Martin at the other. Lucy, Beatrice, Sara and Kestrel's young daughter by his first marriage occupied other seats. They all had full plates, and Kit had interrupted a lively conversation with his arrival. Martin Kestrel was reading through a pile of papers on the table. He glanced briefly at Kit with eyes that were far too shrewd, but said nothing.

Harriet gestured toward the chafing dishes on the sideboard. "Have something to eat." She looked over his disheveled state critically once more, and added, "And tell us what you've gotten yourself into—if it isn't too scandalous for the girls to hear."

"I can't stay," he answered, but he did cross the room to pour himself a cup of coffee from a tall silver pot. Then he snatched up a fresh-baked roll and stuffed it into his mouth. He looked down the long, fragrant line of dishes, and quickly ate two slices of thick-cut bacon. Dinner was a long time ago, and he felt like he'd been through a war since then. He gulped down the strong coffee, sighed happily, and turned back toward the table. Everyone was staring at him.

He shrugged, but didn't offer any explanations. He needed to get out of there quickly. He had to get back to Lily. Kit reached into his coat and brought out the documents he'd stolen. He went to Beatrice and handed them to her. "Aunt Phoebe will want you to help her with these," he told his code-cracking sister.

With his mission accomplished, Kit turned to his

youngest sister. "May I have a word in private, Sara?"

She promptly rose to her feet. "Of course."

Harriet rose as well. So did Lucy. "What are you up to?" they asked in unison.

"Training exercise," he answered, and swept Sara out of the room and hurried toward the front hall, hoping that the others would not follow. "Come with me. I have a carriage outside," he told Sara as they went.

"Where to?"

He put a finger to her lips. "No questions. You have to learn to obey orders without asking questions."

Sara looked at him with the sort of skepticism only a sibling can manage, but she also had the light of excitement in her eyes. She was a MacLeod through and through, and hurried away with him before older, more sensible sisters could interfere with her chance at adventure.

"Will she live?"

"As far as I can tell all she has is a slight bump on her forehead, a badly twisted ankle, and that bruise on her jaw. Nothing life-threatening, certainly."

Kit breathed a sigh of relief, and patted his medically minded little sister on the shoulder. "Thank God."

"Mmm . . ." Sara responded.

There was a great deal of meaning in that sound, much of it disapproving. "You sounded just like Da there," he told her. "What's the matter?"

Sara looked from the unconscious woman on the bed to him, her big blue eyes widening as she said, "Well, I can't help but notice that my patient is wearing nothing but a torn nightdress."

"Yes?"

"And that she's tied to the bedpost."

He couldn't help but tease. "You find that unusual, do you?"

Sara twisted her hands together nervously, and looked everywhere but at the bed and Kit. "Well," she said at last. "I don't think I'm supposed to know about that sort of thing yet."

"Really?" he asked, all innocence. "What sort of thing would that be?"

"Aunt Phoebe hasn't had 'the talk' with me yet."

"It's not just a talk," he said. "She has books too. With pictures."

"Oh." She twisted her fingers together, and blinked rapidly. "Oh, dear."

He watched Sara blush a deep scarlet and decided it was time to back off on teasing. "Never mind, sweetheart. I don't mean to embarrass you."

"You do," she snapped.

He held his hands up before him. "No more. I promise. You're the youngest, sweetheart, I know that's hard. If we aren't smothering you and being overprotective we're making your life miserable with teasing. It's because we love you best, you know," he added.

His words coaxed a smile from his youngest sister, but she said, "And to think I used to wonder what Mum meant when she said butter wouldn't melt in your mouth. Really, Kit, I think you are the definition of incorrigible."

"Perhaps I'll end up in the dictionary."

"Prison, more like, Mrs. Swift says."

"She's always had such kind things to say about me."

"Well, she says it with pride. She's always saying such odd things about all of us. She reckons Lucy's bound for a convent, for example, which I don't understand since we're members of the Kirk." Sara knelt to take a closer look at Lily's swollen ankle. From that spot she said, "Speaking of Lucy and ages, which one is elder, you or Lucy? I once heard Mum say that you were such a scrawny little thing when she found you that she wasn't sure what your age was."

Annoyance flashed through Kit, but he tried not to show it to Sara. He'd been reminded of his origins a few too many times lately, and the allusions were beginning to rub him raw. To Sara he said, in as offhand a way as he could, "I'm definitely the eldest member of the clan. I have memories of the first time I saw Lucy and Harriet, and I was definitely older and wiser. Harry was in nappies, and

Lucy still sucked her thumb. I was an experienced, streetwise gutter rat and man of the world. If Lucy and Harriet hadn't walked in on me when I was robbing Aunt Phoebe's house, I'd be king of the thieves' guild by now."

His sister didn't hear the bitterness. "There's no such thing as a thieves' guild."

"I would have founded one."

What an odd family," Lily thought. And *what sort of pictures?*

Lily's head hurt. So did quite a bit of the rest of her. There was a rather massive ache in the vicinity of her right ankle. She knew her hands were tied to the bed because she'd come awake about the time the girl with Kit mentioned it. Having heard the voices she'd remained still and kept her eyes closed, and listened carefully. She'd expected to hear about a nefarious kidnapping plot and hoped to find out what they planned to do with her. Instead she'd been treated to a discussion about sex manuals and family history. She'd found it all frightfully interesting, and it gave her a great deal to think about, but she still hadn't learned anything that might prove helpful to her situation.

Well, she'd learned that her escape attempt had failed.

Then again, maybe the conversation between Kit and the girl was some sort of elaborate code . . .

"You have to leave now," the girl said.

"Why?" Kit asked.

"Because I need to get a proper look at your young lady. She needs a more thorough examination."

"Oh, no you don't!" Lily declared, opening her eyes and struggling with her bonds. "I've had quite enough of medical exams to last a lifetime, thank you very much!" Her vehemence was enough to cause both Kit and the startled girl to step back from the bedside. "You're from the park," Lily said, recognizing the pretty adolescent. "The one who was reading *Wuthering Heights*."

Sara stared hard at Lily for a moment, then recognition dawned in her expression. She turned to Kit in outrage. "What on earth are you doing with a princess in her nightgown? Does Aunt Phoebe know about—"

Kit took Sara by the arm. "Time for you to go, sweetheart."

"But—"

"I've been kidnapped!" Lily called after them as Kit hustled the girl through the door. "Help me!"

Lily continued to struggle for a few seconds after the door closed behind them, but her captor knew how to tie a knot, and her headache and bruises quickly got the better of her. So she lay there, aching, miserable and resentful for what seemed like hours before the door opened again.

"Where have you been?" she complained when Kit came back in and closed the door behind him. "It's been hours. I could have . . . bled to death."

"You aren't bleeding anywhere."

"That's not the point!"

Kit made a show of checking a pocket watch. "I've been gone five minutes. It's boring being a prisoner, I know," he told her. He pulled up a chair and sat by the bed. "I'll untie you as soon as you promise not to try to escape again." He glanced toward her aching ankle. "Not that you'll get far on that if you try. I've promised Sara that I'll let her come in and have a good look at you and bind up your wounds as soon as you both calm down."

"I have no intention of calming down." Lily would have tossed her head proudly for emphasis, but lying flat on her back put her at a disadvantage for head-tossing.

"You could have been killed, you know," he went on reprovingly. "You're lucky to have only a few bumps and bruises."

"I'm unlucky that I hit my head on the rain barrel and that the blasted drainpipe came away from the wall when I was still a story off the ground," Lily countered. "At least I landed on my feet." Her ankle throbbed as if in reproof. "Briefly."

"You're lucky the drainpipe held that long. I was seven when I gave up shimmying up and down those things. They can only take so much weight"

"Thank you for your professional opinion."

"You're welcome." He smoothed hair off her forehead. His touch was warm and gentle, and unexpectedly calming. "Girl, you gave me a fright."

Lily's first reaction was a suffusion of pleasure at his concern. Then she recalled that she was valuable to him for some reason or this self-styled king of thieves would not have abducted her in the first place. Of course he wanted her to stay alive. Gregory wanted her to stay alive too. No one wanted her dead. She was reassured in some ways.

"Ransom victim or broodmare," she muttered. "What a choice."

Kit sat back and crossed his arms across his chest. He gave her his familiar teasing smile, and asked, "How much ransom do you think you'd bring?"

"I knew it! You swine."

"A curious swine. Just how valuable are you?"

"Depends on who you're asking, doesn't it?" she replied angrily.

He nodded, still smiling and obviously unaffected by her annoyance. "True. Good answer, Lily Princess." He leaned forward a bit. "Tell me, how much are you worth to *you*?"

With his face closer to hers she considered spitting on him. It wasn't the sort of thing she'd ever done before, but it was the kind of gesture of bravado that this sort of situation always called for in melodramatic stage plays and novels. Of course it was also dreadfully rude, disgusting, and foolhardy. And what a waste it would be of such closeness when she already knew how lovely it was to be kissed by—

"You look like you want me to kiss you, but know it's not the right thing to want."

"You think you know me so well, don't you?" she snapped at him, and felt her cheeks heat with embarrassment at having been caught out in her ambivalence.

"I don't think I know you at all," he answered. His lips were close to hers and he kissed her—a quick, gentle touch, like a promise of delight. Before she could even fight off the urge to ask for more, he sat back in the chair. "It might help me to get to know you if I know what you think you're worth."

Why would he want to know her? And what an odd way to find out. The man made her head spin. Perhaps that was from the kiss. Or from hitting her forehead on the rain barrel. "I have a headache, you know."

"You're avoiding a perfectly legitimate question."

It was neither legitimate nor reasonable, but it seemed he wasn't going to be put off. "Well . . ." Lily considered. "My personal wealth consists of two properties in the north and several thousand head of sheep." She glared at him with all the contempt she could muster, which she suspected was nowhere near enough to dent his insouciance. "Would you like to be paid in wool, mutton, or the whole herd? I'll throw in a few border collies, if you'd like."

"What about the Bororavian crown jewels?"

"Not mine to give. Besides, they're paste except for the brooch and ring. It's been very expensive for Gregory to stay in power." Lily realized what she'd said, and gasped. "Oh, bother, now I've given away information to a spy when I vowed not to do any such thing. I should bite my tongue."

He waved her confession aside. "My dearest Lily, what sort of successful thief would I be if I didn't recognize the quality of jewels when I see them? How much is Gregory willing to pay for you?" After a moment he asked, the words sounding bitter for some reason, "What drew you to Gregory in the first place? Do you want to reclaim the throne? To simply marry a king? Or is it Duke Michael that you prefer?"

None of this was any of his business, though she found herself wanting to justify herself to him. To tell him the truth. To ask him for help. Lord, what a foolish thought, for it was Kit who'd stolen her and the documents away from the embassy. It was Kit who currently had her tied to a bed and was asking her questions. She did not know in what way the British Empire was trying to use her father's country in its Great Game with the Russian Empire. She'd been born and reared in England, but though she considered England home, she was a Bororavian princess. She didn't know the people of Bororavia, but that didn't excuse her from an obligation to protect them if she could.

She gave Kit the haughtiest look she could manage. "Bring on the pinking shears and knitting yarn. You'll have to torture me to find out anything more."

"Fair enough," he agreed, and rose from the chair. "I'll have to send to Scotland for Mum's sewing basket. But until it arrives, how'd you like that ankle looked at and a hot bath?"

With that he untied her and left the room, taking the rope with him. A few moments later the girl returned with a basket of bandages and medicines, and a bucket of hot water.

And Lily was left more confused than ever. But she did recall that he'd untied her before she'd made any promise not to try to escape. So at least he couldn't accuse her of lying when she ran off again at the first chance she got.

Chapter 19

When Kit drove Sara back to Kestrel House, he made her promise not to say anything about her errand with him. "It won't be easy," he warned. "But keeping the princess's whereabouts secret is very important."

Fortunately, Sara hadn't asked him why before dropping her off at Harriet's door. Because if she'd asked, then he might have been tempted to tell his sister that he was a reckless, thoughtless idiot who'd made a hideous error in judgment and didn't have the faintest idea what he was going to do about it. He knew he couldn't let Lily return to a place where one man struck her and another had tried to abduct her. At least not until he found out why these things had happened, and was certain they would never happen again. Maybe her safety wasn't more important to her than marrying a knight or duke, but it was to him, unworthy street rat though he was.

He didn't want to ask himself why Lily's safety was so important to him. He knew the answer to that question led down a shadowed path he couldn't afford to take. Christopher Fox MacLeod was too devil-may-care to allow his heart to be broken or to make a fool of himself suffering from unrequited love. Everybody knew Kit was too much the frivolous rascal to ever fall in love for more than a day or two.

"Everyone knows but Kit, it seems," he muttered as he drove the stolen carriage into the stables behind the isolated safe house.

He tried not to think about Lily, or anything beyond the necessary routine of unhitching and caring for the tired pair of horses. Fortunately, the house was always stocked with food and the stable with hay and oats for the infrequent and always unscheduled secret visits from various members of the family.

It was not until he was done with the horses that it occurred to Kit that he had not yet offered a bite of food to his unwilling guest.

"Idiot," he grumbled as he hurried toward the garden door. He was furious with himself, for Lily had been through quite enough without his also unintentionally starving her to death.

Once indoors Kit headed straight for the kitchen. Only to stop outside the kitchen door when the mixed aromas of strong tea and eggs frying in butter stopped him in his tracks. His stood in the hallway, alert, wary and confused. His first thought was that Lily had somehow picked the lock on her bedroom door, and hobbled downstairs to fend for herself. He didn't discount the ability of a princess who claimed to be a shepherdess to know her way around a kitchen.

No. It wasn't possible that it was Lily in the kitchen. If she'd managed to break out of her room again, she'd be hobbling her way to London rather than stopping for a meal first. He didn't know why she wanted to return to her awful family so much, but she was determined to return. Probably something to do with a crown and visions of being addressed as Queen Lily.

Of course, lingering out in the hallway wasn't going to help him find out who was in the kitchen. But it wasn't particularly wise to rush into a room and demand who was there and what was going on. Discretion—which was not Kit's strong point—sometimes needed to prevail. So, Kit began to back silently away from the kitchen door.

Only to have it open wide before he took more than a step back. The dark-haired man who stood framed in the doorway wore wire-rimmed glasses and a frown. "Uncle Andrew," Kit said, with a sigh of relief. "What are you doing here?"

"I could ask the same of you," Andrew MacLeod replied. "You have a woman upstairs," Andrew went on before Kit could reply. "At first I made the assumption that one of Court's sons—probably you—had decided to use the place we call the safe-house for a good reason—as a personal brothel. But since I found the nightgown-clad young woman pounding on a locked door and shouting for help, I came to the assumption that she was not here of her own free will." Kit opened his mouth to explain, but Andrew went on in his most dry, professorial way. "After she cursed you soundly and I indicated agreement and a long acquaintance with your depraved behavior, she came to the conclusion that I was some sort of accomplice and decided not to speak with me anymore. Personally, I prefer quiet women, so I did not see this as a setback. I thought it best to retire from her presence and await an explanation from the culprit in this scandalous affair. That would be you," he added, stepping back and gesturing Kit into the kitchen.

Andrew went to the stove, turned the eggs cooking in the iron skillet, drank deeply from a large mug of tea. "I assured the young woman that I would not harm her as I had received neither orders nor payment to do so, but that did not seem to reassure her in any way."

"You didn't."

Andrew glanced Kit's way, and gave one of his rare, slight smiles. "I told her I'd bring her something to eat."

It was always hard to tell when Uncle Andrew

was joking. He was many years younger than his brother Court MacLeod. In fact, Andrew was probably only a couple years older than Kit, though he gave the impression of being older. They'd played together as children, but Andrew had always been serious, and Andrew's profession was making him more dour by the year. It was time for Andrew to get out of the Game, Kit thought, but he wasn't going to be the one to bring it up. A long, soul-searching talk about the future with one of the most dangerous men alive was really more Da's sort of specialty.

"Thank you for looking after Lily in my absence," Kit said, and moved to fill a cup for himself from the large blue earthenware teapot left to keep warm on the back of the stove. "What brings you here?" he asked when Uncle Andrew gave only the slightest of nods in response.

"What brings any of us to the safe house?" was Andrew's cool answer.

"It was ridiculous of me to ask the question," Kit admitted.

"I suspect that you can be accused of a great deal of ridiculous behavior of late."

Kit opened his mouth to argue, but his annoyance changed to an ironic shrug. "Have you been talking to Aunt Phoebe, then?"

That got him. Kit couldn't keep from smiling when Andrew turned a sharp look on him. "Your great-aunt Phoebe may believe that her side of the family, the Gales, has the monopoly on intelligence gathering, but I have my ways."

Kit took a seat at the battered old kitchen table. He drank his tea while he watched Uncle Andrew place fried eggs, toasted bread, and grilled tomatoes onto a pair of plates. Silence drew out in the room.

Finally, Kit gave in and asked, "What have you heard?"

Andrew turned, holding a plate in his hands. "I've heard that the king of a certain minor Baltic country has offered a reward for knowledge of the whereabouts of a missing mistress and the captain of his personal guard. It seems the couple disappeared from their London embassy last night—taking something with them he wants returned very badly."

"Really?" Kit asked, sitting up straighter. He was quite pleased by this news. "So Cherminsky and the countess ran off together—and Gregory thinks they took Lily with them."

"And I take it you wish to keep it that way."

Kit nodded. "Oh, yes."

"So the king's missing item and the girl upstairs are one and the same."

"She's not an item, she's a princess."

Andrew looked very seriously at Kit for a few moments. Finally he asked, "What are you going to do with a princess, Christopher?"

Kit bounded to his feet. "Feed her," he announced, and took the plate from his uncle. He snatched a spoon from a drawer and headed for his captive princess's tower.

"Where have you been? What took you so long?" Lily hated to admit that she'd been terrified during Kit's absence. She'd fought a growing fear that she'd never see him again. The fear came out now as sharp demands. "Who is that man? What is that wonderful smell?"

"Ambrosia, my princess," Kit answered her last question first. He bowed before her and presented her with a steaming plate.

"Oh, thank you!" she said, gladly accepting the meal. "I'm so hungry I wouldn't care if this was drugged."

"Poison isn't Uncle Andrew's specialty," Kit replied.

Lily did not ask for an explanation of this. She was too hungry to explore more information about Kit Fox's family at the moment. "It's not ambrosia," she said, in between bites. "It's eggs."

"Shall I take it away?" He pulled a chair close to where she sat on the side of the bed. "Would you rather have caviar from the Black Sea. Truffles from Provence?"

"A bit of marmalade from Glasgow would be nice," she confessed after swallowing a bite of bread. "But otherwise, this is perfect. Thank you,"

she added, because even though she was a captive
she had been taught to always be polite.

Kit ducked his head and looked up through thick
dark lashes. "Normally I'd accept your thanks, but I
think you're making an honest man out of me. It's
Uncle Andrew you have to thank for your luncheon."

"Make an honest man of you?" she asked. "Is
that possible on such short acquaintance?"

"No. I imagine it would take a lifetime," he admitted.

His words sent a wave of wonder through
Lily—wonder at what a life with this man who
made her smile even when she was furious at him
would be like. Reforming him might be a lifetime
project, but it would certainly have its rewards.

"Before meeting you I didn't think there could
be anything more interesting than sheep," she
told him.

He sat back in his chair, looking puzzled.
"Should I be flattered by that?"

"Or assume that I've led a very quiet life." She
set her empty plate on the bed beside her, folded
her hands in her lap, and asked, not for the first
time, "What are you going to do with me?"

"You could go home to your sheep," he suggested.

Oh, how she wished that were true. "I must return to Gregory." She hated saying it. She hated the
necessity of it. "I have no choice."

He stood up, suddenly quite angry. "You don't have to go back to that life. Not if you don't want to. But of course . . ." His voice grew bitter. "What woman would give up the glory of being a princess?"

Lily stood up as well, though her ankle hurt when she put weight on it. It was partly the pain that fueled her irritation. "I didn't ask to be a princess."

"Of course not—you were born to it, weren't you?"

"You sound like that's my fault."

"Isn't it?"

They'd moved closer to each other while they bickered. By now they were toe to toe, practically eye to eye. When Kit put his hands on her shoulders, Lily asked, "What are we arguing about?"

"I don't know," he answered. The anger cleared from his expression. "How's your ankle?"

"Aching."

The next thing she knew he'd swung her up in his arms and was walking toward the door. "Care for a tour of the house?"

Lily very much wanted out of the confines of the room. "But I'm not dressed," she pointed out.

"You weren't dressed when you tried to escape," he reminded her.

"That was desperation."

"This is sight-seeing."

She laughed. "Yes, I suppose so." She clasped her hands behind his neck and rested her head on his shoulder. If he was going to carry her about, she might as well be as comfortable as possible. Besides, it felt so very good being held by him, even if he was the villain of the piece. If Kit's so bad, she wondered, why was she rubbing her cheek against him as though she were a big, affectionate cat?

"How odd. Gregory's a villain, but I wouldn't like being carried about by him," she murmured, her face turned toward Kit's chest. She breathed in the scent of him, liking it very much.

"What's that?" he asked.

Lily lifted her head. "Nothing." Kit was carrying her down a long flight of stairs. "Can you manage this?" she asked, noting that the bare treads were narrow.

"You're light as a feather," he answered. "Light as a lily. Parlor's the first room at the bottom of the stairs," he added. "There's a chaise in there where you can rest with your foot up. I have instructions to soak your foot in warm water as well."

"How thoughtful," she said.

"Ever the gallant, that's me." They reached the parlor. He opened the door and swept them into the room—only to stop at the sight of a man sitting by the window reading a newspaper. "Still here, Uncle Andrew?" he asked. Kit did not sound pleased.

The man looked at Kit reprovingly over the top of his glasses, then went back to his reading.

Lily felt very vulnerable in front of this Andrew person. A nightdress was hardly appropriate attire in front of anyone, let alone a pair of men. Why, she might as well be naked—and here she was clinging to Kit, with their bodies so close that she could feel his muscles and the warmth of his skin—and she didn't have on a corset or drawers or . . . anything!

"Breathe, Lily," Kit advised as he gently lowered her onto a green velvet chaise lounge. "Are you all right? What's the matter?" She pointed at a knit throw draped over a chair, and Kit quickly snatched it up and spread it over her. "Are you cold?" he asked.

Lily pulled the covering up to her nose and glared over it at Kit. "Do you have any concept of modesty?"

He appeared thoughtful for a moment. "Some," he answered. "I have sisters, you know."

On the other side of the room Uncle Andrew cleared his throat. "You have no concept of discretion, certainly."

Kit turned to the disapproving man. "Lily's already met most of the girls."

Andrew looked past Kit to gaze coldly at Lily. "Then I suppose we'll have to kill her," he said.

A stab of terror shot through Lily as Kit quickly turned back to her. "He's joking! Don't mind Uncle Andrew. He's really a very mild-mannered fellow with an odd sense of humor. He's a librarian," Kit added, as though the knowledge of this odd uncle's profession would somehow reassure her.

"Archivist," Uncle Andrew clarified. "Researcher."

Also armed and unarmed combat expert, Kit added silently. And professional assassin. "And a very fine cook," he told Lily.

"So you said before," Lily said, pretending that the exchange between Kit and his odd uncle had not strung her nerves even tighter. "Thank you for providing my breakfast," she said to Andrew.

The man nodded, folded his newspaper neatly, and rose from his chair. "Hear that?" he asked Kit.

"Yes," Kit answered.

Lily noticed that both men stood very still, and that they were looking out the parlor window. Then she heard the sound of horses approaching the house.

Chapter 20

"**U**ncle Andrew, what are you doing with that pistol?"

"Holding it on you, Beatrice," was Andrew's calm answer.

Kit, standing on the opposite side of the door-way from Andrew MacLeod, noticed that their uncle did not lower the weapon as Beatrice came into the front hall.

Beatrice was not so foolish as to pay it no mind. She kept her gaze on the gun while she carefully undid the strings of her bonnet. She was wearing a fashionable riding habit, with a fitted navy blue jacket that made her look far too much like a grownup to Kit's disapproving eye.

"You are wondering, Uncle," she said, her voice carefully casual, "that perhaps we were followed. I assure you, that is not so."

"We?" Kit asked.

Beatrice still didn't look at Kit. She did look from the gun to Andrew's expressionless face. "Sara is outside with the horses."

"Sara! What is she doing here?" Kit demanded. "What are *you* doing here? She promised me to keep quiet about—"

"Something's come up," Beatrice interrupted. "I'll explain directly—but first I have to convince Uncle Andrew not to do some dreadful thing like lock me in the root cellar while he looks for another hideout. Isn't that so, Uncle?"

Andrew gave a barely perceptible nod. "Explain how you know you weren't followed, Beatrice."

"Sara and I borrowed horses from Lord Martin's stable on the pretense that we wanted to go riding in Rotten Row. We did ride in the park until we were certain no one was watching us. Then Sara directed me here. We took several detours along the way just to be certain." Beatrice looked up and down the entry hall, which contained no furniture or decoration. "I've never been here before. It's quite nice, though far plainer on the inside than out. The horses need attending to, Kit," she added. "Are there any grooms, or servants at all?"

Andrew slipped the small pistol back under his jacket. "I'll look after the animals." He went to the door and said, "Sarabande Margaret MacLeod, get you in here this instant."

Sara came in a moment later, also dressed for

riding. She carried a carpetbag with her. "Clothes for the princess," she said when she noticed Kit looking at the bag. "I don't know why you didn't think of it, Kit."

Kit considered answering that comment honestly, but Sara really wasn't mature enough for that information. Besides, the fact that he preferred Lily without any clothing on was not information he'd share with anyone other than Lily. Possibly not even Lily if he were going to behave like a gentleman should.

When Sara turned to go up the stairs, Kit said, "Wait." He pointed toward the parlor door. "She's in there."

"Wait here," she ordered, and marched into the parlor.

Beatrice followed her, so Kit had to assume the command had been for him alone. "Fine," he grumbled, and settled onto the stairs to wait.

A few minutes later Beatrice stuck her head out the parlor door and said, "You may come in now."

"Fine," he grumbled again, and ambled into the room. The first thing he noticed was Lily standing by the chaise lounge, propping herself up with one hand on the carved wooden back of the chaise. She was wearing a dark red dress decorated in black piping and hints of lace on the collars and sleeves. It was a very respectable dress, with a high collar and full sleeves. Nothing provocative about this outfit at all. He sighed, much preferring Lily in revealing ball gowns if she must wear anything at all. "That frock looks familiar," he said. "Did you borrow it from Lucy?"

"Yes," Sara answered. "But don't worry, I didn't ask her permission. I didn't tell anyone but Bea that you had the princess here."

Kit clasped his hands behind his back and turned a fiercely annoyed look on his youngest sibling. "And why, pray tell, did you tell Beatrice?"

Sara winced.

"She didn't break her promise lightly, Kit," Beatrice told him. "If you wish to be angry at anyone, then pick on me. By the way," she added, "the princess was trying to get the window open when we came in. I don't think she wants to be here."

"You don't have to speak as if I'm not here," Lily spoke up. "I am, you know." She glanced toward the window. "Though I'd rather not be."

"Why are you keeping the princess here?" Beatrice asked Kit.

He sighed and ran a hand through his unruly hair. "It's a long story."

"One I would very much like to hear," Lily told him.

Kit almost muttered *me too*, but he remembered how Cherminsky had drugged Lily, and how her cousin had verbally and physically abused her. "What I'd like to know, is why you want to go back." The words tumbled out before he could stop them.

"I don't want to, I *have* to." Her quick answer was just as rash, and she pressed her lips together in a tight, thin line after she spoke. Then she gave a weary sigh, and sat down on the chaise, her gaze going to some place far beyond the room.

Kit didn't know what she was thinking about, but he could see that she was terrified. It occurred to him that he'd been asking Lily the wrong questions. In fact, at the moment, he wasn't sure if he had asked her any questions at all. The first thing he wanted to do was take her in his arms and soothe away her fear. Then he wanted to find out what frightened her. Of course, it was perfectly possible that he and the situation he'd put her in frightened her, but he was suddenly certain there was something deeper going on. Was she so afraid of losing her chance at wearing a crown? Was it something to do with King Gregory? Did she fear for her country if she did not become his queen? Or was there some other threat hanging over her lovely head?

He doubted he could get her to open up to him while his sisters sat there and gawked at them. So it was best to find out what they wanted and get them to leave as quickly as possible.

"Beatrice," he said, trying not to sound as irritated at the girl as he felt. "Why did Sara bring you here? What do you need me to do?"

"I don't need you to do anything," Beatrice

replied. She took a leather document pouch out of Sara's carpetbag and set it on the marble-topped table in front of the window. "The papers you liberated from the Bororavian Embassy are in here. They're written in Bororavian," she added.

"Fancy that," Kit said.

Beatrice removed the folded newspaper Uncle Andrew had left in the chair and took a seat. "I always assumed whatever papers you found would be in Bororavian," she explained calmly. "I also assumed they would be in code. I am perfectly prepared to decipher any code, but it has to be in a language I can understand. Aunt Phoebe and I have been making discreet inquiries for a translator. Bororavia is a small, isolated country. Though until the 1830s, the ruling family had always asserted that independence, it was a duchy successively claimed by Poland, Lithuania, and Russia. After the Bororavians won a decisive battle against a superior Lithuanian force, Maxim IV declared himself king rather than grand duke, and Russia backed up the country's right to be called a kingdom. Very interesting history. You aren't interested, are you?" Beatrice asked after Kit yawned.

"Not at the moment, Bea. What's your point?"

"The point is, very few people outside the country know the language. Aunt Phoebe's network did find information about two Bororavians living in

England. The first choice was a linguistic specialist working at Oxford named Constantine Verkovari."

"I know Constantine," Kit spoke up. "Nice man. A bit put upon, but hard-working. I stole those papers from his office."

Beatrice nodded. "Then you see our problem. Mr. Verkovari has been drafted by the Bororavian government to act as their embassy's social secretary. We can't very well approach him to translate documents stolen from his own office."

"Might be awkward," Kit agreed. "Who is the second person?"

"That would be Lady—"

"Lily Bancroft," Lily interrupted. "Which would be me."

"That makes it even more awkward," Kit said.

"Not really," Beatrice answered. "Well, normally it would, of course, since Lady Lily turns out to also be Princess Lily, but since you've"—Beatrice paused, possibly aware that there was more awkwardness to the situation than she had at first taken into account—"acquired," was the word she finally chose, "the princess—um—" She held the papers out to Lily. "Would she mind translating these for me?"

Lily ignored Beatrice. She directed her answer to Kit. "I believe the schedule for my helping you will go into effect at about the same time they have snowball fights in Hades."

Lily would have liked to use much stronger language on Kit, but didn't feel right about using what few curse words she knew in front of the girls. True, the young women were as much a part of the madness as their brother and uncle, but Sara had seen fit to bind Lily's wounds and provide her with clothing. Lily wasn't going to repay Sara by being crude in front of her.

"Does that mean she won't help?" Beatrice asked.

"Why don't you ask her yourself?" Kit responded to his sister.

Lily watched as Beatrice's eyes grew round with shock. "I can't talk to a princess!"

"Oh, good lord," Lily said. "A cat can look at a king . . . why can't you talk to a princess? I'm not much of a princess, anyway," she said, and added with more sarcasm than she intended, "Bororavia's only a little country, after all. Certainly of no importance to anyone but the Bororavians."

"It's important enough for my brother to have risked his life to acquire these documents," Beatrice shot back, looking directly at Lily for the first time. "British Intelligence needs to know what awful things the Bororavians are up to."

Lily smiled, admiring the girl's concern for Kit. They were an odd family, but they certainly cared for each other. Unlike her own, odd, Bororavian relations. "I suppose it was quite brave of your brother to risk life and limb for *his* queen and country," Lily said to Beatrice, carefully not looking at

Kit when she spoke because she was certain her words brought a smug smile to his face. "But what he did constitutes hostile actions toward *my* country. The last thing I am going to do is help Britain spy against Bororavia. That would make me a traitor to my father's homeland."

"That is a valid point," Sara spoke up. "But it might also be a specious one."

The girl caught Lily's attention. "How so?" she asked.

"Well, it's not as if you're really Bororavian. Your name is Bancroft, isn't it? You were raised in Yorkshire. Aunt Phoebe's information says you're from Harelby."

"I happen to be the heir to the Bororavian throne." Lily did not normally take this royal connection seriously, but being told she wasn't really Bororavian felt like a smirch on her beloved father's memory.

"But your father abdicated, didn't he? I'm not sure if his children can inherit." The girl shook her head. "I'm not certain about that, but it seems logical. Law and heraldry aren't my specialties. I'm going to be a doctor."

"You were born in England, weren't you?" Beatrice persisted. "Doesn't that make you a true and loyal subject of the Queen?"

"Queen Victoria is my godmother," Lily answered, and wished she hadn't, because both of

Kit's sisters suddenly looked very triumphant. Lily looked at Kit, as though for help against his siblings. "They're . . . they're . . ."

"MacLeods," he said, looking thoroughly pleased with the pair. "That's our family name, by the way. We haven't been properly introduced."

"Should you let her know that?" Sara asked.

Kit shrugged. "Might as well. She's met rather a lot of the family in the last few days." He looked at Lily, and she was struck by the combination of teasing, tenderness, and fire in his eyes when he said, "I believe at one point that I mentioned that my given name is Christopher?"

Lily blushed, growing warm all over with memories of the night he'd entered her room. "You are trying to distract me," she accused.

He shook his head. "Not distract. Put you off balance." He smirked. "Remind you that a life with King Gregory would not be as pleasant as another option you've considered."

"Considered and rejected," she reminded him. "Twice."

His smirk blossomed into a full-blown, irritatingly charming smile. "Third time's the charm, sweetheart."

She couldn't help but answer that taunt with a slow, seductive smile of her own. It was ridiculous, considering that they were in the middle of an argument about her betraying Bororavia—and she was his prisoner, to boot—but here she was once again allowing her emotions concerning Christopher MacLeod almost overwhelm her reason.

Guilt stabbed her, for she knew she must always say no though it broke her heart. She should not lead him on in any way—but she wanted to say yes!

Lily glanced from Kit to the teenage girls, who were avidly trying to follow the conversation. "And little pitchers have big ears."

"We cultivate eavesdropping in my family."

"Some things are not meant to be discussed in company," Lily reminded Kit.

"You two have gotten far off the subject," Beatrice spoke up.

Kit sighed. "I'm beginning to wonder what the subject really is." His gaze bored into Lily's. "I begin to think that I'm the one who has been listening without any understanding. You keep saying that you don't want to return to the embassy, but you have to. I don't think you have any loyalty to King Gregory, do you Lily my love?"

Lily started to say that she was not his love, but with him looking at her so intently, almost as though he were searching her soul, the denial simply would not come out. Keeping herself from answering with the words *Kit, my love* was so difficult her throat ached and it seemed like a fist tightened around Lily's throat. Her answer came out in a strained croak. "Of course I have no loyalty to Gregory." She couldn't say anything but the truth with Kit looking at her like that. She realized that she was looking at Kit just as intently. The world consisted of the two of them and the barriers that separated them. But those barriers were nothing but smoke and shadows, weren't they? Surely she could step through them, meet him somewhere where flesh and spirit and mind joined beyond all the necessities of family and duty, honor, and country.

"Why isn't there somewhere where we could be only Kit and Lily?"

Lily's hand clapped over her mouth. Good Lord, had she actually said that? How could she have?

"You can't take it back," he told her. "Once words escape they are out in the world and they do what they do. Sometimes they fall on deaf ears." He crossed his arms. "Sometimes they change the world. Dangerous things, words."

"Yes," she agreed, dropping her hand once more to her side. "Very."

"For instance, I am just now recalling some words I should have heeded during a conversation with a friend of your mother's. She said she knew your mother didn't want you consorting with the Bororavian royal family. She said she wrote your mother asking what was going on—but your mother never answered." Lily's alabaster skin was going paler and paler with every word he spoke, and fear blazed in her eyes. She clutched her arms tightly over her stomach. Kit stepped closer to her.

"Why didn't your mother answer the letter, Lily?" She turned her head away. He grasped her chin and made her look at him. "Where is your mother?"

She would have answered, Kit was certain. But the door opened before Lily had quite worked up the courage, and in barged Lucy, followed by Uncle Andrew.

"I knew you'd be here," Lucy announced. Kit had never seen her look so fierce as she took a sweeping look around the room. "All of you." Lucy pointed at Lily. "That's my dress—and leave my brother alone."

Beatrice and Sara jumped guiltily to their feet. Kit stepped protectively in front of Lily.

Uncle Andrew said, "Now that most of the clan's gathered, why don't we call for pipers and Highland games. Better yet, let's put a sign out front announcing this as the Hotel MacLeod." The utter disgust of his tone drew everyone's attention.

"We won't be staying," Lucy answered him. "I've come to collect the girls." She turned her attention back to Bea and Sara. "Harriet's frantic, you know. She can't imagine why you aren't home yet from what was supposed to be a short ride in the park. She's a good lass, but not the most devious member of the clan."

"We didn't mean to upset her," Beatrice said. She and Sara were looking at the rug rather than their annoyed sister.

"Me, I'm devious," Lucy went on. "First Kit made off with Sara. She came back all excited and secretive. Then the pair of you go off by yourselves, but don't return when you promised you would. I began to wonder why Kit would need our would-be doctor. He certainly looked fit enough when he showed up at Harriet's. Then when I went to change into riding clothes to help hunt for our overdue bairns, I found my dress missing. Who would need my dress? Let's see, hasn't Kit taken a fancy to a most unsuitable lady of late? Where could he take the current conquest? Why would she need clothes? I didn't want to think too hard about that." She turned a glare on Lily. "I'm not at all pleased to see my suspicions were correct."

By this time Lily had moved from behind Kit to stand by his side. Their arms were around each other's waists. For support both moral and physical, he told himself. Lucy could be a formidable wench.

"Well, she only had a nightgown," Sara spoke up. "And she was injured."

"So you abetted them in the game they're playing?" Lucy asked. "Kit exposed you to his bad habits?"

"You don't have to make it sound so salacious," Lily defended herself. "I didn't ask to be here. It's not my fault my ankle's injured. Or that I needed something to wear." She looked to Beatrice and Sara. "I'm grateful to the girls for helping me."

"Actually, the ankle is your fault," Kit corrected her mildly.

She turned an annoyed look on him. "Is not."

"Who does a man have to shoot to get a bit of peace and quiet around here?" Uncle Andrew's question got everyone's attention. He stood with his back to the closed door, looking even more irritated than usual. "Lucy, take your argument and your sisters elsewhere," he ordered.

Lucy drew herself up, not in the least bit intimidated. "That is precisely why I am here. We're going. Back to Scotland," she added. "Sara and Bea have had quite enough of the corrupting influence of city life. We're leaving on the evening train." She gestured toward the door. "Come along."

Sara hurried to obey.

"But"—Beatrice said, looking at the papers on the table—"Aunt Phoebe . . ."

"Go with Lucy," Kit said. He drew Lily closer to his side. "I'll take care of it."

Lily stiffened, and Beatrice gave a wistful look before heading toward the door with Lucy and Sara. Uncle Andrew opened it for them and waited in the hall for them to pass.

Lucy, however, could not resist a parting shot of animosity toward Lily. "Red's not your color, lass," she told the princess. "Not with that hair. Though I suppose it goes well enough with being a scarlet woman."

"Why you—!" Lily began, but Kit held her back when she tried to get at Lucy.

Lucy slammed the door after this insult, leaving Kit to deal with the furious princess.

Chapter 21

"**A**t least she didn't ask for the dress back," Kit joked once they were alone, and Lily had stopped banging her fists against his chest. He agreed that she had every right to be annoyed at Lucy—in fact, he was feeling less than charitable about his eldest sister himself. If he hadn't wanted to get rid of them, he might have given Lucy a piece of his mind in defense of Lily's honor. "She had no right to speak to you that way," he told Lily.

"She doesn't like me," Lily concluded, forcing her frayed temper under control. Her feelings still stung as she looked questioningly at Kit. "Why doesn't she like me?"

Kit gave a faint chuckle. He didn't loosen his hold on her, but drew her into a comforting embrace. "For a girl born in London, she's the most dour Highlander I've ever met. Lucy's protective," he explained. "She fears you'll be a bad influence on me."

"I'll be a bad influence on . . . ?" Lily tried to fathom this upside-down logic of the MacLeods, but it made no more sense than anything else that had happened in the last few days. She rubbed her forehead against Kit's shoulder, but instead of wiping away the cobwebs from her confused brain, it only made her more aware of him. "You're all mad," she said.

"Mad as hatters," he agreed. "It's like going down the rabbit hole living with us. But we're never boring," he added, as though this was a plus.

It would have been so easy to snuggle closer to him, to stop thinking and simply be with him. She might have given in to the urge, but the ache from putting weight on her ankle was growing. It reminded her that her duty was to get away from Kit MacLeod even though her other senses screamed for her to stay.

As though reading her mind, Kit lifted her and set her down in the nearest chair. She found herself sitting by the table on which the stolen documents were spread. She carefully kept her gaze from going to the pile of papers.

Kit took a step back. "What do they say?"

The steel in his voice was frightening. Lily looked up at him. He looked grim and purposeful. It made her remember that he really had risked his life to obtain the papers, and in the process saved her as well. At least from Cherminsky and Irenia's machinations. She was grateful for Kit's coming to her rescue, even though there had been self-interest on his part, because he might have been caught if he hadn't taken her with him. And she would have been killed if he hadn't. She couldn't help but believe that Kit did essentially mean well.

She tried to tell herself that her judgment and wits were addled because she was so attracted to him. He was good-looking. He was charming. He made her feel like a woman, and a person, and a friend. He made her feel wanted and safe. And thoroughly exasperated, and angry and alive. She wanted to throw herself into his arms, and into his bed and stay there forever.

"Talk to me," he urged. His steely expression had turned to something softer, more familiar, but he still looked determined. "What's going on in that pretty brain of yours?"

"Brains aren't pretty."

He shrugged. "Sara would tell you different."

"Sara wants to be a doctor."

"And will be, too. She has pretty brains."

"You don't object? To women doctors?"

"Would I dare? You've met some of the women in my family. I'd like to meet some of the women in your family," he went on before she could respond. "Perhaps you could introduce me to your mother."

Lily nervously bunched the heavy material of her skirts in her fists. She glanced out the window to discover a faint mist falling outside. The garden was covered in crystal beads of water. "My mother would like you," she finally said, though her throat was tight with fear. She wanted to cry. The sky was crying, why couldn't she? Because crying did no good, of course.

She wanted her mommy.

Lily sighed, and knew all her anxiety could be read in the sound.

While she continued to stare out the window, Kit's fingers touched her cheek. "Lily?" The word was spoken with such tender concern she couldn't help but turn her gaze up to his. "Where's your mother?"

"I don't know." She spoke before she thought. Then fury blazed through her as she realized how easy it had been for him to worm this admission from her.

She didn't have to say a word for him to step back in response to her angry look. He held his hands up before him. "You need to talk about this. You truly do. I can see that you're being eaten by worry. And don't go on at me about how I'm an English spy and a thief and trying to get you to betray your homeland," he warned before she could do just that. "It's not true and we both know it."

"That you're a thief and a spy?"

"That you give a damn about Bororavia."

"I do!" she shouted at him. "I—"

"Why?" he demanded.

"The people—"

"You know nothing about the people."

"I know they deserve better than Gregory!"

His expression turned triumphant. He took another step back and pointed a finger at her. "Now you've spoken a true thing. Gregory is the gist of all our problems. Your problems. Bororavia's. England's."

She was well aware of Gregory's heavy hand in her life, and in the lives of his downtrodden subjects. "What problem, pray tell," she inquired sarcastically, "does England have with my petty dictator cousin?"

"Anarchists," he answered.

"Anarchists?" she questioned back. "Aren't anarchists in the business of overthrowing monarchies?"

"My comment exactly when I first heard the term mentioned in connection with your cousin." He gestured toward the stolen documents. "I was sent to find out why King Gregory is consorting with anarchists. Apparently they've sneaked into England with his help. We need to know where they are and what they're up to. So, you see, British security is very much at stake. This is *my* country, and I do what I must to protect it."

Kit began to pace the room. Giving her time to think, she supposed, to ponder the dire possibilities of the situation. She couldn't help but watch him restlessly stalking the parlor, and her mind did race, from one awful scenario to the next. She didn't doubt that Gregory was capable of anything. Look at what he'd done to her mother, to her. He'd driven her father out of Bororavia, and sent assassins after him for years—until the British government made it clear that King Maxim was a welcome guest in the country and attempts on his life would lead to Britain's cutting off vital trade relations with Bororavia. Queen Victoria's sponsoring Lily at her baptism had been a part of Britain showing favor to Bororavia's ex-king. If for no other reason, Lily supposed she owed the British government for helping her father.

Outside, the mist had turned into heavy rain. As the sky had darkened so had the room. Lily stared into shadows and grew colder by the moment.

Lord Ornov had taught her that international politics was played on many levels. He'd told her that Gregory had not come to London simply to marry her and oversee the trade negotiations. Was Gregory involved in some conspiracy to overthrow the British monarchy? Was he a cat's paw for a Russian plot?

"Is Gregory going to kill Queen Victoria?" The words came out as a frightened whisper.

Kit crossed the room and lit a lamp on the table, chasing away some of the shadows. "We have no idea what Gregory is up to." He swept the papers into her lap. "Not until we find out what those say."

Lily riffled the pages; they were dry as autumn leaves. She looked up at Kit, who hovered uncomfortably close to her chair. There was no getting away from him until she did as he wanted. "I am so sick of men ordering and threatening and forcing me to do whatever they want. I have a will of my own, you know."

Kit knelt in front of her and took her hands in his. The papers in her lap wrinkled beneath their clasped hands. Warmth spread through her at his touch. "I have never made you do anything against your will, now have I? All right, I abducted you, but that doesn't count. Have I forced you in other ways? Have I imposed my desires on you?"

She almost smiled. In fact, Lily almost laughed, not in mockery but at the formality of his tone, and because the truth of what he said sent a calming wave of reassurance through her. Despite the fact that being alone here with him in this house totally besmirched her reputation in the eyes of the world, she knew she could trust Kit MacLeod with her honor. But that was between them. How far could she trust him outside the bedroom?

"All right," she said, wanting to give more, but unable to make promises that might affect others. "I'll read the documents." She could tell from the way his dark eyes narrowed that he noticed that she didn't say she would translate what she read.

But he nodded and rose to his feet. He took a step back after moving the lamp closer to give her more light. She was far too aware of his silent presence as she picked up the paper on the top of the pile, straightened it out, and looked at the words. Bororavian was not her first language, though she'd certainly had ample opportunity to brush up on speaking it lately. Still, making out the words came haltingly. Lily had to go over what she read slowly, several times, at least for the first page or two. Then, as she continued to read the world began to spin around her and grow brighter, but that was not because of the proximity of the lamp or that it had stopped raining outside.

"What's the matter?" Kit asked. She didn't answer. "Can you make out the words? Are they in code?"

Lily finally responded to his question. "Nothing's the matter." She couldn't conceal her joy when she looked up at him. "I can make out the words. They aren't in code." She threw her head back against the high back of the leather chair and her laughter filled the room.

At first Kit thought Lily sounded relieved, but as her laughter went on and on it began to sound slightly hysterical. When tears began to appear in her eyes and her shoulders began to shake he couldn't take it anymore and drew her up out of the chair and into his arms. Mindful of her sprained ankle he made sure her weight rested against him as he held her close. Her arms came around his shoulders, and she pulled him even closer as she began to sob.

"Tell me," he whispered, running his fingers

through the hair that fell loosely around her shoulders. "It's all right. Whatever it is, I'm here for you." The words poured out of Kit. He wasn't even sure what he said, only that he meant every word. All he wanted to do was protect her, help her, keep her safe. She was his Lily and nothing was ever going to hurt her again.

Good God, when had he become a knight in shining armor?

"You don't have to cry," he said, after Lily had cried so long and so hard that his coat, his shirt, and his shoulder were damp. She lifted her head from his shoulders. Her face was red and blotchy, her eyes bloodshot and almost insanely bright with tears. "You're beautiful," he told her.

And that was when she kissed him, tasting of salt, and sharing exultation with the frantic urgency of her lips and tongue. Kit's senses caught fire with swiftness that left him shaking, and shaken. His hands were all over her in an instant and she arched eagerly into every arousing touch. He very nearly lay her down on the chaise and had her then and there.

He wasn't sure what it was that kept him from picking her up and carrying her the few steps, and he cursed the sanity that abruptly returned, but he finally was able to pull away from her. "I think we're celebrating something," he said, after taking a few breaths to calm down. "Before it goes any further, would you mind telling me what?"

"Me mum," she answered, her Yorkshire accent suddenly so thick he could barely make out what she said. "I've found me mum!"

This time Kit did pick her up and set her down, but he took a seat next to her on the chaise lounge, curiosity getting the better of lust for the moment. He took Lily's hands and squeezed them gently. "Your mother has something to do with those documents, is that it?"

She nodded. "And the anarchists."

Kit didn't ask. Instead he nodded encouragingly, and waited for Lily to tell him whatever she wanted.

"You see," she began. "A few weeks ago a group of men came to Harelby House in the middle of the night. They made my mother and I pack our bags and took us away. I was brought to London. I had no idea where they took my mother. I was so frightened," she admitted. Lily paused for a moment, and he could almost visibly see her push away the impulse to show any fear or self-pity. "Gregory was waiting at the embassy in London. Gregory and his stupid plan," she added angrily.

"Plan?" Kit asked quietly. From her expression he thought she might be about to go off on a diatribe against the king. While a bit of cursing the black-hearted bastard might do Lily good, Kit was anxious to hear her story.

"He's a childless widower and sits rather shakily on the throne. The nobles back in Bororavia are in factions. This is my guess, but I believe that there's a group scheming to put Gregory's half-brother Michael on the throne. And there is possibly another group who wants me on the throne. I'm only guessing this in hindsight. My mother had very firm ideas about my learning about politics and court intrigue, and I've come to think she was mistaken since I've had to learn how to scheme and be distrustful from scratch." She took a deep breath. "Gregory's idea was to marry me himself. I'm pretty sure Bishop Arkady wants me to marry Michael. I don't want to marry either of them, but what I wanted didn't mean anything to anyone inside the embassy. Normally I wouldn't be very good at being a pawn, but Gregory had my mother. He wouldn't tell me where she was, only that he would kill her if I didn't do as he said. And I believed him. I was trapped inside the embassy, Kit, with Gregory threatening and bullying me. There were guards. I wasn't allowed to write to anyone. If Gregory hadn't decided he wanted to take part in the London social season, I doubt I would have ever seen anyone. I was expecting to be shipped off to Bororavia at any time as the newly wed consort of the king."

Kit grew thoughtful even as he wanted to take Lily in his arms and comfort her for the weeks of terror. He began to see why she had responded to his flirtation. She'd used him—playing on Gregory's jealousy to try to save herself from an abhorrent marriage. How could he blame her? She hadn't thought he was serious. Which, he had to admit, he hadn't been.

Not at first . . . *Am I now? God, yes!*

That realization hit like a flash of lightning. But this was not the time to declare himself. There was a mother to deal with. And the matter of the anarchists. He could not afford to forget his assignment.

When he forced his thoughts away from his feeling for Lily, a theory began to dawn. "It's not that easy for even a king to get away with kidnapping and murder, Lily," Kit said. "Especially not in a foreign land and with a court full of conspiracies. That's where the anarchists come in, isn't it?"

"You're so clever." She reached forward and ruffled his hair.

He barely stopped from catching her hand and kissing her palm. "Tell me what you learned."

"I found correspondence between Gregory and several people involved in the conspiracy. Gregory made an agreement with a pair of political prisoners to release several of their accomplices if they would carry out a very secretive assignment for him in England. Gregory didn't involve any of his own officers, diplomats, or courtiers. The anarchists report directly to him, but kings don't pay their own bills. Gregory did have a clerk performing that mundane task, and the papers you stole are records of funds that were issued to these people. And"—she grinned—"most important of all, I found a rental agreement among those papers for the house where my mother is being held!"

"Follow the money," Kit said, with a nod. "Always follow the money trail. It's one of the first things we learn in spy school," he told Lily. "Where's the house?"

"In Scotland," she answered. "Do you know the town of Fort William?"

He didn't answer immediately, nor was he completely honest with his answer. "I've heard the name." Everyone had heard of Fort William. It was a famous resort town at the foot of Ben Nevis, the tallest mountain in Scotland. The Queen had made the place popular back when Prince Albert was alive.

Lily clutched his hands tightly, imploringly. The expression on her face was one of earnest trust that twisted his heart. He knew what she was about to say, and almost winced when she did. "We have to leave immediately. We have to save my mother. You will help me, won't you, Kit?"

"I'll see what I can do," was the best he could answer. For as impulsive as he was with his personal life, Christopher Fox MacLeod never played fast and loose with an assignment. He'd been told to acquire the papers, and he had. He'd told Beatrice he'd find out what was in them, and he had. Now he had to report that information.

After that duty was completed, then he'd see what he could do about making the sun shine once again in Lily's world.

Chapter 22

"**N**o. Absolutely not. I forbid it."

"Aunt Phoebe . . ." Kit smiled, though he gritted his teeth beneath the pleasant attitude, trying to hold on to his growing anger. He'd rushed to her flowered, feminine sitting room and told her everything. As he spoke he watched her expression grow darker with every word, and now he deeply regretted sharing confidences with her. "It's the right thing to do. Surely you see that. A woman's life is in danger. We need to rescue her. You, of all people, must have sympathy for a woman alone in the world, and in danger."

The iron-willed old woman shook a finger at him. "Don't try to wheedle compassion out of me, lad. It doesn't work."

She was a small woman, and he was a tall man. The differences in their sizes didn't keep Kit from feeling like a small boy who'd been called onto the carpet to endure a tongue-lashing after being caught being naughty.

"In the first place," she went on angrily, "you had no business taking this girl away from the embassy. In the second, all you have to do is return her, and her mother will not be in danger."

"Lily was about to be murdered."

"You don't know that."

"I don't . . ." Kit shook his head in disbelief. "I was there. You weren't. A field operative knows when to use his own best judgment."

"Your judgment's addled with lust."

He didn't feel like a little boy anymore, but he was a very angry man. He pointed at his great-aunt. "Not another word about Lily," he warned. "What's between us is no affair of yours."

"Not of mine," she agreed, "but of your government. She's not a private citizen, lad. She's a princess. We have uses for princesses."

The level of Kit's indignation soared skyward. Such callousness was not to be tolerated! His hands balled into fists. "Not my Lily, you don't."

She shook her head in disgust. "It's worse than I thought, isn't it? You're in love with this woman." The words were an accusation. She glared closely at him for a good minute, and Kit glared defiantly right back. "Tell me you're not so far lost to duty that you've told the princess how you feel." The words came out more as an order than a question.

Kit's heart sank, and his anger grew from heated to bleakly cold. "Of course I would not dare voice such presumption, Lady Phoebe."

Aunt Phoebe crossed the distance from where she stood next to her embroidery frame to join him in front of the empty fireplace. She touched his arm, though he shied away from the contact. "Kit, lad, I hate to see your heart broken, but this woman is not for you. You are my favorite thief of hearts." She shook a finger under his nose. "But this is the one thing I cannot let you have. She must return to Bororavia."

"She's never been to Bororavia. She doesn't want to go."

"She has no choice in the matter. Neither do you."

He had always known his great-aunt was tough as steel, but he'd never known her to be heartless before. "How can you speak so? You, who have always championed a woman's right to live free and as she chooses?"

"Because this isn't personal. There's nothing I can do about this. There's no help for it. At this moment policy dictates that there be a stronger British presence in Bororavia. Princess Lily will provide that presence. Simply by marrying the king she will strengthen diplomatic ties between our countries." Kit stood stiff as stone and made no comment. He noticed that Aunt Phoebe was becoming uncomfortable having one of the family not only questioning her, but angry with her. "Haven't you guessed the game by now?" she demanded after a drawn out silence. "Someone within the Bororavian court caught wind of the king's consorting with anarchists and passed their suspicion along to us. We found the evidence that Gregory brought foreign criminals onto British soil. That evidence will be used by us to pressure the Bororavians for more trading concessions and a stronger diplomatic presence. This weakens Gregory, while the new queen is not only English in temperament and sympathy, she is also the true heir to the throne. We weaken Russian influence in the Baltic and Lily gets her throne back. The girl is the victor in this, Kit. Surely, you see that."

"It's not a victory if she doesn't want to be a queen."

"Wearing a crown is her right, and her duty. She isn't the same as you and I. She has no choice in who she loves, where she goes, what she does. She must do what is right for her country. Royals must be held to a different standard. A harder standard, perhaps, but that is the way of the world."

He could see that Aunt Phoebe truly believed what she said. Perhaps she was right, though everything in him cried out to believe her words were lies. He knew it wouldn't do any good to argue the point anymore. "All right, I understand." The words tasted like dust when he said them. "But what about her mother? We know where she is. We can save her."

"No," Phoebe said again. "Absolutely not. I forbid it."

"But—"

"The matter is no longer up for discussion." She returned to her seat, and pulled the large embroidery stand to her. She picked up her needle and began to stitch. "Thank you for visiting me, Kit," she said, cool and aloof as ever, not even looking at him. "You must come again very soon." She shot him a commanding look. "And bring Princess Lily with you." She gestured toward the door. "Good day."

He stalked out, still seething with fury. But once outside his aunt's home he stood on the street and watched traffic going by on the cobbled street and had no notion where to go or what to do. His mind was blank. All he knew was anger, failure, and the pain of his heart burning down to ash.

She couldn't pace, and she wouldn't cry, but Lily did force herself to read the newspaper Kit had left with her when he locked her in the upstairs room once more. It had not been the most exciting news day. There was no mention of a frantic manhunt for a kidnapped princess. She wasn't sure how she felt about the fact that no one had reported her missing—though it's a very exciting story, she thought.

Perfect for the scandal sheets, what with the hours the princess spent only wearing a nightgown, and the lack of chaperones for much of the time. Shocking. And adventurous. Of course, readers would think the part with the drainpipe made me look like a fool.

Still, it would be nice if someone knew or cared that Lily Bancroft was missing. Again. And had been missing for weeks before this second, much preferred abduction. Paramount among all her ambivalent feelings was fear of Kit getting into any trouble for what he'd done. There was also the continued, constant fear for her mother's safety.

She also supposed there was something perverse about sympathizing with the man who held her prisoner, but there it was.

"Besides, if anyone does him an injury for his crimes, it is going to be me," she said as she finished the paper and put it down on the table beside the bed. After that, there was nothing to do but wait.

Day turned into evening, and the silence in the house turned nerve-rackingly ominous.

What was the matter with Kit? She kept asking herself as time dragged by. Why hadn't he told her where he was going? Or taken her with him? Why was she still here? Was he going to help her or not? Why was she still a prisoner? All these questions were disturbing, but most disturbing of all was how much she missed him.

By the time the door opened she was ready to scream, but kept stiff and silent out of pride. Kit stood in the doorway and watched her for a moment, one arm full of packages; a lamp illuminating his face was held up in his other hand.

Lily moved to sit on the side of the bed, crossed her arms when he stepped inside. She waited until Kit had put the lamp on the table and the packages beside her before she spoke. "I hope you have brought something to eat with you."

"Straight from Fortnum and Mason." His smile was strained, but he presented her a small basket with a graceful flourish.

She opened it to find fruit and biscuits, also fancy sandwiches of cucumber, cress and ham, and a pair of delicate little cakes. She didn't offer to share a bite of it with him.

They sat in silence while Kit watched her wolf down the food. When she was done, he said, "I think you're annoyed at me."

"How observant of you."

"I brought you presents."

Lily tried not to be curious, not to be interested, not to be pleased. "What sort of presents?"

"Shoes," he answered. "Silk stockings. And garters. And other pretty things."

"Shoes." She stuck her bare feet out from under her skirt. "Show me the shoes." She inspected the brown leather, high-button shoes carefully when he handed them over. "Tortoiseshell buttons," she observed.

"Only the best for a princess." While his tone

was cheerful, there was a dark undertone to his words that made her uncomfortable.

"You make me feel like Cinderella." She expected him to rise to this invitation to tease, but he didn't respond. "This will definitely fit my good foot."

"The swelling will soon go down in your ankle. Both shoes will fit fine; you'll just have to fasten one a bit looser for a few days."

"You sound like an experienced ladies' maid."

"I have wide experience with ladies' apparel," he answered.

She glanced sideways at him, and saw the faintest of smirks hovering on his lips. She fought hard to hide a smile of her own, and a not at all faint stab of jealousy at the thought of his giving other women such intimate presents. "I suspect your shopping experience has little to do with your sisters."

He suddenly stroked the hair that fell loose around her shoulders and ran his fingers lightly down the side of her throat. Lily shivered, and Kit said, "I have a great deal of experience in pleasing ladies."

He touched her, and she melted. "If you stop touching me I could remain angry with you."

"I know." There was sadness in his voice that frightened her.

Lily had no idea why she wanted to comfort Kit,

and fought off the urge to do so. "What about my mum?" she asked instead.

"I've reported the situation to my superiors. I brought you a frock, as well," he said, and pushed the largest of the packages toward her while she tried to understand the nuances of what he'd said.

Lily ignored the box. "What does that mean? That you've *reported the situation*? Are you going to help my mother or not?" She heard her voice going shriller with each word, but was powerless to keep her nerves under control.

"The matter is not in my hands." Kit stood very quickly, and all his muscles were stiff as he looked down at her. His face was expressionless as was his voice.

"I am such a fool." She'd never been more stunned in her life. For an endless moment the world went blank, numb, colder than the Arctic north, as all the while she searched a beloved face that was empty of emotion, with dark eyes as distant as the moon.

He was not going to help her. If there was any one truth in the world, it was that Kit Fox was not now, nor had he ever been, on her side. She'd called him thief, liar, spy, scoundrel and more, but deep down she'd instinctively believed him to be a hero, her champion. He was every wicked thing she'd ever called him, and nothing more. Finally, she believed it.

"What are you going to do with me?"

He remained silent as he walked to the door while she stared, her heart breaking. Lily held her breath, hoping he'd turn, say something witty and sweet and make all her confused pain go away. Instead the door opened, then closed, and she heard the key turn in the lock.

Her breath rushed out, then, in a screech, she let out the voice pent-up and threw a shoe against the door with all her might.

Outside in the hall Kit winced as the loud thump sounded through the heavy wood of the door. That had definitely not gone well. Of course, he didn't know what he'd been trying to accomplish. Maybe he should have just marched in and announced, "All right, that's it. It is back to prison and a forced marriage for you, my lass. I am so sorry."

But how could he do that to her?

Because he must.

Kit banged his head against the nearest wall a few times. Of course, that did nothing but give him a headache. Didn't even put a dent in the sturdy wall. He considered banging a fist through the plaster, but his hands belonged to the service of the Queen, now didn't they? Couldn't risk injuring his clever thief's hands.

"If you're going to stand there and feel sorry for yourself all night, I might puke."

Kit turned his head in the direction of the disgruntled voice. "Hello, Uncle Andrew."

"I take it you've been to see the auld besom,"

was Andrew's acrid reply. "And she's talked you into giving the girl back to her barbarian cousin. I can tell you've agreed to the sacrifice by the slump of your shoulders."

Andrew MacLeod stood at the other end of the hallway, just at the top of the stairs, his tall form outlined by moonlight streaming in an octagon window above his head. He looked as grim as the angel of death, which was, frequently, his profession.

"Normally I'm fond of you, Uncle," Kit said, coming slowly toward the other man. "But today you have been far more sarcastic and annoying than I can stand."

"And you've been more obtuse and foolish than I can believe," was Andrew's sour reply. A bit of moonlight glinted off his glasses as he tilted his head to one side. "If there was one thing I never expected from you, Christopher, it was that you'd be taken in by one of Lady Phoebe Gale's complicated, cold-hearted schemes."

"I don't think it's her scheme, this time," Kit said. But he didn't deny that his great-aunt was being harder than he'd ever known she could be. "She's carrying out her orders. *I'm* carrying out her orders," he corrected bitterly. Then his spine stiffened. "And what do you mean I'm being 'taken in'? What are you talking about?"

Andrew leaned back against the stair railing. He looked deceptively relaxed. "Did she give you a speech about duty—yours and the princess's?" Kit nodded. "She's very good at making speeches, is Phoebe Gale. Everything is acceptable for the good of the Empire, is her philosophy. Has it occurred to you that she's wrong?" Andrew said, his tone far gentler than Kit was used to. "It's not like you to let anyone else make your decisions for you, lad. Not like you at all. There's doing what's right. There's following your instincts. And there's doing what you're told no matter what you think about it. It's up to each man to decide what he's going to do every time something hard is put before him. It's your choice, Christopher MacLeod," Andrew said, his piercing gaze locking with Kit's. "Yours. Not Phoebe Gale's or anyone else's. Ought to be the lass's choice as well, I think."

With that, Uncle Andrew turned and went back down the stairs, leaving Kit to ponder what he'd said.

Kit let out a long, deep sigh that rattled him to his bones. He rubbed his palms wearily against his eyes. This was just what he needed, another voice chiming in opinions to muddy up his thinking on what had been the hardest decision of his life. "Right. Wrong. Instinct. Duty." Each word came out with growing fury, and seemed to swirl around him with dizzying speed while his rage grew to the point where his body swirled around in a tight circle and he drove a fist with all his might into the stout wall.

"*OW!*"

Kit swore, bending over double as he grasped his injured hand against his chest. In the distance, beyond the pain, he was faintly aware of Lily banging on her prison door.

"Kit!" she called. "Kit, what's wrong? What happened? Are you all right?"

How could she be concerned? How dare she be concerned? Didn't she remember what a bastard he was?

"Oh, God, Lily," he said, and saying her name brought the world into focus.

It took a moment to fumble the key out of his pocket. Hand still throbbing, but head suddenly crystal clear, he fit the key in the lock and opened the door.

"Lily my love," he said, gazing with his usual rakish smile into her startled, concerned face. "How would you like to take a quick trip up to Fort William with me?" The next thing he knew she had limped into his arms and held on to him with a terrible fierceness that left him breathless.

"Thank you, thank you, thank you!" Lily said, in between kissing him, on the cheeks, on the nose, on his throat and forehead, and finally, wonderfully, getting to his mouth.

The kiss went on for a long time, the intensity they shared sending Kit into a tumult of need, and burning away any last faint doubts that he was doing the right thing. Finally, before the urge to sweep everything off the bed and lie Lily down beneath him on the soft mattress overpowered him, Kit managed to get himself under control. "Rescue," he said, running his hands through her lovely copper hair. "We have to plan a rescue."

"Yes," she agreed, breathless and bright-eyed. "Yes we do. This is no time to think about us. We have to go."

Kit swallowed hard. He could almost hear the frightening peal of wedding bells in the air. But—he'd never planned—he wasn't—"Us?" Lily didn't notice his faint whisper. She was looking around frantically. "What's the matter?" he asked her.

"My shoes," she answered. "We can't go anywhere until I've found my shoes, now can we?"

"No, of course not." He answered. "And besides, I'm sure they'll come in handy for you to throw at me in the future."

Chapter 23

"Most men would say that this is no place for a woman."

"Most men don't come from families where sharing ammunition is considered a romantic gesture."

They were seated at a small table on the verandah of an inn, and though Lily's words had been for Kit, she cast a wary glance at the man who had spoken. She was relatively relaxed with Kit's uncle, but she still didn't know what to think of Andrew MacLeod, other than that he made an odd chaperone. She had found Andrew's company far more stimulating than Lady Ornov's in the two days it had taken them to reach Fort William by train. He didn't ask her to do embroidery, but he didn't give her a chance to be alone with Kit, either.

They had checked into the inn on the outskirts of Fort William only an hour before, and met on the porch to make plans while having afternoon tea. Ben Nevis loomed above them, the mountain's skirts were green with summer foliage, but its heights were wreathed in thick mist. Clouds scudded by overhead, but the day was mostly fair, though it was cool enough for Lily to be glad of the plaid wool shawl Kit had acquired for her. Lily sipped from a red china cup full of strong, fragrant tea, and even though she was flanked by her two dangerous traveling companions at the small table, this was the least she'd felt like a prisoner for a long time.

"I'm glad you chose to come along, Uncle Andrew," Kit said, though he smiled at the frustrated look Lily gave him. "He's quite handy to have around," Kit told her.

"As muscle," Andrew added. He looked from Kit to Lily. "As well as keeping an eye on the pair of you."

Uncle Andrew was not only acting as chaperone, he was opposed to every sensible plan Lily suggested. She wasn't sure whether he was playing devil's advocate, or merely intent on bedeviling her with his objections. "We know exactly where they are," she pointed out. "Let's go."

"But we still haven't reconnoitered the place," Kit answered. He gently took her teacup and set it down on the table. Then he held her hand and looked into her eyes. "I understand your concern."

"No you don't. Your mother's never been kidnapped."

Kit started to answer, but Andrew cleared his throat significantly, and Kit closed his mouth and patted Lily's hand reassuringly. She didn't want to be reassured. She wanted action!

"I still don't see why we can't call in the constables to come with us," Lily said, not for the first time. "I know you don't want to cause an 'international incident.' Frankly, I don't care if Gregory gets in trouble for abducting my mother. I want her safe and sound and at home."

"I don't care about international incidents, either," Andrew said, keeping his voice low even though they were the only people on the wide, white-washed verandah. "The men we're going up against are dangerous. More dangerous than any local peacekeepers can handle. I don't want amateurs hurt. I don't want your mother hurt. We have to take the opponent out quietly and secretly or we have a strong possibility of casualties. Do you understand?"

Lily's mouth went dry at this blunt explanation. No one had brought that up before. Maybe she shouldn't have taken this for granted. There was no use complaining that she wasn't an experienced international espionage agent. "I think I've led far too sheltered a life," she said. "But my grasp of politics and the spy game is expanding."

"You are a fish out of water," Andrew acknowledged.

"But one that's adapting quite well," Kit hurried to add.

"You're still patting my hand," she told him, and gave him a smile. "Stop being sympathetic and re-assuring and tell me what we are going to do."

"We are going to have a look at the house while you have a rest," Kit told her.

Her quarters were on the ground floor of the inn; a pleasant suite with a bedroom and sitting room. A petulant part of her wanted to point out that she was only being banished to yet another prison, but the sensible part of her pointed out that it wasn't really like that at all. Sometimes she hated her sensible side. Lily didn't want to have a rest. Her ankle was much better and she was growing increasingly restless. She wanted to get her mum from the clutches of evil men. She also knew that arguing with a pair of 'professionals' wasn't going to get her mum to safety any faster.

"Fine," she said. "Go. Do whatever it is you do. But hurry."

"Dogs," Kit muttered into the darkness. "Why did it have to be dogs?"

Lily my love, this had better work. He was alone, crouching in a small stand of trees just within the grounds of the isolated property where Lady Eleanor Bancroft was being held. Earlier reconnaissance had shown that there were at least three large dogs patrolling the grounds around the house where Lily's mother was being kept.

"Kit, you're white as a sheet!" Lily had said when he walked into her sitting room after returning from the outskirts of town. She sprang up from her chair, her expression showing only a minor twinge of pain. *"What's the matter? Is Mum all right?"*

How could he tell the woman he cared for so deeply that the man she depended on to help her was worried about a few vicious, snarling hounds from hell? *"Nothing's wrong at all,"* he had said, and kissed her. The touch of her lips made him feel better.

But it didn't do anything about the dogs.

Of course, it was Lily who came up with the plan once she found out about the guard dogs.

"What sort of dogs are they?" she had asked. *"What do they look like? What were they doing when you saw them? Roaming about the property? Sleeping by the house?"*

"I saw them from a distance," Kit had told her. *"Didn't want them barking to alert anyone inside."*

"Ah, but perhaps you do want them barking."

"What are you thinking?" he had asked worriedly. She was bright-eyed and eager. He found her beautiful in her excitement, but it concerned him greatly. *"You're not thinking of letting them chase you or anything foolish like that, are you?"*

"Let her talk," Uncle Andrew had said. *"And tell her about the dogs."*

So he'd told her, and she'd laughed and clapped her hands with devilish delight. Then he and Andrew MacLeod, a pair of hardened secret agents, listened and agreed to a scheme thought up by a country girl with no experience at all in covert operations.

But she knew sheep, and she knew dogs. Or so she claimed. And here they were, three people sneaking about an isolated property on a chilly, cloudy night. Three people, and a farm cart full of sheep, Kit amended.

Kit was tense as he waited for the signal to move. He didn't know where his uncle was, but it wasn't necessary for Kit to know Andrew's movements. It was Andrew's job to deal with the anarchists. It was Kit's job to get in and get Lady Eleanor out. It was Lily's job to create the diversion that would set both Kit and Andrew's actions in motion.

Kit cursed himself for letting Lily talk him into this. He cursed Andrew for agreeing this was their best plan. Why had he let her come along? It was dangerous. What if she was captured? What if she was hurt? What would he do then?

What would I do without her?

The question froze him down to the soul.

But before any bleak pictures could form of this horrible future, sheep began to bleat and dogs began to bark, and Lily shouted in the distance, "Help! Help! Is anyone there? My cart overturned! Get your dogs away from my sheep! Help!"

Kit sprang to his feet and ran across a broad lawn suddenly swirling with the chaos of panicked sheep being chased by suddenly alert canines. The big dogs took no notice of him, for they had far more interest in the four-legged intruders than any two-legged one.

"*Ha,*" Lily proclaimed after he described the dogs. "*Prick-eared and long-bodied, you say? With long rough coats and a loping run? Look something like a wolf, do they? Dangerous-looking fellows, but those are Belgian herd dogs or I've never chased a stray ewe across the moors. I've heard that some shepherds were importing Belgians into the Highlands. I'd wager your anarchists paid a pretty penny to some local herdsman, but they didn't get what they bargained for. Set them in a herd and I'd love to see how they work.*"

It looked like the lass was getting her wish. Kit chuckled at his princess as he ran through the stampede and circled around the back of the house. He caught sight of men pouring out the front door as he passed, but they didn't notice him. He also caught the hint of a shadowy figure moving silently to intercept the men who came out of the house. He was more than confident that Andrew MacLeod could manage a mere three-to-one odds, and concentrated on his own specialty.

While carefully not looking at the snarling, barking wolflike creatures milling about the yard.

It was quiet at the back of the house. Kit found no

guards posted back there when he took a quick look around. He did notice a light in the second-floor window. He took a chance and tossed a rock at the window, then ducked behind a bush to wait. After a few seconds a woman peered out. Kit caught a glimpse of reddish hair, and a face that was as lovely as Lily's, though decades older. He was half-tempted to show himself and ask her to jump down into his arms. It was more practical to go in and get her.

So Kit raced for the rear door, changed his mind when he got there, and broke a window instead. He opened the back door once he'd crawled through the broken windowpane, leaving the escape route ready for use. Then he ran up the back-stairs but found Lady Eleanor's door locked, yet unguarded. A lockpick from the supply in his vest pocket soon took care of that problem.

"Lady Eleanor," he called as a precaution before opening the door. "I've come to rescue you." After all, you never knew when the person behind the door waited nervously to smash an intruder over the head with whatever came to hand. "We must hurry."

The door swung open before he could turn the knob. The woman who faced him was indeed a slightly faded copy of his own Lily, dressed all in mourning black. "Who are you?" she demanded.

"Christopher MacLeod," he immediately answered. "From the Foreign Service." He held his hand out to her. "Please come with me."

"Hmm . . ." She tilted her head, listening to the noise coming from out front. "Is that my daughter I hear shouting at sheep?"

"Yes, my lady. It's a diversion."

"Sounds like a typical day at home to me." She stepped forward, waving aside his offered hand. "Lead on, Mr. MacLeod. I want to see my daughter."

"Well, we've had enough excitement to last a lifetime, haven't we, my girl?"

Lily squeezed her mother's shoulder and answered, "Yes. Yes, we have." She said the words to be comforting, but the truth was, she'd had a marvelous time tonight.

Could it be that some people were made for adventures, and she'd missed her calling until Kit Fox showed up and asked her to dance? Good Lord, but what a merry dance he'd led her on since she'd glanced up and saw his dark eyes smiling down at her!

"Well, it's over now," her mother said, and patted Lily's hand. "And we're safe at last."

Lily did not feel the least bit safe. Physically she knew she was, but emotionally she was . . . She didn't know how to describe what she felt, other than that she was about to fly out of her skin. Oh, she felt very safe, very comfortable—very happy, ecstatically happy as a matter of fact.

After a tearful reunion on the road outside the house where her mother had been kept, Lily, Kit, and her mother had hopped into the farm cart and Kit drove back into Fort William while she and her mother hugged and kissed and caught up with what had happened to them in the last several weeks. Lily had kept out some of the more scandalous bits, such as she and Kit's constantly meeting in bedrooms and abductions featuring her dressed in a nightgown. She'd heard Kit occasionally chuckling over her careful editing, but he didn't add anything to her story. In fact, the only comment he'd made was in reply to her asking about Uncle Andrew.

"He makes his own arrangements," was the ambiguous answer. "You don't have to worry about him."

Since Kit seemed certain his uncle could take care of himself, Lily dropped the subject. Once they arrived at the inn, Kit escorted them to Lily's rooms, kissed both her and her mother's hands, and told them he'd see them in the morning. Lily hadn't wanted him to go, but he was gone before she could say so. Besides, he was right, she and her mother did need time alone together.

Now Lily and her mother were seated side by side on the sofa in their sitting room, sharing a pot of tea and enjoying each other's company. They were washed and rested and fed, dressed in nightgowns and robes and warm slippers. A banked fire glowed in the grate, fending off the chill of the Highland evening. A pair of lamps with pink-tinted glass shades lent a mellow light to the room. Lily was supremely happy—or would have been, if only Kit were there.

She wondered how it was that she could miss the man so much when it was no more than an hour or two since she'd seen him last.

"Handsome, isn't he?"

"Oh Lord, Mum, you don't know the half of it."

Lily blinked in sudden confusion, aware that she'd answered a question while staring into the glowing embers of the fire. She'd been looking at the fire for a long time, she thought, half asleep, with her head resting on her mother's shoulder. She stayed that way while the confusion cleared, then she sat up, blushing as she recalled what had been asked, and what her answer had been. When she looked at her mother, she was silently laughing.

"Mum!"

"No need to be ashamed, lass. I've got eyes. Any woman who doesn't look twice at your Mr. MacLeod has likely been dead for some time."

"I've looked," Lily answered as her mother rose to her feet and looked toward the bedroom door.

"Happy as I am to be with you again, my darling, I'm weary and must get some sleep. Let's continue talking about your Mr. MacLeod in the morning."

"My Mr. MacLeod," Lily said, and smiled at the

notion of Kit being hers. It was a fiercely possessive smile, and she knew it. An image of Kit, bare-chested, his dark eyes almost glowing with arousal, sprung to her mind. Memory of his kiss teased her lips. Memory of his arousing hands sang across her skin. "Mine," she said, the whisper barely audible.

"Coming to bed, dear?" Mum asked as she walked to the bedroom door.

Yes, but not here. Lily was looking at the fire, wondering if it was anywhere near as hot as the blood rushing through her. "Not just yet," she answered. "Sleep well . . ." she added, and waited until the door closed behind her mother before rising silently to her feet.

Chapter 24

Kit stepped from the path onto the verandah, going up the stairs with his usual silent grace. But instead of going into the inn, he took a seat at the corner table where they'd sat earlier in the day. He wasn't ready for bed yet, not with the excitement of the evening still pumping through him. He hadn't minded the walk back to the inn in the cool evening after returning the cart to the farmer from which they'd rented it, and the half dozen sheep. Kit had paid the man extra to go out and collect the sheep and dogs. Lily had made him promise to make sure the animals got home safely. He smiled on a wave of deep fondness at the way Lily loved animals.

And he sighed with contentment that the rescue was successfully completed, and basked in the sights, sounds, and smells of the night. He loved the Highlands. The air was clear and clean, fresh with scents of pine and water. The stars shone bright as candle flames, when they could be seen at all through swirling mists and racing clouds. Despite all the time spent in the great cities of Europe, and two years in America, the Highlands were home.

Not that he necessarily wanted to live at home, he reminded himself. He was a man of the world and could never be content, say, running a sheep farm, the way his princess could. There might be a certain contentment in coming home to that sort of place every now and then, but—

Had it come to this? Was he actually fantasizing about settling down?

Now, that was the sort of thing he'd always thought was all right for his parents, and Harriet seemed to be taking to matrimony like a duck to water, but for Christopher Fox MacLeod? Maybe for Christopher, he conceded. Christopher was a civilized sort—but what about Kit Fox, adventurer, scoundrel and gentleman–thief? What was a gentleman–thief, anyway? Someone who absconded with other people's property without getting his hands dirty?

Or his heart engaged?

Kit sighed, and decided he was tired after all. His heart suddenly felt heavy, and his soul weary. He must have been thinking too much, and that was never a wise thing for him to do. Living on instinct and impulse was enough for him.

Except it didn't feel like it anymore.

His step was not exactly sprightly when he went upstairs to his room. He supposed he needed a good night's sleep, but it wasn't going to change the fact that he had no idea what tomorrow would bring. The girl, the mother, and the day were all saved, but what came next?

Lily would want to go home and get her life back, of course. This was the thing he dreaded—that she'd bestow a chaste peck on his cheek, a heartfelt thank-you, and then he'd wave good-bye from the station platform as her train chugged off toward Yorkshire. Then he'd get back to his life.

"Such as it is," he grumbled, walking into the dark bedroom. Being an international thief and spy didn't seem at all exciting at the moment.

He had not paid much attention to the furnishings of the room when he'd left his things in it earlier in the day. He wondered why he had not noticed the bed before, for the heavily carved, canopied four-poster loomed up out of the darkness like a huge reminder of medieval times. The thing looked like it must have been ransacked out of some ancient laird's castle for it certainly belonged in a grander setting than a quiet resort-town inn. Layers of diaphanous lace draped down from the canopy like wedding veils, and fluttered ever so gently, giving the bed an air that was sensuous, beckoning, and mysterious.

Seems a shame to only sleep in it, Kit thought, and lit a candle to undress by. With the light came an awareness of shadows through the gossamer draperies, caught out of the corner of his eye. A glint of muted copper caught the light. A hint of a long, slender waist and rounded hip, and a shadow that might be a smooth, bare shoulder tantalized Kit into breathless stillness. The young woman seated on the bed turned her head a little, revealing a long neck; the mass of shining hair rippled down her back as she showed her delicate profile without giving away the details of her face. She lifted her hand, the graceful gesture beckoning.

Kit could not help but take a step forward.

He blinked, mind unbelieving, while his body tightened, aroused by the erotic way the layers of bed curtains played with light and shadow and imagination.

"Lily?" Her name came out as barely a whisper. He took another step. Then he shook himself out of what seemed like an erotic dream, and came around the bed to the other side—where the naked woman looked at him with a smile that was part welcoming, part trepidation, and part irritated.

"What are you doing in here?" he asked.

At the same time she asked, "What took you so long?"

She sat there, back straight, with her hands resting on the mattress on either side of her. She was framed by tied-back white bed hangings, and looked for all the world like a prize in a sultan's harem waiting to be claimed by her lord and master. He supposed the gentlemanly thing to do would be to drop his gaze, but she had lovely breasts, and it was very hard for a man not to look at them. They had a lovely roundness that would fit beautifully cupped in his hands. What pretty pink nipples, he thought, hard and thrust out as if begging for a touch, or a taste.

"I've grown rather chill waiting for you," Lily said.

"Why are you waiting at all?" he asked.

He very nearly put his hands out to touch her, but thrust them behind his back instead. He noticed her nightgown and robe puddled on the floor. The robe was aquamarine silk; he'd been thinking of her eyes when he bought it. He'd also been thinking of her naked beneath the clinging silk at the time. He thought that returning to that pleasant imagery would be far safer right now.

He picked up the robe and draped it about her shoulders. Strands of silky hair clung to his fingers as he pulled the robe closed, and the back of his hands brushed the tops of her breasts. He had to swallow hard before he could say, "Is that better?"

"No."

She shrugged off the silk. It flowed off her like water, mesmerizing him, drawing his eye down from her breasts to her stomach and the juncture of her thighs.

"How did you get in here?" he asked, when all he wanted to do was lie her back on the bed and have her.

Lily laughed softly at Kit's consternation. "What? Not used to having your room broken into, Mr. MacLeod?"

"I've never broken into your room naked," he answered.

"Neither did I." She gestured toward her abandoned nightclothes. "A person can't go sneaking around the corridors of a proper establishment wearing anything less than that. And I didn't break in, the door wasn't locked."

"You shouldn't be sneaking around any corridors late at night. You're a nice girl," he proclaimed.

"I shall still be a nice person in the morning," she answered. "I simply won't be innocent. One cannot stay innocent forever, Christopher."

Had she ever called him Christopher before? He couldn't recall. And why did it please him to hear a naked princess calling him by that name?

"Besides," she went on. "I'm getting used to sneaking. It's quite a lot of fun, isn't it?"

"You're enjoying having adventures, aren't you?" he accused. "Does your mother know you're here?" The look she gave him told him she thought him barking mad to ask such a question. He was the one who ended up blushing while she sat there cool and calm and naked as the day she was born.

"I suppose that was a silly question."

"Yes." She rose to her feet.

Kit looked her up and down, from her pretty pink toes, up long, shapely legs, his gaze lingered at the crisp penny bright curls at the juncture of her thighs, her slightly rounded belly and flat stomach. He admired the way her narrow waist flared into the curve of her hips. His hands still begged to cup her thrusting breasts. Her shoulders and neck were particularly . . .

"I could turn around if you like," Lily offered.

His arousal was becoming almost painful. He made himself look her in the eye rather than continuing to rove over her particularly lovely body. There was a significant hesitation before he managed to say, "Don't."

She arched a brow, and the teasing look in her eyes challenged his control. "You sure?"

"No, I'm not sure."

She raised her arms, slowly, and stretched. The movement drew his gaze to her breasts again. The air in the room burned his lungs. Then Kit realized he was holding his breath. He wouldn't move, he told himself. He wouldn't grab her around the waist and throw her under him on the bed. He was hard as a rock.

"Lily."

"Yes?"

"You had better leave."

"No."

"I'm not a saint."

"I should certainly hope not."

"You don't understand."

"You want me, lad."

"Of course I want you!"

"Well, then—"

"This isn't right!" What was he saying? When did propriety begin to matter to him? Here was a young, extremely beautiful woman blatantly offering herself to him.

"Are you saying no to me?" She spelled it out for him.

He very nearly whimpered. His cock pressed hard against his fly, begging for release. His fists were balled so hard they hurt. "I'm trying."

Lily was actually rather pleased that Kit was playing hard to get. It showed her how much their relationship had changed, and for the better. "You set out to seduce me, as I recall."

"Yes. But—I didn't know you then."

He looked infinitely surprised at his own answer. "So . . . I was merely a challenge? You were only interested in turning up my skirts, making a check on the bedpost, and moving on."

He blushed. "I'm sorry."

His sudden contrition made her love him more. And she did love him very much or she wouldn't be here. "I knew. Not at first, of course, for I was dreadfully naïve, but you know I didn't mind once I figured it out. I was quite flattered."

"Then why'd you keep saying no!"

"Because, as you've stated, I'm a nice girl."

Kit looked her over once more, the hunger in his eyes sending waves of heat through her. "Nice girls don't—"

"Yes, we do. When we can give ourselves freely. I wasn't free before, Kit. I owe my freedom to you."

His face changed abruptly from a look of desire to one of anger. His eyes hardened. He retreated, backing up against the thick curve of one of the carved bedposts. She saw the effort it took him to lean casually against the post, and force a thin smile. Had she not been *aware* of him deep in her blood and bones and racing heart Lily might have been fooled by Kit's effort to strike a casual pose. His eyes still burned with need, though there was hot fury in them, and a deep hurt she did not understand. His muscles were tense, and the bulge in his trousers told her that his body still wanted her despite whatever fool notion had suddenly lodged in his head.

Men, so Lily had been lead to believe, were easy.

And sometimes, you had to know when action was more important than words.

Lily took a step forward, and ran her hand along the quilted bedspread, before she reached up to undo the top button of his shirt. She felt his breath catch, and he leaned forward into her touch, though he withdrew quickly.

"Turnabout is fair play, is it not, Mr. MacLeod?"

"Mr.?" he asked while she undid another two buttons. "Why so formal, princess—at a time like this? Is this an act of noblesse oblige?"

She didn't bother to answer, but briefly kissed the base of his exposed throat instead, then looked up at him. She had no doubt that he craved more, but his hand covered hers before she could unfasten another button. She let her hand rest against his chest for a moment, until he relaxed slightly, then slid her hand beneath the cloth of his shirt.

He gasped. "Lily!"

She smiled. "That's much better than being called princess." She pulled his arm down, then placed his fisted hand on her chest. The tensed fingers loosened and curled around her breast. She arched against him. "As you can see, I'm not wearing a crown."

He knew he should pick her up and toss her from the room. Well, *after* he'd made her cover her nakedness. Of course, the only thing he wanted covering her nakedness was him.

"I don't want you because you're grateful!" The words burst out of him before he could stop himself. His trembling hands grasped her shoulders, so angry and aroused he could barely stop himself from shaking her. "Stop torturing me, woman, and get out while you can."

"You're not getting me because I'm grateful, you fool!" Lily shouted at Kit. She was almost frightened at his fierce reaction, but his touch sent a roar of excitement through her. Excitement fueled by a snap of anger. "If it was about gratitude I'd send a thank-you note."

"Hush!" he commanded. "Do you want someone to hear?" He looked around as though expecting the door to burst open on them at any moment.

"Let them hear," Lily answered. "Maybe they'll listen to what I say instead of making assumptions!"

He glared at her. "Is there no way to shut you up, woman?"

"I can think of a way."

He laughed, the sound edged with anger. "So can I."

He finally pulled her close and kissed her, his mouth hard and hungry. This was exactly what Lily had had in mind, but his intensity was still overwhelming. She was shaken in a way that closely resembled standing too close to a lightning strike.

One shouldn't tempt the lightning—but Lily liked it.

He groaned, with his tongue deep inside her mouth and she responded by pressing herself closer against him. The sensitized tips of her breasts rubbed against the material of his shirt. It sent sparks of excitement through her, but she wanted the touch of his skin.

She was vaguely aware of cloth ripping and buttons popping when she ripped open Kit's shirt, but she was more interested in the sensations as contact was made between them.

Kit broke the kiss to mutter, "Woman, I didn't bring that many shirts with me."

Lily leaned her face into his shoulder and laughed, shaking with a combination of amusement and need. "You're not supposed to notice that sort of thing in the heat of passion."

"We're not yet in the heat of passion," he told her. "We're just warming up. Besides, beneath my polished exterior beats the heart of a frugal Scotsman."

Liar! he thought. He was a London street urchin with no right to be here, doing this. God, but he needed her! He took her lips again, then moved with swift kisses down her neck and to her breasts. Tasting her, touching her, knowing he was the first to be with her made him forget everything but the moment, and the growing pleasure.

She peeled the sleeves of his shirt off his arms and tossed aside the ruined clothing. Kit's hands smoothed down her back. "If this isn't heat—" she began.

"Hush." He cupped her buttocks and ground his hips against hers.

Lily made a small, pleading sound, and her fingers dug convulsively into Kit's shoulders. "That feels so—wonderful."

"This is nothing, sweetheart," he promised. "We haven't even gotten to the bed yet."

"I would very much like to be lying down with you. For I don't think I can stand much longer. I'm all—melted."

She leaned her entire weight against him. Kit had never been more aware of anything than he was of Lily's nakedness. The way she aroused him was driving him deliciously mad. "The bed's fit for a princess," he told her.

"Then it's time the princess and her love get into it, I say," was Lily's enthusiastic answer.

"Very well."

Kit picked her up and took the few steps to the bed, laying her down on the turned-back sheets. Lily held her arms out to him, but he fetched the candle and its gold light spilled over her long limbs and soft curves.

"Let me just look at you," he said. His body raged against this romantic nonsense, but his soul wanted this moment to last forever.

Lily, however, said, "Oh, do put that down and take your clothes off."

Kit laughed, and put the candle on the bed table. "I am yours to command, princess mine."

Lily rose up on her elbows. "Now, there's a dangerous thing to proclaim. Though I'm not sure what sorts of commands to make. I'm new to this, you know. I trust to you to turn me into a shameless wanton—any day now," she added while he continued to stand there, still mostly clothed.

Kit finally gave in to her urgings and his own

need and quickly stripped off the rest of his clothing. "How's that?" he asked once he was naked.

He put a knee on the edge of the mattress, but Lily held up a hand before he could climb further into bed. "One moment, please." He waited, breath held, while she sat up and ran fingertips up his thigh. He whimpered when she delicately touched the tip of his straining penis, but Kit stayed as still as he could. "So, that's what men look like without the fig leaves," she said, almost conversationally. "Amazing."

"Thank you," he ground out from between clenched teeth. Then curiosity managed to make some headway through his seething senses. "Fig leaves?"

"Oh, do come here," she insisted, and grabbed his hand and pulled him down.

He landed on top of her with a loud, "Umph!" and they tumbled backward, sharing laughter, then a breathless kiss. From her lips, Kit worked his way with light and tender kisses down to her breasts.

Lily's head rolled back on the thick pile of pillows. Her eyes drifted closed and her fingers slowly began to move through Kit's hair, over his shoulder and down the long muscles of his back. Touching him was so very necessary, as necessary as the building pleasure his every touch brought her. The pleasure that rippled through her when he began to suckle her nipple nearly turned her inside out.

"Oh, my . . ." she breathed.

She was only able to speak incoherent gibberish after that and she didn't mind that Kit chuckled at her . . . as long as he kept doing what he was doing. Which he did, for quite a wonderful time, while the aching, yearning pleasure in her grew and grew. His hands moved over her, lower with each stroke, until his fingers began to comb through the now moist curls below her belly. Lily thought she could go on forever like this, until the yearning got out of hand. She felt her thighs open, and her body rose to press against his hand. Her skin was hot and sensitized to the point that she was ready to scream. Or explode.

"This is—is—so—"

"I know," he whispered. "It'll be better soon."

"Better? How could it be . . ."

His fingers moved into the cleft between her legs, stroked soft, sensitive flesh, drawing all the fire building in her down to this newly discovered center of her being.

Kit watched with fascinated pleasure and nearly overwhelming need as Lily responded to his touch. His erection pressed hard against her thigh, and every little movement she made sent demanding desire through him. He craved to mount her, to feel her heat surround his cock, but she needed this release before they could go any further. He continued to tease and stroke, watching her face change, her breathing grow more and more ragged. She became more wildly beautiful with each passing second as the fire he stoked blazed to a shuddering crescendo. Through his own aching hunger he watched her first climax with a kind of awe and possessive pride that he had brought her this much deserved pleasure.

He put his lips close to her ear and whispered, "Didn't I tell you it would get better?"

When he kissed her sweat-damp forehead her arms came up around his neck and traced down his back in a long, slow, languid gesture. Lily's eyes, still huge and dark with desire, focused on his face. "I love you," she said. "I hope you don't mind."

Kit's heart clutched painfully in his chest, whether with pleasure or fear he didn't know. His body didn't care; primal need was clawing to get the upper hand over any rational reaction. "Why would I mind?" was the most coherent answer he could manage. His hands moved over her body, down to her thighs. "Lily—I have to . . ."

"I know," Lily said, and stirred out of the sea of bliss in which she was floating. She shifted her position slightly, raised her legs, and opened them to him. Kit moved to position himself, kneeling over her, hesitating still, though she could tell by the way he trembled that this was the hardest thing he'd ever done. "You don't have to be afraid of hurting me," she told him. "I want you inside me—only you."

Only you forever.

Lily dared not speak what she felt. She already knew he was frightened enough—that she only did this from gratitude, that she might crave commitment. But what they did tonight was a gift for both of them. She put no strings on it. On him. Or on herself. Here and now, in this bed, for this night, they were both free.

She put her hand on his penis, tentatively taking wondrous pleasure in stroking the hard, hot length. Then she guided it to the entrance of her vagina. "Please come inside me," she said. *Please don't ever leave me.*

And the only sound she made was a moaning gasp as he slid up and into her. She'd expected discomfort this first time, but it felt too right to call the sensation painful. His hardness complemented and completed her. This was the place she needed him to be. There was one sharp prick of pain that lanced through her before turning into a sweeter sensation as Kit stroked inside her. Lily knew he was trying to be gentle, to go slowly when he wanted to race. She watched his face, saw the mixture of fierce pleasure and how he fought for control. There was fire in his eyes, fire for her that sent wonder and love through her. She drew his head down into a hard kiss, demanding and sharing passion. She arched against him, her own desire spiraling through her again, meeting him, matching his rhythm. When had her legs wrapped around his waist?

She grabbed him by the shoulders and demanded, "More!"

He threw back his head and laughed, though the sound was half-howl. And he obliged her.

Lily lost herself completely after that. She became a part of the storm that raged through and around and fulfilling them. And it was wonderful.

Kit had no recollection of collapsing onto the bed when he finally came to his senses, nor did he know how long he and Lily had lain together, limbs tangled, sharing warm, sated exhaustion. Since he knew a night like this might never happen again, he lay still and savored the moment. He realized that he felt more than satisfaction. He was happy, content, at peace from his innermost soul out to his sweat-damp skin. He'd made love many times with many women. He enjoyed pleasuring his partners. He enjoyed the chase, he enjoyed the act. He enjoyed sex. What had happened with Lily went far beyond mere enjoyment. He'd set out to seduce her. It had not been a callous decision, but it had been a casual one. What had happened between them went so far beyond casual that he was quite lost to define what it was.

Or so he lied to himself. He knew exactly what it was. He simply wasn't going to name it. Lily had said the word. She was far more courageous than he was in that way. Did he have more to lose than she did?

Yes, he told himself, a bittersweet ache replacing his contentment.

"It's growing late," Lily said. She stirred beside him. He reluctantly let her sit up. "I must go."

He wanted to ask her to stay. He did ask, "Why?"

"Well, I suppose we *could* let Mum find us like this," she answered. "But do *you* want to face the fuss?"

He grew cold as she slipped out of the bed. God, but he wanted her to sleep beside him! He sat up, and kept this longing to himself as he watched her don her nightclothes and slippers again. "Wait a moment," he said when she started toward the door. "I'll walk you to your room."

She turned back to him, her smile radiant in the candlelight. "If I wait a moment longer I will have to come into your arms and kiss you—and then it will start all over again."

He crossed his arms over his bare chest. "I'd like that."

"So would I, of course," Lily answered. "But . . . Mum . . ."

"You've just gotten her back, you wouldn't want to upset her," he said, sounding understanding, when he wanted to demand *his* woman return to *his* bed this instant.

"Exactly," Lily answered. She put her hand on the doorknob, but hesitated a moment longer. "Thank you," she said at last. Then blew him a kiss, and was gone.

Kit sighed and settled back on the bed to keep from staring at the door and wishing for her to open it and run back to him. Instead, he stared at the ceiling, remembering, and doubting he'd get any sleep through the rest of the night.

Chapter 25

"**G**ood morning, Nephew."

Kit looked up from the full breakfast plate a maid had set before him only moments before as Andrew MacLeod crossed the otherwise empty dining room.

"Join me, Uncle." He gestured at the seat beside him.

Andrew pulled out the chair, and they waited in silence while the maid bustled in and out to take Andrew's order.

She came back almost instantly with the toast, marmalade, and clotted cream Andrew requested for his breakfast. Kit concentrated on his own choice of kippers and grilled potatoes.

The day was typically gray, with rain pattering against the dining-room windows. A cheerful fire burned in the grate, the décor of the room was bright and welcoming, with starched white linen covering the circular tables, and botanical prints on the teal green walls.

It was just after seven in the morning, and Kit fought hard not to yawn. He hadn't expected to spend most of the night making love when he'd agreed to meet Andrew first thing in the morning. It annoyed him that he'd done no more than doze fitfully after Lily's departure.

Andrew checked his pocket watch. "We've a few minutes before the rest of the guests bestir themselves." He spread sticky orange marmalade on dry toast while he looked Kit over critically. "Would you rather have slept in?"

"I would always rather sleep in," Kit answered.

"With a young lady beside you, no doubt."

Kit did not react in any way to this comment. "It was a strenuous evening."

"It was a farce with livestock, but it worked out well enough. The ladies are well, I trust?"

"Lily and her mother are delighted at being reunited." Too delighted, Kit thought, disgruntled that Lily had returned to her mother instead of staying with him. He knew his attitude was petulant and ridiculous, but that didn't change it. Perhaps another cup of strong tea would. He carefully poured from the huge blue earthenware pot and stirred in several spoonfuls of sugar. "How are you this morning, Uncle? Not up too late with our foreign friends, I hope. Where are our friends from the house?"

"Where they won't bother anyone," Uncle Andrew answered this reference to the anarchists. "Not dead," he added in response to the sharp look Kit gave him. "There are some friends of mine who want to question them. After that, if they're cooperative, they'll likely be deported. Speaking of my friends," Andrew added. "I've got some news on other international matters you'll want to know about."

"What did you do, break into the telegraph office last night?"

"As a matter of fact, yes. Do you want to hear my news or not?"

A stab of fear went through Kit. "Does this news involve Lily?" he asked. Were they coming to take her away?

"Involving Bororavian politics."

Kit stabbed a kipper forcefully with his fork. "Someone assassinate King Gregory, I hope?"

"Not yet," was the calm answer, "but there has been a small revolution within the embassy."

Kit's head came up sharply, his heart suddenly hammering in his chest. "What happened?" *Please, God, don't let them have proclaimed Lily Queen.*

"It seems the lass's abduction was the last straw to the lot that were already planning to overthrow Gregory. They used the outrage, along with the information about Gregory consorting with anarchists that our government provided them with, to arrest Gregory and put his brother Duke Michael on the throne."

"Michael?" Kit searched his memory. "Isn't Michael the drunken milquetoast Gregory's always ridiculing?"

Andrew took a sip of tea. "Not drunken, nor a milquetoast. Apparently he's been working toward a bloodless coup for years. He's proclaimed himself king, and Gregory's being sent into exile."

Kit sighed. "Then Lily's safe."

"Safe from what?" Andrew questioned. "The situation's hardly stable with the Bororavian government. I have no information about what *King* Michael wants done with his only rival for the throne. If I was your Lily, I wouldn't be rushing back to London just yet, or to a sheep farm in Yorkshire."

"She was kidnapped from her home once before," Kit agreed.

Where could he take her to hide? Where would she be safe? The answer was obvious, of course, considering where they were. "We're not far from Skye."

"Finish your porridge."

Lily glanced almost covertly at the skinny, iron-haired, stone-faced, ramrod straight Mrs. Swift who stood over Lily's place at the table. Lily was tempted to hunch her shoulders and murmur a respectful, *Yes, Mrs. Swift,* but she guessed from the way a number of Kit's siblings were watching her that this encounter at the breakfast table was something of a test.

Since arriving yesterday evening at Skye Court, the MacLeod family's Highland home, Lily had only had the chance to form brief impressions of the place and the people. Though Mrs. Swift had been introduced as the housekeeper, she was actually more of a force of nature, and definitely a person to be reckoned with. She had flat-out stated that she didn't like visitors when she answered the door, but then she'd seen Kit, and a smile had almost broken over her stern countenance. Mrs. Swift had welcomed him home, and lugged his traveling case upstairs despite his protests. At the time Lily had been amused.

Right now she refused to give in to the housekeeper's daunting presence. She gave Mrs. Swift a polite nod, and a firm, "No, thank you. I am quite full."

"You're wasting good food," Mrs. Swift countered. "Skinny thing like you needs filling out."

"I am not skinny," Lily replied. "I have a very talented corsetmaker."

Lily noted a few faint smiles from the watchers around the table, but no one dared show open amusement. Mrs. Swift sent a basilisk look around the table that would have done the most draconian school mistress proud. Then she picked up Lily's half-full porridge bowl and stomped out of the dining room.

"She likes you," Kit announced.

Lily's gaze flew to her lover. "What?"

His dark eyes gleamed with amusement. "She didn't *accidentally* spill anything on you, now did she?"

At the head of the table, Kit's father clapped. A few of his children joined in. "You have faced down the family guardian," he told Lily. "Congratulations and welcome."

"Thank you for your hospitality," Lily answered. She smiled at Sir Ian MacLeod, who had already told her to call him Court. Then she looked at Kit's mother, seated to Court MacLeod's right. "Thank you, as well, Lady Hannah."

"Happy to have your company," she answered. Lady Hannah looked down the long, crowded table to Kit, who was seated between Beatrice and one of the twin brothers, Lily wasn't sure which yet. "Thank you for providing an excuse for Christopher to come for a visit, my dear. Did you have a good journey?" she asked, looking back to Lily. "Skye Court can be a bit daunting to get to."

"Isolated is just the way we like it," Court MacLeod added.

"It was a pleasant journey," Lily's mother spoke up from the far end of the table.

Conversation continued around her, but Lily's

gaze fixed on Kit, who looked her way as well. They shared a secretive, frustrated smile. Oh, it had been a pleasant enough journey by coach from Fort William to Kyle of Localsh, a ferry across from there to the Isle of Skye, and the MacLeods' old carriage waiting for them at the docks. Apparently Uncle Andrew had sent word of their arrival, though he'd chosen not to accompany them on the journey. Lily was rather glad of that, for she found Andrew MacLeod disconcerting. She rather wished her mother hadn't accompanied them as well, for Mother made far too good a chaperone. And frankly, Lily wished the trip hadn't led to Kit's family home. While she was happy to meet more of his large, eccentric clan, what she really wanted was to run away somewhere deliciously private with him and indulge in an eternity of sensually scandalous behavior. Seeing Kit naked again was her fondest wish. Being naked with him and making love was an even fonder desire.

Of course, she'd settle for a chance to be alone with the man, if only for a chaste hour or two.

Lady Hannah must have been a mind reader, for she got Lily's attention by saying, "Kit, since Lady Lily is finished with her porridge, why don't you show her around the property. I'm sure she's bored sitting here waiting for the rest of us to finish."

"Yes, Mum!" was Kit's swift answer. He was out of his chair like a shot.

Lily rose quickly to join him when he came

around the table. Lily was so anxious to make her escape with Kit that she barely noticed her mother command, "Take a shawl," as they hurried from the room.

She really should have brought a shawl, Lily thought, as love was not guaranteed to keep one warm in Scotland, even in the summer with the arm of the man you loved snugly around your shoulder. *The man I love.* Lily sighed happily as she thought these words. It was quite true. She was mad for the man.

She hadn't a clue if he felt the same. She had hopes. But she wasn't sure at all how to go about asking him. She knew he cared for her, or he wouldn't have saved her from Cherminsky. He wouldn't have helped save her mother. He wouldn't be going out of his way to hide her from her Bororavian relatives.

"Of course, we can't hide forever," she heard herself say as she looked down from a ruined hill fortress on a shepherd working a field full of Shetland sheep. "Nice herd," she added.

"We're not hiding," Kit countered. "We're on holiday."

She relaxed against him. "It certainly feels like a holiday."

They were seated close together on a broken wall, content to sit in silence for a while. He had showed her through gardens, where they'd spent time kissing behind a huge rose bush full of fragrant pink blossoms. They'd kissed when he showed her the streams and the fields and stands of trees. They hadn't kissed while they'd made their way through the pasture, for she'd taken the time to admire the Shetlands and the border collie herd dogs, and to have a conversation with cousin Huey, the shepherd. Finally Kit grew impatient, snagged her hand, and led Lily up here to the ruins that crowned the hill.

The day was chill, gray, and windy. The weather was especially unpleasant up here on the hilltop, but Lily had no intention of complaining. She loved being outdoors. And she loved being with Kit even more. She was happy to risk pneumonia for the chance to be alone with him.

"If you could be anywhere in the world, where would it be?" he asked, finally breaking the silence.

"Here," she answered truthfully. "Well, not necessarily *here*, in this exact spot," she admitted. "But with you." There. She'd given an honest answer. He had asked. Lily waited tensely to see how he took it. His arm tightened around her. She reveled in the close embrace. And the shared body warmth. It took Lily a while, but she finally stopped being nervous about his reaction and let her curiosity get the upper hand. She turned her head to look up at his still profile. "And where would you most like to be."

"Somewhere warm," he answered. He turned his head to smile down on her. "Making love to you."

That smile and those words were all the sunshine Lily needed. Warmth suffused her on this cloudy day. Warmth and utter joy. She put a hand up to cup his cheek. "You could kiss me again, you know."

"I could," he answered. "But your lips are so blue I doubt you'd feel anything."

"I'd warm up soon enough." She glanced behind them, into the depths of the ruined medieval fortress. "There must be somewhere in that pile of rock where we could—"

"No."

"Why not?"

"Because if we dared try it, one of my family—my father most likely—would be sure to catch us. It's happened before," he added.

She sighed. "But I want you. You've no idea how much I've changed since we made love. It was an eternity ago." She tried to look winsome. "Can we do it again, please?"

He chuckled. "You'd become a wanton if I'd let you, wouldn't you, lass?"

"Oh, yes, please!"

"I'm not against it," he told her. "In fact, I'm all for making love to you as often and as much as I can. It gets better with practice, you know."

"I suspected as much."

"And there's a great many variations that can be tried."

She nodded. "I would very much like a peek at your aunt's picture books."

A sudden frown creased his brows. "How do you know about that?"

"I woke up when you were discussing them with Sara."

Kit was taken aback by this admission from Lily. If she'd heard about the books, what else had she heard? Did she know about his history? Would she care? Stupid question. What woman born with the bluest blood imaginable in her veins would consider marrying him? Maybe he should tell her. Maybe she wouldn't care. Right now the fear that she would care and repudiate him froze his tongue. He had never been so insecure with another woman, probably because no other woman had ever mattered.

He cleared his throat. "I think Mum might have copies of the books hidden somewhere in the house." Lily leaned her head against his shoulder. He put his hand up to stroke her long throat, and couldn't help but continue down to cup her breast. He felt her nipple press against his palm through several layers of clothing. "You want me, lass."

"So I do," she answered. "But that's also from the cold."

He stood, and put his hands around her waist to help her to her feet. He left them there once her feet were on the ground. "We should go back to the house."

"And sneak into an empty bedroom?" she asked hopefully.

"With Mrs. Swift forever on the lookout?" He shook his head. "I'd gladly protect you from fire and storm and evil cousins, but I draw the line at Mrs. Swift."

She cupped his face in her cold hands. "You are a wise man, Christopher MacLeod."

"No one's ever called me that before."

She drew his head down until their lips were just a whisper from touching. "No one's loved you like I have," she said, and kissed him before either of them could respond to the shock of her words.

He kissed her like he had never kissed anyone before, passionate, tender, giving and demanding all at once.

It was quite an experience, and it might have led to his leading Lily farther into the ruins of the fortress, but she broke the kiss after a too brief eternity. "I shouldn't have said that," she told him. "I'm not sorry, but I had no right—"

"You have a right to say whatever you feel," Kit answered. Elation warred with his fear of rejection. He didn't know that he had the right to say what he felt. "You're always going to be a princess," he said. "We can't change that."

"But, what's that—?"

"Let's go back to the house." Kit took her by the

hand. She started down the hill with him, but he felt the reluctance in her steps. "Tell me what you'd be if not a princess?" he questioned, keeping his tone light.

"I've never had any interest in being a princess."

"Would you go back to your sheep farm?"

"No." She came to an abrupt halt, refusing to budge when he tried to tug her forward.

Kit looked at her face and saw the surprise registered there. It made his heart sink. "Did you just discover that deep down you really do want to be a queen?"

Lily gave him a very annoyed look. "No. I just discovered that deep down, I want to run away from home. I mean, I've had this very nice life. A nearly perfect, pastoral upbringing. A way of life I thought I wanted to last forever, full of everyday challenges, pleasures and disappointments. Then my father died, and then Gregory made a mess of things, and then I met you and started feeling like a woman, and having adventures. I haven't had time to think anything through yet." She looked him squarely in the eye. "I don't know what I want to do, but—"

A voice calling "There you are!" from the bottom of the hill interrupted what Lily was going to say. Kit fervently hoped that she'd been about to proclaim *I want to do it with you*, but her lips closed as she looked past him and raised her arm to wave. Kit turned to see that Lady Eleanor Bancroft was halfway up the hill. She didn't look at all pleased that Kit was holding Lily's hand. She held up a red wool shawl, waving it at Lily.

"Hello, Mum!" she called back.

"You two must be freezing," Lady Eleanor answered. "Hurry along. Mrs. Swift says she won't hold lunch for God, man, or Kit Fox MacLeod. So, if you want to eat—"

"We're coming," Lily said, and took her turn pulling Kit down the hill.

Chapter 26

"**I** am so bored," Kit complained.

He was standing at the bay window in the front parlor. It was raining outside. He could see Michael and Gabriel seated before the fire, playing a game of chess. Alexander was seated in a wingbacked chair, smoking a cigar and reading a book. Kit loved his brothers, but was disgruntled to be spending the afternoon with them when Lily was somewhere nearby—equally surrounded by MacLeod women, and her eagle-eyed mother. This had been going on since Lady Eleanor had come to fetch them from the hilltop ruins. It had been days. It felt like months.

In the three days since they'd arrived at Skye Court, Kit had come to believe Lady Eleanor did not approve of him. He didn't blame her much. If he was Lily's mother, he knew he wouldn't approve of Kit Fox MacLeod courting his daughter.

Courting his daughter?

Good God, when had it come to him thinking like that? Of course, considering what he and Lily had done together, they were well past the courting stage. In fact, if his Da knew about his and Lily's intimacy they'd be standing at the altar, with Da performing the service. Kit supposed he should be horrified at the thought of this scenario, but he actually found it quite pleasant.

"How the mighty have fallen," he murmured.

"What?" Alexander murmured behind him.

Kit didn't bother to answer, but Michael chimed in, "He's pining for the princess. It's part of the courtship ritual," he added.

Kit didn't bother answering that jibe, either. Brothers were a vexation even worse than sisters when it came to teasing. But the funny thing was, he and Lily really were engaging in a relatively normal courtship ritual. They spent a great deal of time together, but none of it alone. Pleasant conversation and meaningful looks had to suffice while desire bubbled just barely under the surface. Yesterday it had been dry, so there'd been a picnic. Evenings were spent with music recitals, singing, reading aloud, and parlor games. There'd been a shopping excursion into Portree. They'd attended kirk, where Da had preached a fine sermon, and they had at least managed to sit next to each other during the service. The worst of it was, *everybody* was aware of the sparks flying between Lily and himself. Except for dark looks from Lucy and a certain stiffness from Lady Eleanor, the household was finding this torture vastly entertaining.

What the MacLeods needed was for some evil mastermind to pose a sudden threat to the Empire so they could concentrate on saving the world and leave Kit's and Lily's private lives alone.

"I am so bored," Kit repeated after staring out the window a while longer.

"Then go for a walk," Alexander suggested. "The rainwater's cold enough to do you some good."

"I think I'll do that." Kit spun on his heel and marched from the parlor. He pretended that he did not hear the twins snickering as he closed the door. He was heading for the front door when he met Mrs. Swift coming down the hall. She was carrying a package wrapped in oilcloth. "What have you got there?" he asked her.

"Package for Lucy," she answered. She held it up, balanced carefully on her palms.

Kit noticed a great many exotic postage stamps covering the top of the parcel. "Looks like it came a long way."

"One of her nasty potions, I'll wager." Mrs. Swift gave an emphatic nod. "That girl's dangerous." Coming from Mrs. Swift this was not a complaint.

"Why don't I take it to her for you," Kit suggested, mostly out of boredom. Time spent in Lucy's laboratory might be more interesting than a walk in the cold rain, even if Lucy did lecture him about Lily. Come to think of it, Kit relished the thought of getting into an argument with his sister. It would help relieve some of the pent-up tension.

"You do that," Mrs. Swift answered, handing over the package. She rubbed her hands on her apron. "Some of us have work to do," she added as she stalked away.

Lucy's lab was located at the back of the greenhouse at the far end of the garden, so Kit ended up going out in the rain after all. But the greenhouse was a warm, colorful haven from the weather. Kit almost forgot his errand when the first thing he saw as he walked in was Lily, surrounded by orchids. She wore a pale purple dress that exactly matched some of the blossoms, and her coppery hair was unbound, flowing around her shoulders and down her back. The sight of her took his breath away.

"Lily, my love," he said, coming toward her.

Her warm smile was all the greeting he needed.

"Ahem," Sara said, before he and Lily actually met and touched.

Sara had been standing next to Lily, with an open book in her hands, but this image did not register on Kit until now. He sighed. "Hello, Sarabande."

"You needn't sound so disappointed," his youngest sister answered.

"Sweetheart, you wouldn't understand."

"Yes, I would."

"Sara was explaining orchids to me," Lily jumped in. "It's quite fascinating."

"I'm fascinating," he said, turning his petulance on Lily.

She did not give him the mocking laugh he deserved, but she did raise an eyebrow and tilt her head as she looked at him. "What's that?"

He hefted the package. "Something for Lucy."

"She's in the back," Sara said.

"Then I'll deliver it and we can be on our way," Kit said, looking tellingly at Lily.

"Yes, let us leave Lucy to her work," Lily agreed. She stood aside and let Kit proceed her and Sara into Lucy's inner sanctum.

Lucy's private work area was a large, well-lit room full of many crowded but neatly organized shelves, tables, and racks. Bunches of mysterious dried plants and flowers hung from the ceiling. There were glass bottles and tins full of mysterious pills and potions and heavy tomes about the healing properties of all manner of nature's creations in many languages to be seen in Lucy's lab. Smoke often filled the place, and awful stenches and rich perfumes. It was the most interesting place Kit had ever seen, mostly because he hadn't a clue to what it was Lucy actually did in there.

Kit expected to see Lucy hunched over a bubbling cauldron engaged in one of her arcane experiments. Instead he, Lily, and Sara entered to find Lucy and Mum seated at a worktable, cups in hand, and a steaming pot of tea between them.

Mum looked them over, and said, "Have any more cups, Lucy?"

Lucy's gaze had instantly focused on what Kit carried. She ignored their mother's question and jumped up to come toward him. She smiled, at the package, not at him. "Oh, good. It's finally arrived."

"What is it, dear," Mum asked. "Who's it from?"

"Where's it from?" Sara asked. "May I keep the stamps?"

"It's a fish," Lucy said.

She took the parcel, put it down on the worktable, and proceeded to strip off layers of protective oiled paper and cloth. Kit gathered around the table with everyone else to watch. He and Lily took the opportunity to clasp hands while they did.

"A fish," Sara said. "What do you want with a fish?"

"It's a special fish," Lucy answered. "Several of them, I should hope, preserved and sent to me by Dr. Pomeroy of Kingston, Jamaica. He and I have been corresponding about the possible scientific causes behind island shamans' creation of zombies. He promised to send me supplies of the extract for my experiments." She smiled happily as the last of the packing material was cleared away, revealing several sealed vials packed in a box of sand. She lifted one of them. "And here we are."

"Zombies?" Lily asked. "What is that?"

"The walking dead," Sara answered. "A creature from the folklore of the Indies. They practice a form of witchcraft called voodoo in the islands," Sara added.

Kit exchanged a look with Lily. "I still don't know what they're talking about, either," he told her.

"Zombies are not legends, they exist," Lucy said. "They aren't walking dead, Sara. Dr. Pomeroy has seen them. He's treated several people who were poisoned with the drug. The poison is an extract prepared from a certain tropical fish. The poison simulates death, but it doesn't create a zombie. To create a zombie—a mindless slave—other drugs must be added to the poison to affect the victim's mental state. It's a cruel custom, but the actual poison taken in the proper doses could prove very useful."

"You're planning on experimenting with that dangerous stuff?" Mum asked. For once even she sounded nonplussed. "Lucy, I don't think—"

"I think I'll start with something small. Sara's cat should do."

"Mum!"

"She's joking, Sara. You are joking, Lucy." It was a command, not a question.

"Mum!" Lucy complained.

Interesting as this exchange was, Kit tugged on Lily's hand and tilted his head suggestively toward the door. She nodded, and they turned to leave. Kit hoped the argument brewing among his sisters and mother would be enough to keep their escape from being noticed.

They might have made it out, but the door leading back to the greenhouse opened before they reached it. Mrs. Swift stood there, and turned her dour look on Kit. "You're wanted in your father's study," she told him. "And *you* are wanted by your mother," she told Lily, then she folded her skinny arms over her flat chest and stepped aside so both could pass. "Now," she added.

Da was not a man you wanted to keep waiting. A summons to the study was serious. If Da was concerned about a matter, he came looking for you himself. If he was angry, he sent Mrs. Swift. Her role was rather like the witches who warned of doom in MacBeth. Even as an adult in his thirties, Kit faced the summons with trepidation. Not because he was afraid of his father's ire, he'd faced that before, and Court MacLeod did treat his children as adults. No, Kit's steps were slow and heavy approaching the study door because he was already certain of what waited within the room.

"Damn," he muttered, too painfully aware that the idyll with Lily was over before it had any proper chance to begin.

Kit was not surprised to see the two men who waited within the study with his father when he opened the door. "Martin." He acknowledged his brother-in-law with a nod. To the other man, he said, "Lord Ornov, am I correct?"

"Indeed," the older man replied, giving Kit a stiff nod. "And you, I am given to believe, are the man we owe for rescuing our beloved princess from a nefarious plot."

"The princess and her mother," Kit elaborated. "Now they are free to lead their own lives."

"Close the door, please, Christopher," Court MacLeod spoke for the first time. "Then have a seat, because we have a great deal to talk about, and I want the conversation to remain civil."

Kit reluctantly did as his father requested. He was certain Da had read his impulse to flee and run away with Lily. She would come if he asked her, he was certain. He was almost certain. He was terrified she wouldn't. His mouth was dry with this fear when he took the remaining chair opposite Court MacLeod's wide desk. Lord Ornov sat in the second chair. Martin stood by the fireplace.

Kit turned his attention on Lord Martin Kestrel. "Traitor."

Martin flinched ever so slightly at this accusation. "I didn't want to come here, Kit."

"How did you even know to come here?" Court MacLeod questioned. "You know we like our privacy, Martin."

Kit was glad to see his father's disapproval turned on Harriet's husband. "In my dealings with the MacLeods," Martin answered, "I've come to believe that when they're desperate, they always run for the shelter of home."

"Desperate?" Kit started to rise from his chair.

"Christopher." Da's voice held stern warning that Kit responded to by settling back into his seat. Da turned his attention to Lord Martin. "He thought the Bancrofts were in danger, so he brought them here as a refuge."

Kit had not explained any of this to his parents. He'd sent a telegraph saying they were coming, then he, Lily and her mother had simply arrived and been made welcome. Neither Mum nor Da had asked questions, but then, they didn't have to; they had all the intelligence sources of the Empire at their disposal. And Mum was incredibly nosey. Who knew what information she'd gotten out of Lady Eleanor during casual conversations?

"A wise precaution," Lord Ornov said. "For which we thank the British government."

Kit saw how this was going. Everyone was going to pretend that the benevolent Brits had heroically stepped in to protect the princess while loyal but beleaguered Bororavian patriots set everything right. "You're about to add that it is now time for the princess to come home, am I right, Lord Ornov?" Kit asked, bitter and cynical. "She doesn't want to go," Kit spoke to his father. "This is your home. You will not allow anyone to be taken from here against their will."

"No," Court MacLeod agreed. "I will not. That is

why I asked you here," he told Kit. "Because these gentlemen intend to leave with your princess, and I believe that she will not willingly go with them unless you convince her of the necessity of taking up her royal duties."

"Da!" Kit did surge to his feet this time. "How can you ask this of me?"

His father looked up at Kit with a calm expression and a great deal of regret in his eyes. "Because I can see that the girl loves you."

"And I love her." He had never said the words to Lily, but Kit had no difficulty in speaking the truth to his father.

"That is impossible," Lord Ornov said.

Court MacLeod looked at the Bororavian diplomat. "Sir, the heart has no concept of what is or is not possible. The mind," he added, looking back to Kit, "tempers the heart. Duty comes first for us."

"It is Lily's life," Kit said. *My life, too!* "Her choice to make."

"She is a princess," Lord Ornov said.

"I've heard this argument before," Kit told him. It always came down to class, didn't it?

"This is important, Kit," Martin Kestrel said. "I wouldn't be asking for your help if it wasn't."

They wanted to take Lily from him—and they wanted him to help them do it? Kit couldn't keep from laughing. "I don't think so, Martin." He rose and walked to the door.

He expected his father to call him back, but it

was Martin Kestrel who stopped him by saying, "I have come directly from the Queen. I am here to carry out her specific orders. Queen Victoria," he added when Kit turned to gape at him. "You are a servant of the Crown, Christopher. Please listen to what I have to say."

Oh, hell. Oh, bloody, bloody hell! Honor. Duty. Oaths to serve without question. Even in his wildest, most self-indulgent moments Kit had accepted these boundaries on his own desires. He served the Queen.

There was not going to be any way out of this, was there? Kit Fox was a slippery devil, quick-witted and sly in getting his own way. Kit Fox was only a persona, though, wasn't he? Christopher Fox MacLeod took his hand off the doorknob and went back to resume his seat.

"Say what you've come to say," he said to Martin Kestrel. God, but he wanted a cigarette.

Chapter 27

Lily looked around the parlor, becoming suspicious when she saw that Kit was the only other person in the room. "The place seems a bit—empty," she observed, stepping gingerly inside.

Kit didn't turn from staring into the fire. He stood on the hearthrug, his long, lean body stiff with tension. His hands were clasped tightly behind his back. "Close the door."

Lily already suspected what was coming. Her mother had told her that several visitors had arrived at Skye Court, but Lily doubted they were strangers to her.

She walked toward Kit, her hands held out to him. She pretended to be bright and cheerful rather than show her trepidation. "Alone at last," she told him. "Not that I'm complaining too much about our having so many chaperones. They're an interesting lot. You have an amazingly brilliant and charming family, but it's like living in Wonderland, isn't it?" She put her hand on his arm, the muscles were hard as stone. She continued chattering while she peered closely at his shuttered profile. "At any moment I expect to see rabbits with watches, or bottles with tags on them that say *drink me*, or to be invited to play croquet using flamingos as mallets."

Kit's voice was flat, but he did say, "It's been raining too much for croquet."

"Ah," she said, squeezing his arm lightly. "So you are listening to me." Since he didn't seem likely to turn to face her so she could kiss him properly, Lily brushed her lips across his cheek. It hurt her heart when he flinched.

"Sit down," he said.

Lily heard the strain in his voice and wanted desperately to take him in her arms and hold him until they both felt better. Instead, she moved to the nearest chair and did as he directed. The air in the room seemed very still and cold, full of shadows and foreboding despite lamps lit on almost every table and the pleasant fire in the grate. There was an aura of pain and resignation around Kit that gave off almost visible waves of misery. All this left Lily's nerves and stomach in knots, but she was determined to face him calmly. If she showed her own fear, she was terrified Kit might break.

Once she was seated, with her hands tightly folded in her lap and her spine very straight, Lily said, her voice shaking only a little, "You may now turn around and deliver the bad news."

He spun around quickly at her words. "Highness," he said, and bowed slightly from the waist.

"Oh, dear." She understood completely. Her fingers were clutched together so tightly the knuckles were white. "Please don't do that, Christopher. I have no intention of returning with them. Who did they send, by the way?"

"Lord Ornov. And my traitorous brother-in-law," he added, relaxing just enough to show some bitterness. "He came in the name of Queen Victoria. You have to return to the embassy with them. You're going to be the queen of Bororavia."

"No, I'm not. I would like to be Mrs. Christopher MacLeod," she added. "In case you haven't sussed that out yet. I was hoping you would bring it up, but it seems my hand has been forced."

She tried so very hard to keep her tone conversational, though the words came out quite rushed at the end. It wasn't easy confronting the man you loved with the knowledge that you loved him when he'd never mentioned the word to you. She'd concluded that Kit was having difficulty wrapping his mind around the notion that he *wanted* to settle down. She had been giving him time to work it out for himself; and her mother and his family had certainly been doing a fine job of giving Kit that space too, since they'd made wonderful watchdogs in the last few days.

He did not act as though her words had any effect on him. "You cannot be Mrs. MacLeod," he said, quite calmly.

Her throat and heart clutched with pain, but she managed to say, reasonably calmly. "Oh. Is your heart engaged elsewhere, then."

Suddenly Kit was kneeling in front of her and his hands covered hers. He'd been standing before the fire all this time, but his hands were cold. "No one but you will ever have my heart. No one."

She wanted to take him into her arms and kiss him forever then, but he backed away when she made the slightest move toward him. Within moments he stood over her, his hands behind his back again. She looked up, and tears spilled over her eyes when she did. Lily pretended they weren't there and let them roll down her cheeks. She had to clear her throat before she could speak. "I take it that we will not be posting banns and issuing invitations?"

He shook his head.

"We could invite the Queen," she suggested.

"The Queen does plan to attend your wedding. You are marrying King Michael. Gregory has been overthrown. You are being restored to your rightful place as queen of Bororavia. Queen Victoria is pleased to give her goddaughter in joyful union with Britain's ally, Michael of Bororavia. The Queen has spoken. We obey."

Lily sat back in the chair. "Well, I don't."

Kit looked at her in complete astonishment.

"How can you refuse a command from the Queen?"

"I say no," Lily replied simply.

"You can't do that!"

It obviously had never occurred to him that one could. Kings and queens of most nations did not say no to the British Crown. If they did, armies might come to call. Lily could not imagine an army marching across Yorkshire to ransack Harelby House, but in the last few weeks she'd learned that anything could happen when dealing with the royalty of the world.

"I suppose there will be repercussions," she said. "Perhaps we shall have to leave the country. Could we become exiles in Paris?" she asked. "I've always wanted to go to Paris."

"We could go to America," he said. "I like it there. What am I saying?" Kit shook his head violently, and a thick lock of hair fell across his forehead. "You must go to Bororavia—and there is not a thing we can do about it."

Lily was cold with fear. He was so adamant. So certain. "I do not want to," she told him. He only looked at her sadly in response. Lily rose to her feet and lifted her chin proudly. "Does asserting my will seem selfish? I don't know why. Listen to me carefully, Christopher MacLeod. I do not want to be a queen."

"What about the people of Bororavia?"

"I am not acquainted with the people of Bororavia."

"Yet you have a duty to them. By birth. By blood. I'm supposed to remind you that Britain graciously allowed your father to reside in England in peace and security, and you owe a debt of gratitude for this generosity."

Lily was outraged at such moral blackmail, and at Kit's mouthing it even at someone else's request. "Tell them to send me a bill," she told him sarcastically.

"This is the bill."

She thought about it for a moment. "Yes, I suppose it is. Well, they'll have to ask for a different coin."

"Blast it, Lily, you *are* the rightful heir to the throne! You have to think of duty first. Marrying your cousin Michael will ease tensions between political factions in the country. The marriage will help secure Michael's claim."

"What do you care about Michael's claim?"

"I don't. I'm repeating what Ornov and Kestrel told me. You must listen to what I tell you. It is important. *You* are important."

"As a pawn, not as a person. I hate that."

He gave her a long, sorrowful, tender look. "You are important to me Lily Bancroft." His expression hardened again, and he went on before she could answer. "The marriage is for the good of Bororavia.

For the good of Britain. For the stability of Europe. You were born to this, whether you like it or not it is in your blood. Besides," he added, with a hint of his usual teasing humor, "What girl wouldn't want to wear a crown? And stand on balconies waving at the adoring masses? And you get to issue proclamations. And cut ribbons at ceremonies."

Lily couldn't bear to tell him that he was making light of a future she found utterly appalling. "I was not raised to fulfill royal aspirations. I have no dynastic ambitions. While my mother's life was in jeopardy, I was willing to put my neck in that noose. I'm not going to marry anyone now but you. If you'll have me."

It was painful to wait for his response to her words. Lily had to fight the temptation to hold her breath. Her muscles tensed as though she were waiting for a blow. The room went very still and quiet.

Kit had never in his life felt so battered and confused. On the one hand, hearing her tell him that she loved him wounded him in ways he knew would never heal, for her words made him admit to himself that he loved her with all his heart. Though he felt as if he were dying, he bore the wounds gladly, knowing they were all he would have to remember her by. He hated himself for accepting the charge to make her accept her royal destiny, but it was for her own good. He was going to have to make her see it before he succumbed to the temptation to run off with her. Not that running away with her would do any good. Kestrel and Ornov had made it quite plain that Queen Victoria and King Michael were adamant about the marriage. If he tried to flee with Lily, they would be hunted down relentlessly.

"What is the matter with you?" he demanded. "Most girls want to be queens."

"I don't mind being a queen," she answered. "You're the king of thieves, aren't you? Make me your queen."

It was like a hot knife going into his heart. "I can't." He shook his head, and it felt like the gesture of a wounded animal. "I can't do that to you, Lily, my love." She looked at him, pale, trembling, trying not to show the fear that filled her eyes. Her pain ground against his soul. "Sit down," he told her. "Please." He wanted to take her by the hand and help her into the chair, but he dared not touch her. He dared not touch her ever again. "I have something very important to tell you," he went on. "Something ugly. Something about myself. I cannot marry you, even if you were merely Lady Lily Bancroft."

Kit looked ill. Worse, he looked trapped. Lily did not want to hear whatever he wanted to tell her, not if it cost him this much. "Don't," she said. Lily made a small, helpless gesture. "Just don't."

He shook his head. "Too late, my love. I should never have let it get this far. I knew better. I was warned. But I'm selfish, thoughtless. Worse, I never thought I would come to love you. If I didn't love you, or you me, it wouldn't matter, because we would never have gotten to this day. I cannot marry you. I would never presume to aspire to marrying you. I should be horsewhipped for daring to think about it. You have no idea what I really am."

"You are the man I love."

"I have no idea who I am," he went on, as if he hadn't heard her. "I do know what I am, and it is very ugly. I am a rat, born and bred in the sewers of London. A rat snatched from the gutter by a good woman. She loved me, educated me, gave me a father, surrounded me with a family—but a rat is still a rat. I have no parents—"

"Then who are those people who—?"

"I have no breeding. I have no place in society. I was already a housebreaking thief when Hannah Gale took me in. I'm very likely the cast-off bastard of a whore."

Lily flinched. Not at Kit's words, but at seeing how much it hurt him to say them.

"That is the real me," he finished.

She knew he hurt, but she couldn't help smiling a little, not mocking, but maybe to ease his pain. "Yes. I know."

"What do you mean you know?"

Lily sat and stared at him for a moment, she even blinked a few times, but Kit's lean, handsome form did not warp and change after baring this secret to her. "I overheard you talking to Sara about it," she told him. "I won't apologize for eavesdropping, as I thought you were my enemy at the time."

Kit sat down abruptly, barely making it to a chair before his legs gave out on him. He buried his face in his hands, his breath coming in hard, painful gasps. Finally he looked up and at her, his eyes full of fire. "You went to bed with me."

It was almost an accusation. "It would have been all right for me to go to bed with you if I hadn't known?"

"Nice girls do not knowingly go to bed with bad men. It's wrong."

"It's problematical, as it's already over and done with. It was wonderful—and I very much would like to do it with you many more times. A lifetime of times," she added.

"So would I." He turned a look on her that was very nearly an annoyed glare. "You are supposed to be shocked and horrified. You are supposed to rush out of this room and into the arms of a king."

"A very handsome king he is, too. Have you noticed that about Michael?"

"I've noticed," he growled.

It was petty of her to be so pleased that Kit was jealous, but so what? This whole situation was ridiculous and impossible. It seemed that no one was going to let her get out of a destiny that everyone thought glorious but her. Even the man she loved. Who said he loved her. Kit was letting her go out of a strong sense of duty and honor, she saw that. She admired him for it. He also infuriated her, because it wasn't *his* duty and honor that was being flung in her face. It was *her* duty and honor that everyone seemed to think was *their* business! People—Kit—kept telling her what was good for her, what was right, what she deserved, what she must do, as if she didn't have a mind of her own.

It made her so angry she wanted to spit. So angry she could barely see through the spreading red wrath.

She rose to her feet, quivering with fury and just about beyond reason. "Marry me, Christopher MacLeod," she demanded, adamant as granite. "Marry me." She pointed toward the door, though her arm shook with the surging emotion. "Marry me, or I walk out of here and straight to the altar like a sacrifice for queen, and country, and my father and everything else that has nothing to do with me. Including, and especially, your damned, stupid, unfounded sense of inferiority!" Her voice had risen with every word, until she was shouting so loudly her throat burned from the strain. She dashed hot tears off her cheeks, tears that were as much from fury as from a breaking heart. "Say you'll marry me—or at least run off and live in sin with me—or I am gone and you will *never, ever* see me again."

Kit looked at Lily in astonishment, aware that he had accomplished what he'd set out to do, but not at all in the way he'd thought he would. He had thought she'd be the one who'd push him away. That was how it was supposed to have worked. Instead she'd surprised him by telling him she cared for him, not for his background. Her declaration took his breath away. It lifted a burden from his heart. And it did neither of them any good at all. He loved her for her acceptance, but he could not say so. Despite that it felt like death to him, letting her go was the best thing for her.

He wanted to say something, but his throat was closed with pain. He could not bring himself to deny what he felt or what he truly wanted. All Kit could do was rise shakily from his chair. He walked to the fireplace; there he stood with his back to her. He stared into the dying fire, with his hands grasping the mantel to keep him upright, or to keep him from turning back to her, he wasn't sure which. He felt like a man who'd bared his back to the lash, and waited for the first blow to be struck.

The first blow came when he heard her say, "Blast and damn you for a fool, Kit MacLeod." He was shocked at how much the words hurt.

But that pain was nothing in comparison to the blow that sent him to his knees when he heard the door slam and he knew she was forever gone.

Chapter 28

Well, now, that was a stupid stratagem on my part, wasn't it? And there's no getting out of it now. At the time it seemed the only thing I could do. Kit was supposed to stop me.

The thoughts kept tumbling over and over in her head, as repetitive as the rumbling of the carriage wheels. It was all Lily could do to keep from crying in front of the people who shared the carriage. A mutter burst out of her instead. "Good Lord, I am an idiot."

"What did you say, dear?"

Lily glared at her mother. She couldn't help it. She'd glared at everyone all the time since she'd stormed out of Skye Court. "You didn't have to come with me, Mum," she said, not for the first time.

"Well, I did anyway," her mother answered,

growing testy at Lily's continued truculence. "So you might as well stop complaining about it."

"I shall complain if I want," Lily answered, leaning back in the well-padded carriage seat and crossing her arms as she pouted. "I am a princess, you know."

"You are a sheep farmer from Yorkshire. The sooner you remember it and forget all this talk of marriages the better off we'll both be."

"I don't want to be here," Lily said. She glanced sideways at Lord Kestrel, who was seated beside her, looking very uncomfortable. Then she looked at Lord Ornov, who was beside her mother on the opposite side of the carriage. "*They* insisted. And I have decided that I am tired of being polite and pleasant to people who make me do what I do not wish to do. That is my royal prerogative, is it not, Lord Ornov?"

He looked very pained as he answered, "Yes, Highness."

Lily smiled, hoping the look was icy and dangerous, though she supposed she could easily look as mad as a hatter. Lord knew that was how she felt, and worse. Through the looking glass indeed. She sighed, and asked, "How's your daughter, Lord Ornov?" Lily fervently hoped she wouldn't have to deal with Irenia ever again. Should she mention to the woman's father that Irenia tried to have her killed? "Did she run off with Cherminsky?" Lily asked hopefully.

"She came back." Ornov looked seriously embarrassed. He cleared his throat. "Irenia went into exile with Gregory. It seems she loves the bullying fool. It's amazing who people fall in love with," he added.

"Yes," she said, the word coming out between gritted teeth. "Isn't it?"

Lily glanced out the carriage window. They had left Skye behind hours ago and it was getting dark. The ride in the well-sprung carriage was as comfortable as it was possible to be on these Highland country roads. She doubted any stops for a night's sleep at an inn were planned for the journey. They were probably afraid she might try to escape, and they'd be right. Trapped again. And this time it was all her own fault.

"You really do think you love that young man, don't you?" her mother spoke up.

Lily turned her glare on her mother once more. "I do not *think*. I *know*."

"Young girls frequently think they are in love with Kit," Lord Kestrel said. "The affliction passes, especially faced with the prospect of such a glorious future. Kit is quite the flighty charmer."

Lily was surprised and pleased when her mother tartly replied, "That *flighty* young man was the only person who bothered to come to our aid."

"I did not say he was not a good person," Kestrel answered.

Lily did not look at Kestrel, nor did she rise to

Kit's defense after her mother had already done so. Lily did notice her mother watching her carefully. For the first time she thought she saw sympathy and assessment in her mother's very discerning gaze. Lily was too sad and heart-weary to hold her mother's gaze for long. It was not only her soul that felt battered; it was as if her body had been pummeled by grief as well. She wanted to escape, but all she could do was close her eyes and fall into a restless, uncomfortable sleep.

"I am an idiot."

"Of course you are," Lucy answered Kit. "What about this time?"

"Lily left three days ago." He had told her about this before, but it had obviously slipped her mind. Lucy was too immersed in her research to let the real world in right now. "You missed the excitement when you dosed yourself, Luce."

"Good. I hate excitement."

"I loved her."

"Hmmm." Lucy's hands continued to be busy transferring a potion she'd just taken off the boil into a row of small clear glass vials lined up on her worktable. She wore a pair of thick gloves, yet her movements were graceful and precise rather than clumsy.

Kit doubted she was really aware he was there. She'd been working feverishly for the last day and a half. Ever since she'd woken up from her experiment. She'd also been lying low, staying more out here in her laboratory than in the house. Kit wasn't sure who was more upset with Lucy for her daft behavior, Mum, Da, or Mrs. Swift, who'd had to halt the funeral arrangements. Mrs. Swift hated when her work went for nothing.

"I've been through hell while you played Sleeping Beauty, you know."

"That's nice, love."

Kit had spent a good deal of time in Lucy's lab since she came out of the trance, mostly because the distracted Lucy was the only one in the family who didn't flash him sympathetic looks every time he appeared. "You really are mad sometimes," he told her. "Going off and doing a fool thing like that."

Lucy put down the last filled vial and turned a hard look on him. "There was nothing foolish about it. It was a calculated risk to try out the fish toxin, with the odds in my favor."

"You upset Mum."

"I left her a note. Besides, she's the one who wouldn't let me use the cats, the dogs, the rabbits, or even the sheep. How can one perform an experiment on a living being without having a living being to work with? There was no one left but myself. It was necessary to know how the formula works on humans anyway. It's all a matter of planning and preparation. It worked out exactly as I planned, didn't it?"

"You put yourself into a deathlike trance for two days."

"And apparently missed out on a great deal of fuss and bother about our former houseguests, which was fine with me. The experiment worked. I don't see why anyone is annoyed with me."

"The scientific mind eludes me," Kit answered.

Her look turned sarcastic. "Planning and preparation have no place in your line of work?"

"Point taken," he agreed. Then he sank back into his own troubles. I am a fool. I've never been so lost and alone, Luce. I'm not used to hurting, to being so empty." This was not the sort of thing one could say to a brother, of course, but as sisters went, Lucy was not exactly the soft and sympathetic type. Not that he wanted tea and sympathy. He wanted—he *wanted.* "I want Lily," he said. "I don't think I can live without her."

"I can't see why," was Lucy's answer. "She's pretty enough if you like the pale, red-haired sort, but you've had prettier girls. What was so special about her?"

"She loves me," Kit answered simply, the words tearing him apart.

"Other women have claimed to love you." Practical, precise, and pitiless, that was his Lucy.

"But this one I love back."

She shook her head. "Didn't I try to warn you off her? Didn't I tell you a princess isn't for the likes of you?"

"So you did," he conceded. "And so I told her." He laughed softly, a sound of mocking pain, not amusement. "She didn't care. I told her everything, and she wasn't the least appalled. She wasn't even impressed. You see, Lucy, she loves *me*. Who'd have thought it possible, eh?"

Lucy rested her hands on her worktable and leaned toward him, her eyes bright. "Let me get this straight, you told her your background, about being adopted?"

"I told her everything."

"And she still claimed to love you?"

"She was actually quite angry that I thought she wouldn't love me if I told her everything. Blistered my ears, she did. Then she told me that if I didn't marry her or run off with her, she was leaving."

"And you let her leave?"

He had never heard Lucy sound so shocked. He stared at her. "You were among the ones who kept ramming it home to me that I'm not good enough for her. She was the only one who ever disagreed."

Lucy shook her head. "Unbelievable."

"Yes, I know. Lily is quite amazing."

"No, I mean your behavior is unbelievable." She peered at him closely, as though examining a specimen under a magnifying glass. "How could you bear to let her go?"

"I can't," he answered, knowing all his anguish was naked on his face. "It's killing me. It was the right thing to do, but it's killing me."

"What was so right about it?"

Kit recalled that Lucy'd been conducting her sleeping potion experiment when their brother-in-law arrived with the Bororavians, and all the family drama since then had centered around Lucy's having experimented on herself. She'd been at the center of her own storm while he'd been going through days of private hell. Well, at least things had quieted down at Skye Court for now. He sat back and filled Lucy in on events involving queens, kings, ambassadors, intrigues, foreign policies and his hidden role in sending his own Princess Lily away.

"Well, that's all perfectly awful and complicated," Lucy said when he was done. "How do you propose to get her out of it?"

"I can't get her out of it," he explained. "I got her into it."

Lucy looked very cross. Sometimes she reminded him of Mrs. Swift. "It must be true love," she concluded, "because you're acting like you don't have a brain in your pretty head. Of course you must get your Lily out. Precisely *because* you got her into it. You're a thief. Go steal her back."

Kit couldn't help but chuckle. "Lord knows the girl is used to being abducted by now. But I can't do it," he added. "I've considered it, of course, but running off together would only cause us more trouble. Both British and Bororavian security is on the alert for our trying to escape. Come hell or high water, Lily is trapped into becoming the queen of Bororavia. Nothing short of an act of God is going to stop it."

"I see," Lucy said. Then she turned back to her work as though the conversation had not happened. She took down a beaker from a shelf, looked through one of her notebooks, and gathered ingredients while Kit watched in consternation.

Finally, he asked, "What are you doing."

Lucy picked up one of the small glass vials filled with the powerful sleeping potion. She turned a really quite dangerous smile on him. "Well, there's nothing that says an act of God can't be manufactured, now is there?"

Chapter 29

"Michael, you are a nice man, but I don't love you." Lily had told him this before, of course. This time she said it as they shared a meal in the small dining room off the private sitting room on the embassy's second floor.

Neither of them had eaten much. Michael, she noted, was drinking water from the crystal wine goblet. Michael, she learned, had not actually drunk spirits of any kind. Though, he promised now to toast his bride with the finest champagne after they signed the marriage contract. She managed a wan smile at this gallant gesture rather than giving in to the urge to tell him not to bother. It was not sensible to be petty and mean to the man she was likely to be spending the rest of her life with. Unlike Gregory, Michael was not a bad man.

He just wasn't Kit.

The servants had been dismissed, and there was a strange quiet about the building. For the first time since she'd met her cousin Michael she was alone with him. In fact, if it were not for the guard dogs setting up a distant racket in the yard, she and Michael might be the only people in all of noisy, busy London. They were alone because they were now formally betrothed, which in Bororavia was almost the same as being married. Besides, he was the king and could order everyone to give them privacy if he wanted to.

"I don't love you, either, Lily," Michael said, answering her for the first time. "That doesn't mean we can't have an alliance that will help our country."

"Marriage should not be about politics," she said. "I know you think that is naïve of me, but I believe it. I love someone else," she went on. "That will always stand between our partnership."

"I love someone else too," he told her. "I won't— can't—let it matter. I have to love my country more."

Lily was rather pleased to find that Michael was already in love. Perhaps this attachment was something she could work with. "You should marry the woman you love. Form a working partnership with her." She gave him a hard look as she went on, "Because if you think I'm going to let you keep a mistress while I'm forced to live in a loveless marriage you are *very* much mistaken. And by the way, I'm not a virgin."

He shrugged. "Neither am I. That sort of thing

mattered to Gregory, not to me. I'll be a faithful husband," he added. He took a sip of his water. "I owe you that."

Lily didn't answer him. Instead she picked up her own wineglass and took a sip. She supposed Michael was being so reasonable because he could afford to be magnanimous. After all, he'd won. He was in complete control. His people loved him. At least everyone at the embassy did. The coup they'd been planning for years had come off without any violence. The British Empire had recognized Michael as legitimate ruler instantly, and was granting concessions in the trade negotiations to emphasize their support. There were even more invitations arriving for the Bororavian royalty to attend parties and balls than before. Responses to invitations to the wedding were pouring in. Queen Victoria was planning on coming to the wedding. Wedding presents were arriving.

The wedding.

It was only a few days away. Bishop Arkady and Lady Ornov, even her mother, were absolutely rapturous about the wedding plans. Well, perhaps Mum wasn't rapturous, but she was engaged in heavy correspondence about the whole thing with her old friend Baroness Mattsam. Mother had even agreed with Bishop Arkady about setting the day for Lily's baptism into the Bororavian Orthodox Church. The day was tomorrow. The wedding would be the day after that.

Lily knew her time was fast running out.

Time for what, she wondered. To be rescued by Kit? Bitterness and anger surged in her at the very notion. Kit MacLeod was the reason she was in this trap. He cared more for his country than for her! Perhaps someday she would see that loyalty as admirable. *No. It was not admirable.* It had destroyed any chance of finding happiness together.

In the ten days since her prison coach had pulled up to the embassy gates at the end of the journey from Skye, she hadn't been able to stop thinking about Kit. Mostly those thoughts were anything but kind. Ah, but it was hard to forget his charm, his teasing, the exciting way it felt to be in his arms while dancing—or making love. She never wanted to forget how it felt *making* love to Kit, but Lily forced herself to hate him, for it was safer than loving him.

"Why don't you marry the woman you love," she tried again. "It's hard enough being a king. Give yourself some happiness in your private life."

He took another sip from his water glass, and looked at her intently over the rim of the crystal goblet. His voice was silky when he said, "Perhaps we will build happiness in *our* private life."

Michael's eyes were dark, like Kit's. He was a handsome man making a stab at getting her interested in him. She felt nothing for him, nothing stirred in her, nothing sparked. Lily even felt vague irritation that her betrothed was attempting to seduce her. "I wouldn't count on it, Michael," she answered him. She stood, then asked, "May I go now?"

He put down the glass, and nodded. "Of course."

A guard, a maid, and Lady Ornov waited outside the dining room to accompany her back to her rooms. They were there for her protection, of course. The guards had been very *protective* since Lily's one abortive escape attempt a week ago. So protective that there was always at least one guard no more than a step behind her. She hated that she was even more closely watched now than she had been while being Gregory's prisoner. The security inside and outside the embassy was more intense as well. The new captain of the Royal Guard took his role far more seriously than Cherminsky had. This man acted as though the embassy could come under siege at any moment.

She'd been assured many times that her life would be far less circumscribed once she was wed, crowned, and whisked off to Bororavia. Of course it would seem less circumscribed, she thought. Then she'd have the entire country as her prison. Pity it was such a small country.

Lily left the trio outside the door to her suite. Lady Ornov wanted to come in, but Lily sent her off to bed instead. She found her mother waiting for her in the sitting room.

"What's all this?" Lily asked when her mother turned from looking at a table full of boxes of every size and shape. Lily gestured at even more parcels on every surface, and even piled on the floor.

"More presents, of course," Mum answered.

Lily met her mother's gaze. "Why?" she asked. "I don't know enough people to account for all these gifts."

"You're going to be a queen," her mother replied. "People like being in a queen's favor. Load of bloody nonsense, if you ask me. I've always thought so. Took me years to bring your father round to my way of thinking. Now it's starting all over again with you."

"No it isn't," Lily defended herself. She gestured, taking in the room, and the world beyond. "You know I don't want any of this. I feel like a bee being slowly covered in sap. Pretty soon I'll be turned into a bug in amber—a smothered thing that people look at and collect. I'm dying, Mum," she finished as she came forward. Her mother met Lily in the center of the crowded room, then held her as she cried on her shoulder. But her mother didn't let Lily feel sorry for herself for long. Gently Lady Bancroft pushed Lily away and handed her a fresh handkerchief to dry her tears.

"I've been going through quite a few of these, haven't I?" Lily asked as she dabbed at her wet cheeks and lashes. "It makes me feel like a weakling."

"I think you are holding up fairly well under the circumstances," her mother replied. She took Lily's hand and led her to the laden table. "Let's have a look at these, shall we? Something here might cheer you up."

Lily doubted that. "All right." Any distraction was certainly welcome. It was either that or go off to her lonely, empty bed to another fitful night's sleep. "I don't want tomorrow to come, Mum," she said. "I really don't."

"I understand, darling."

Lily shook her head. "No."

"Yes," her mother countered. "You aren't marrying the man you love . . . and you think death might be better than life without your Mr. MacLeod."

Lily considered this for a moment. "That is how I feel," she agreed. "Then I recall that it was Kit who sent me away—and I want to pummel the man senseless."

Her mother smiled. "I see that it really is true love. Darling, there were times I wanted to wring your father's neck, and he mine, but we always worked it out after a bit of shouting. The times after the shouting tended to be quite pleasant," she added with a reminiscent smile. "Never mind that," she went on. She opened the lid of a red gilt box. "Have a look at these. Perfume," she added.

Lily glanced down at a delicate crystal flagon

nestled in a bed of copper-colored velvet. The liquid in the lovely little bottle exactly matched the color of Lily's eyes. Lily picked up the perfume bottle. A small, folded square of parchment was tied to the bottle with a flamingo-pink satin ribbon. There was something about it . . .

She looked at her mother. There was something about the look in her mother's eyes . . . "Who sent this? . . ."

"I'm going to bed now, Lily, my love," Mum answered. "Read the note," she added as she turned and walked to the door.

Lily opened the tiny square of paper. The note read: *Drink me.*

Lily's fingers opened with the shock, but she managed to catch the bottle just before it crashed onto the table. Breathing hard, she clutched the small bottle to her bosom, holding it tightly in her closed fist. She knew it was her imagination, but the thing in her hand felt warm and alive and full of dangerous promise.

Drink me. How often had she compared her life of late to the works of Lewis Carroll? She remembered that her last conversation with Kit had started with her saying "—*but it's like living in Wonderland, isn't it? At any moment I expect to see rabbits with watches, or bottles with tags on them that say* drink me, *or to be invited to play croquet using flamingos as mallets.*"

"Good Lord," she murmured, and looked nervously around the room. What was this? What was going on? What was she supposed to do?

Her head began to swim with the possibilities.

Kit. It had to be Kit. Of course it was Kit.

"Kit," she murmured, and was astonished at the rush of emotions that welled up at saying his name. Anger mixed equally with elation. And there was suspicion as well. What was the king of thieves up to? What was his true motive? Was this an attempt to rescue her? Or did he have something more devious in mind? If he was trying to rescue her, why did he send her away in the first place? Did he truly love her?

Drink me.

She sighed. She held the bottle up and studied the aqua liquid in the lamplight. What would it do?

Drink me.

"And find out."

It all came down to the matter of trust, didn't it? It was dangerous, wasn't it, whatever this potion was? Dangerous. A leap of faith. Like love itself.

At this point it also came down to the question of did she truly love Kit MacLeod. Love and trust were the same thing, weren't they?

"Oh, bother," Lily muttered, and carefully eased the stopper out of the little crystal bottle.

"Drink this."

"Drink what?" Her head hurt.

"Open your eyes and find out."

She did not want to open her eyes. She wasn't sure she could lift her heavy lids. Good God, but her head hurt. Her mouth tasted of—dead fish? "Have I thrown up recently?"

"Twice now."

Twice was not enough. She gagged, and gentle hands held her head.

"Do you remember your name yet?"

She became aware of a rhythmic, rumbling sound. She knew she was lying down, but she was also swaying ever so slightly back and forth. It was a familiar feeling. So were the sounds. Train. She was on a train.

"Do you remember your name?" the persistent man asked again. He had a nice voice. She'd heard it somewhere before. It made her feel good. Well, actually she felt terrible, but there was something about his voice and touch that soothed her, made her know she was warm and safe.

She thought about the question for a while. Things began to come back to her. "Lily," she said finally. "Lily Bancroft. Who are you?"

"Try to remember on your own," he urged. Hands cupped her face, then smoothed down her throat and over her shoulders. His touch felt marvelous. "Would you like a drink of water?"

"Oh, yes. Very much." The words came out a whispered croak. Her throat hurt, but not as much as her head.

"Then you have to open your eyes."

"You're mean to me."

A kiss brushed like angel wings across her forehead. "Oh, no, Lily, my love. Never."

Lily, my love. Now, who called her that? No angel. Someone—wonderful. "Rascal. Rogue. Adventurer. Lover."

"I'm glad you remember that."

"I remember now." Lily opened her eyes. Her lips formed a weak smile. "Kit."

There he was, smiling back at her, with deviltry in his dark eyes. "Here's your water," he said, and held a glass to her lips.

She drank it all down eagerly, and asked for more while he held her propped up on his arm. When done with the second glass of water, Kit helped her to sit up the rest of the way. The world reeled and wheeled around her, colors and shapes mixing up and swooping in and out of her vision. This was not a pleasant time, but she did manage not to throw up again. It felt like a victory.

After reality had settled down into something that looked and felt like an ordinary train baggage car, Lily said, "Why are we in a baggage car?" Then she took a closer look at something she'd noticed out of the corner of her eye, a long, boxy shape that took up quite a bit of space at the other end of the car. "Is that a coffin?"

His arm was around her shoulders, and it tightened comfortingly as he answered, "Yes. Yours."

"Oh." She and Kit occupied a long padded seat

at the other end of the car, with small windows on either side of the bench. She glanced out a window, and noticed the countryside rolling by. She saw fields and pastures separated by dry stone walls, woods, and farmhouses, and a great many sheep and cattle in the pastures. "It looks very rural out there."

"London is far behind us," he agreed. "So is everything Bororavian. Forever."

"Good." Lily blinked in confusion, and rubbed her aching forehead. "My coffin?"

"Lucy assured me that it will all come back to you. It did to her."

"It?" Lily settled closer to Kit, content for a bit to rest within the comfort and strength of his embrace, content to let his warmth and scent permeate her senses. She was with Kit. She was all right. She didn't know how or why, but she was with Kit. Finally, after a few blank but utterly comfortable moments, she giggled as a memory emerged. "There was a message in a bottle," she said. "Or something like that."

"Something." He helped her straighten up so they could look at each other face-to-face. He took her hands in his, squeezing them reassuringly. "It's rather melodramatic, I'm afraid."

Lily glanced at the coffin. "You mean it's rather gothic, don't you?"

He grinned, eyes alight with mischief. "It could

have been much worse. I had this grand scenario planned out where I rescued you from your crypt, but your mother insisted that she wasn't putting her daughter through any more distress than necessary to convince everybody that you were dead."

"My mother?"

"Oh, yes. Your mother made all the funeral arrangements."

Lily spoke slowly and reasonably. "Of course she did."

Kit laughed. "I'm not mad, at least for a MacLeod. We get embroiled in all sorts of nonsensical schemes. This was one of them." Then his look turned very serious, and full of longing. "Perhaps we'll save the explanations for later," he said, and drew her to him.

He kissed her then, tender at first, then full of demand and passion. Lily had not felt alive until their lips touched, and their souls touched, and she suddenly felt like she was Sleeping Beauty awakening at her prince's kiss. It was the most wonderful moment of her life. But when their lips parted and their gazes met, she did not regret that the kiss ended. She knew from the fire their look shared that their lives would be filled with many more such rapturous moments.

"I was so worried for you," he told her. "I had to trust it would work, but I was terrified every moment you were in the trance."

"Trust," Lily repeated—and suddenly the memory of what she'd done came back to her. "Trust." She grabbed Kit in a tight embrace. "I trusted you. I'll always trust you."

"Thank you," he answered, holding her with equal fierceness. "Thank you. I am so sorry it was all I could do. I love you so much—I couldn't bear to lose you."

He loved her. He'd come for her. They were going to live happily ever after. Or she'd know the reason why. She smiled, full of the most utter contentment a woman could know.

"I love you," she told him. Then she sat back and said, "Tell me everything."

"Couldn't we kiss for a while first?"

He looked for all the world like an impish boy pleading for a sweet before he ate his dinner. Lily shook her head, only getting a little dizzy from it. "Be brief. Then we can kiss."

He straightened his shoulders, and took a deep breath. "The only way we could prevent you from marrying the king was for you to die. Lucy concocted a serum from the Jamaican zombie formula that simulates death and tried it out on herself. She certainly looked dead for a couple of days. When she woke up we decided to send some of the potion to you. We couldn't make direct contact with you, so we contacted a friend of your mother's and the two of them exchanged letters explaining the details of the plot. Your mother was reluctant at first, but she became convinced it was the only way to get you away from the embassy. So, the perfume bottle containing Lucy's potion was delivered. You drank it. There was a great fuss about your having committed suicide. The wedding was canceled."

"I should think so."

"Hush, I'm trying to do this quickly."

"Sorry. Go on."

"Your mother made a great fuss about taking your body home. She made sure there were air holes in your casket and loaded you on a train for Yorkshire. I was waiting in the baggage car. I opened the casket. After a while you woke up and threw up on me and proceeded to do so several more times until we reached this moment. In the near future we shall leave the country under assumed names." He cocked his head to one side. "May I have a kiss now?"

Lily held up a hand. "In a moment. I remember hearing the guard dogs that night. Was that you breaking into the embassy?"

"Yes." He pushed up his coat sleeve to reveal a healing bite. "I'd do anything for you."

"You broke in to leave the perfume bottle?"

"No. I sent that through the post."

"Then why—"

He grinned, and a ring appeared on his palm, as if by magic. It was a small silver ring, set with a small, insignificant yellowish orange citrine. It was the Bororavian royal wedding ring. She looked from his palm to his smiling but serious face. "I thought you might like this. For you truly do deserve to be a queen. Be my queen."

She couldn't say a word. She had never been more amazed, and pleased, and touched by anything in her life. She had not thought she could love him any more, but she did. Tears stung her eyes and her throat. Without any conscious thought, Lily held out her left hand. He tenderly placed the ring on her finger. She wasn't surprised that it fit perfectly.

"Your queen of thieves," she said, and, "Good Lord, Kit. Of course I couldn't bear to be anything else."

And *then* they kissed.

Forget the chocolate this Valentine's Day ...
dally with sexy heroes from Avon Books!

BORN IN SIN by Kinley MacGregor
An Avon Romantic Treasure

He is the infamous "Lord Sin," a mysterious stranger whom everyone fears. He despises his Scottish heritage, but now, to unmask the king's enemies, he will return to the Highlands and wed a bewitching lass whose flaming red hair matches the fire of her spirit ... and whose beauty and grace awaken a perilous need he's never known.

STUCK ON YOU by Patti Berg
An Avon Contemporary Romance

Trouble bubbles over the day Logan Wolfe arrives in Plentiful, Wyoming. One look at this gorgeous hunk was enough to knock Scarlett O'Malley off her sky-high heels, but she is sure this stranger is up to something. Logan doesn't need a screwball sleuth dogging his footsteps, but when her wacky investigation takes a surprising turn, this ex-cop finds himself glued to her side, keeping her out of trouble—and falling in love.

INTO TEMPTATION by Kathryn Smith
An Avon Romance

Julian Rexley, Earl of Wolfram, knows Lady Sophia Aberley is the "anonymous" author of a tell-all about their scandalous past. Though she refuses to admit that *he* was the wronged party, Julian still aches for the exquisite lady. But he is determined to resist the intoxicating lure of her kiss, for they both know the kind of trouble *that* can lead to!

INNOCENT PASSIONS by Brenda Hiatt
An Avon Romance

Dashing Noel Paxton has taken on the guise of the legendary Saint of Seven Dials to expose a dangerous spy in London. Is country beauty Rowena Riverstone in league with his prime suspect? Noel longs to discover if her enchanting innocence is real ... and release her passionate fire with a sensuous kiss.

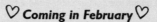

Coming in February